I told h

He eyed

We argue

ever kept up with me.

We talked about everything. And then we talked some more.

When we heard the alarm clock go off in the room next door, we were still sitting on the couch as we had been at the beginning of the night, only my sandals were lying on the floor. We were facing each other, our heads leaning close together. Our hair may have even been intertwined.

Nick stared at his watch in disbelief. "Oh God, I really didn't mean to keep you up all night." He gave me one of those puppy-dog looks that could make any living, breathing woman forgive any transgression he might ever decide to commit, including any one of the mortal sins.

"Don't be silly. Despite the sleep deprivation, I had a great time," I said softly. (Besides, I had some great concealer to take care of all that.) He got up, and I walked with him to the door. Was this it? Should I say something? I really wanted to kiss him . . . or more accurately, I really wanted him to kiss me . . .

"I *loved* getting the inside scoop on the fashion world. I wanted to *be* Alex and be allowed to go to Chanel for a couture fitting—but if I can't be her, reading about her fabulous life is the next best thing. Readers will devour details about going to the shows and the sample sales."

—Marian Keyes, bestselling author of
The Other Side of the Story* and *Sushi for Beginners

Some Like It Haute

Julie K. L. Dam

WARNER BOOKS

NEW YORK BOSTON

This book is a work of fiction. Names, characters, places, and incidents are the product of the author's imagination or are used fictitiously. Any resemblance to actual events, locales, or persons, living or dead, is coincidental.

Cover design by Anne Twomey
Cover photo by © Howard Berman / Getty Images

Warner Books

Time Warner Book Group
1271 Avenue of the Americas
New York, NY 10020
Visit our Web site at www.twbookmark.com

Printed in the United States of America

First Trade Printing: February 2006
First International Mass Market Printing: March 2006

10 9 8 7 6 5 4 3 2 1

For my mom

Acknowledgments

To my agent, the incomparable Marianne Gunn O'Connor, a million thank-yous. This book never would have happened without your flash of inspiration that morning in London—and your continued support and advice. (And thank you to Lainey Keogh for bringing us together in the first place, all those years ago!)

I want to thank my parents, for encouraging the smart side and humoring the shallow. Thank you, Julie Gold, for being my first reader and a great friend. And thanks to Caryn Karmatz Rudy and Emily Griffin at Warner Books.

Last but not least, thank you to my very own Khaki Guy, David Wadler, for learning to embrace his inner fashionista (or at least pretending to, just to freak me out).

Some Like It Haute

Chapter One

Oh my God. Oh my God. Where were those shoes? Oh God, not the Manolos!

It was Fashion Week in Paris, and if it was Tuesday, it was Chanel. And if it was Chanel, it was my new black Manolo slingbacks with the two-and-a-half-inch kitten heels, to go with the charcoal-gray tweed A-line skirt I got at the Chanel sample sale last season and the perfectly Coco-esque black boiled-wool jacket with the delicate grosgrain trim that I had slipped out of my mother's closet years ago. It said so right there on the daily wardrobe schedule I had meticulously entered into an Excel spreadsheet last week: Chanel skirt, trusty black jacket. Black La Perla bra, the one with the light padding. Matching thong. Tahitian pearl choker. Mabe ring. The black Balenciaga bag. (The brown version was slated for Thursday.) Manolo slingbacks. Only on this Tuesday morning the shoes were nowhere to be seen among the contents of the three suitcases scattered around me.

What a disaster. This would throw off my week's schedule completely. I mean, I suppose I *could* switch over to the Wednesday outfit, but then I'd be wearing vintage Yves Saint Laurent—and we're talking Monsieur Saint Laurent himself, not the Tom Ford era—to a Chanel show, and that just wouldn't do. Not given the history between Saint Laurent and Karl Lagerfeld. I'm not stupid. I know better than to do that. And forget about the Thursday outfit. God and Anna Wintour know better than to wear Stella McCartney to Kaiser Karl's show. Nope, it was Chanel or bust. And without those Manolos, I was utterly, absolutely, fabulously screwed.

Never mind missing an appointment at John Galliano's showroom or getting lost in the stampede of fashion editors in black town cars herded from Celine to Louis Vuitton. Or even accidentally leaving my goodie bag under the seat like I did that one time at Fendi in Milan. Or, heaven forbid, being seated in the third row at Prada. That—that I could just almost deal with. Forgetting my slingbacks (or, my thoughts darkened, having them filched by some shoe-connoisseur bag handler on the Eurostar!) and messing up my entire week's wardrobe: this was unacceptable.

The Chanel show was scheduled for eleven o'clock, but with all the air-kissing and gossiping, followed closely by backbiting the very same people you'd just been kissing, it wouldn't start until noon at least. And you wonder why you almost never see watches featured in runway shows? If I found it in myself to be decisive in the next, oh, fifteen minutes or so, I could probably run over to the Bon Marché a few blocks away, pick out a new pair of pointy-toed black slingbacks without too much of an ordeal, and then make it on time to the show at the Chanel boutique next door to Coco Chanel's original *maison* on the rue Cambon. After a minute and forty-two seconds of indecision—a record low for me, I could be, well, almost sure—I gingerly tiptoed my way through the minefield that was my hotel room floor, trying not to step on the thousands of dollars' worth of Prada, Marni, Dior, and McQueen strewn here, there, everywhere.

Now, where did I put the Wednesday shoes? I slipped them on and—mortified as I was that the three-inch heels were way too high for the outfit—took one last glance at myself in the full-length mirror in the absurdly large bathroom. From the ankles up, anyway, that was one full-fledged fashionista looking back at me. Not bad for a Texas girl with big hair and blue eyeshadow in her not-so-distant past. I grabbed my scheduled Tuesday handbag and was off.

I checked myself out again in the ornate mirrors in the lobby of the old-world-posh Hôtel Ste.-Claire. Ever since my first visit to Paris just out of college, when my editorial assistant's salary made a slightly shabby (bohemian, I thought at the time) little hotel in the Latin Quarter my only option, I had loved staying on the Left Bank. It wasn't always convenient for the shows—but then again, the avant-garde designers made a point of putting on shows at locations that weren't particularly convenient to anywhere. Leave the grand hotels on the Right Bank to the tourists. I'd take the narrow cobblestoned streets, alleys really, that revealed hidden gems of boutiques to the determined shopper. Of course, it didn't hurt that a Prada boutique was also right around the corner.

Once through the doors of the Bon Marché, I could finally let out a sigh of relief. The sight of the pretty little trinkets ripe for the buying—the sparkly lipstick-size Judith Leiber handbags side by side with some delicate jet-beaded earrings I could most definitely fit into my Thursday ensemble—reminded me that I was in my element, indeed my natural habitat. Surely Marie-Claude, my favorite saleslady largely because she deigned to understand my timid French, could find something just right to replace my misplaced shoes. And surely, I reassured myself, my editor would forgive me for expensing them.

I expertly maneuvered past the busload of Japanese tourists manhandling the Vuitton bags on the ground floor, circumvented the perfume spritzers and makeover artists, and sprinted upstairs to my most favorite section of the store—of any store, anywhere. Literally anywhere. A few years back I managed to wangle a trip to Vietnam to do a story on the textiles made by a northern hill tribe that had inspired Donna Karan's resort collection, and I scored some intricately embroidered slippers from some cobblers five villages away. (Daniel Day Lewis, eat your heart out!) My seldom-tested journalistic ingenuity kicked in when in pursuit of one thing and one thing only.

It wasn't my fault; I inherited my weakness for shoes from my mother, who bought me my first pair of girly Mary Janes when I was two and went back to the store to buy herself a matching pair that same afternoon. And from my father, who has been known to order three pairs of the same shoe at once. I was doomed from the start.

Oh, the many incarnations and variations of that most miraculous of inventions, bunions and fallen arches be damned. Dainty mules and sturdy-soled boots. Sexy stilettos and practical brogues. Manolo makes 'em and I buy 'em. How perfectly the world turns.

Or so I thought, until I scanned the third floor and there was nary a sign of the saleswoman's severe black bob and perfect posture. Marie-Claude was missing. Just like my poor slingbacks. Disconsolate, I imagined the shoe-connoisseur bag handler stuffing his big smelly feet into my beautiful shoes and prancing around Waterloo Station in them. I shuddered.

In Marie-Claude's usual corner I spotted from behind a dark-haired man in a Savile Row pinstripe suit and what I could tell were hand-tooled Italian loafers. I perked up. A salesman wearing hand-tooled Italian loafers couldn't be half bad.

"Excusez-moi, monsieur?" I said with a nervous smile.

When he turned around, I noted how his brown hair faded to gray at his temples and how the tiny wrinkles around his cornflower-blue eyes crinkled when he smiled back at me. There was something very familiar there.

"Oui, mademoiselle?" he said. Our eyes locked for a split second, and he paused as he registered my baffled stare.

"Mr. Billings? Monsieur Jacques? Eastview High School? Sixth-period French class? 1990? What on *earth* are you doing here?"

He stared back, did that thing he did with the crinkling eyes, and then burst into a hearty laugh. "Saints alive," Mr. Billings—Monsieur Jacques to his pupils—said in his Texas drawl. "Well, if it isn't my star student, Alexandra Simons."

I cringed. Prize pupil I might have been, but I'd figured out pretty quickly my first time in Paris that all those French pop songs we sang in class didn't help much when it came to asking a Parisian for directions to the Hermès store. But I would let Monsieur Jacques believe what he wanted to. "Oh, you're such a kidder," I said, pretending to be modest.

"Well, just look at you," he said, sizing me up and smiling appreciatively. "What a gorgeous skirt. Chanel?"

"As a matter of fact, yes," I said, certain I was blushing from head to toe. That was part of his charm. He always did notice one student's new haircut or another's favorite pair of shoes. I added hurriedly, "I haven't exactly kept in touch with anyone from back home. I didn't know y'all finally upped and moved to Paris."

I did a mental double take at myself. Did I just say *y'all?*

"Oh, well, you know, my wife and I split up last year," he said. "I was ready to start fresh, and I always did dream of livin' here, so I decided, by gum, I'd do it."

Monsieur Jacques was the most popular teacher at Eastview. His class was always overbooked with besotted girls—it reminded me of that scene in *Raiders of the Lost Ark* when the student in Harrison Ford's class had I LOVE YOU written on her eyelids. Only instead of being rough-and-tumble like Indiana Jones, Monsieur Jacques was as suave as you could ever imagine in suburban Dallas, Texas. He didn't reek of Old Spice like the other teachers, and he most certainly would never have been caught dead in the polyester pants and pocket protectors favored by our physics teacher. No, Monsieur Jacques was cosmopolitan. He wore these expensive custom-made shoes that glided down the hallways without so much as a squeak. His suits were bespoke before I knew what bespoke was. He smoked Gauloises out back behind the gym between classes. He spoke *French*, for God's sake! How he could have emerged from the primordial ooze of Houston, I could never figure out. His only fault, in our adolescent eyes, was his beautiful, sloe-eyed painter wife who would pick him up after school in her vintage red Mustang convertible. His tie finally undone and his hair flopping in the wind, they'd speed off into the sunset, or at least to some smoky salon gathering of artists and philosophers that we had only read about in French novels (in translation, of course).

He couldn't have been older than twenty-eight or twenty-nine then, I guessed, which put him in his early forties now and, I supposed, my demographic-group peer. I had reached that awkward age when it was technically proper to call my parents' friends by their first names, and maybe even socialize with them, but I would certainly never dream of it. Same situation with Monsieur Jacques. Here we were, both grown-ups, both single. So I had a mad crush on him back then, and the thought of his touching my feet, I will confess, might have once been the subject of a daydream that spanned sixth-period French class all the way through seventh-period chemistry. But put that in the context of his helping me buy some shoes—well, it kind of broke the spell, didn't it? And now . . . and now all I could really think about was whether it would be okay to *tutoyer* him. It was just one of the many existential issues plaguing me in my beginning-adulthood crisis. And let's not even mention the fact that my parents already had two kids by the time they were my age. Of course, had I never left Texas after high school, that would've been all taken care of by now. I could've probably thrown in a divorce or two to boot.

"I'm sorry to hear about the split, Monsieur J—" I stopped myself mid-Jacques and laughed.

"You can call me Jack. Or Jacques. Conveniently interchangeable," he said.

"Well, *Jacques,*" I said, "it is so good to see you here. I really do want to catch up, really . . ." I looked down at my shoddily shod feet. "But I really, *really* need a new pair of shoes. I'm fixin' to go to this fashion show"—a quick glance at my watch might have left me panicked had I not been distracted by my use of the word *fixin'*—"oh my God, in, like, twenty minutes. Could you help me, please?"

"Well, aren't you livin' the glamorous life," he said, his eyes filled with laughter and what I, momentarily regressing to my girlish crush, giddily registered as impressed approval.

"Oh, you know," I said, grinning stupidly, "it's just a job. I've been covering fashion for *The Weekly* magazine for the past couple of years. I'm based in London." And for the benefit of my parents who paid for my $120,000 college education, I added dutifully, as was my wont, "I did hard news before. You know, earthquakes, transit strikes, the Winona Ryder trial."

I glanced at the dozen and a half marginally different variations of pointy-toed black slingbacks daintily displayed on the white Formica tables around me, and nodded at the one closest to me. "Now, do you think that Louboutin heel is too spiky for this skirt length?"

Fifteen minutes later, I left the Bon Marché with my Wednesday shoes in a shopping bag, some utterly demure black Louboutin slingbacks on my feet (I would have gone for something a little sexier, but somehow I thought that would embarrass Monsieur Jacques . . . or maybe just me). And oh, yes, Jacques's cell phone number in my Palm. If the girls from Eastview High could see me now . . .

. . . fighting for a taxi with a little old Parisian lady. Armed with a baguette fresh from the boulangerie, she was clad in beige Chanel tweed and D'Orsay pumps, a cigarette dangling from her scarlet-painted lips. I'd spotted her from all the way down the block, and between us was a man stepping out of what seemed to be the only available taxi in the arrondissement. As he paid the driver, I made my way, as quickly as I could while still taking care not to get my new heels caught in any grates—or more likely, dog poop—that might have been in my path. I never let Chanel Lady out of my sight. Oh, I could tell that she saw me, too. Our eyes locked at twenty paces. I sped up. She sped up. I flashed her my best Intimidating American look. She shot back a Haughty Parisian. If Coco Chanel had been looking down from heaven, she would surely have been tickled to see that two women wearing clothes bearing her name were playing chicken over a taxi.

In the blink of an eye—that is, had either of us wimped out and blinked—we both lunged at the door handle, as if it were the one and only Birkin bag left at the editors' preview night of the Hermès sample sale.

Luckily, I was younger—and more desperate. I felt the weight of the bread beating against my back as I slipped into the cab and locked the door behind me. Chanel Lady—and as it turned out, I had used that word loosely—was spitting venom at me. I tried to read her lips. Did she really just call me a *putain*? I have always been convinced that the ability to curse at someone in another language was the best measure of fluency, and now I was wishing more than ever that Monsieur Jacques had taught us something really useful. Instead, I did something almost universally understood: I stuck my tongue out at her and waved.

What a harridan, I thought to myself as I brushed the baguette's flour off my jacket. Catching my breath in *my* cab, I took a moment to contemplate how, in Paris, there really was no going gently into mumsy housedresses and early-bird specials. Women there would give up their cigarettes and red wine before they relinquished short skirts, lipstick, and heels (but no pantyhose, perish the thought). Chanel Lady, at least, had impeccable taste.

"Numéro vingt-neuf, rue Cambon, s'il vous plaît," I told the driver. I could have sworn that was a lascivious look he gave me. No matter. I had become accustomed to being chatted up by taxi drivers during fashion weeks in Paris and Milan. More than one had asked me—all 5'5" of me (in three-inch heels)—if I was a model. They must figure that one day they'll hit the jackpot. Usually I just played along to practice my French or Italian. But there was no time for pleasantries today, not when the show was about to start and I was still across the Seine. *"Je suis en retard,"* I told him, trying my most flirtatiously pleading face.

He stepped on the gas. I could see his smirk in the rearview mirror. *"Et vous êtes mannequin, n'est-ce pas?"*

I tried, I really tried, not to roll my eyes and instead just gave him a tight smile. I guess my smackdown of Chanel Lady had only increased my standing in his eyes.

I avoided his gaze and just looked out the window as we weaved through the Paris streets, past the students loaded down with backpacks, the couples strolling hand in hand and the tourists with their noses in *Time Out Paris* guides, past the pensioners braving the March chill to while away their morning over a café au lait and a brioche at a sidewalk café. They were all the sights that once filled me with *Breathless*-fueled thoughts of romance, and that I now rarely had time to notice when there were catwalks and catfights to write about.

We inched our way across the river and past the obelisk in the place de la Concorde, down the Faubourg St.-Honoré to the corner of rue Cambon. I hadn't noticed in a long time just how pretty Paris was.

I stepped out of the cab a few minutes past noon. Outside the entrance was the dramatic tableau that had become so familiar to me: A scrum of fashion students, paparazzi, wannabe modelizers and assorted other hangers-on were all pushing and grabbing at something, nothing, everything. False-alarm star sightings were met with a flurry of camera flashes until word spread that it was someone who simply *looked* like a C-list celebrity. While several beefy men, clad entirely in black and wired with those Secret Service earphones, handled crowd control, the far more imposing-looking PR girls did the real dirty work: checking tickets and cross-referencing the guest list.

I waved my invitation at them and they let me pass, handing me a goodie bag (No. 5 eau de toilette, I guessed) on my way in. The music—unrecognizable bubblegum pop—was thumping, too loud for me to ask for help from the ushers who were in any case too busy ogling the sprinkling of French film starlets in technicolor dresses cut down to there and up to here, who were at the show in search of a touch of class.

I had no idea where to find my seat in the maze of rooms and doorways. One room led into another, and on and on. On either side of each room, three rows of white-satin-cushioned chairs had been tightly plotted like a zero-lot suburban subdevelopment. A narrow corridor in between the two banks of seats served as the runway, winding through a doorway and into the next room. The lack of a real catwalk—the models just strolled casually through the boutique—gave the show an impression of intimacy. A false impression, of course, considering there were probably four hundred people gathered there to see the glamazons in various stages of undress. But the setup did make for a wise seating plan: More front-row seats meant fewer miffed editors.

Dressed to kill in this season's Chanel, the usual suspects formed a murderers' row front and center. Wait a minute. What was *Moda*'s editor-in-chief doing still wrapped up in her full-length fox fur, slumped in her seat? Could it be? That not only was she wearing the identical blood-orange tweed minidress, fringed jacket, and logo boots as someone else in the room—but her twin was the mere fashion editor of *Max Mode*? I would just about die if that ever happened to me, I thought, as I joined the chorus of titters in the room. Apparently the paparazzi had already had their field day when the doppelgangers—who was whose double would surely be the subject of some debate at the Valentino dinner tonight—crossed paths on their way to their seats. I could just make out the details from some stylists who were whispering nearby. Damn my replacement shoes. I couldn't believe I had missed the action.

In their place of dishonor in a cordoned-off corner of the first room, two dozen photographers were busy elbowing each other to stake their claim to the best vantage point—the one where they might, if they were lucky, capture on film some naive new model adjusting her G-string. They'd obviously been forced to wait too long; they were starting into some World Cup soccer chants. In the back rows the newbies were poised on the very edge of their seats, soaking in every detail of the room, their neighbors, the lights, the music. This place was about to burst.

I made my way through the room, pausing here and there for an air kiss—a long-distance air kiss in some cases. Way in the back of the *maison*, I saw some camera flashes go off, and then a blur of long legs and the snap of some hundred editors' notebooks opening, pens at the ready. The show must have just started. Great. I had to hurry. I wandered through the room and paused in the doorway into the next. I checked the seating assignment written on my invitation again. What on earth did Dc2vii mean?

"Excusez-moi." "Excusez-moi." "Excusez-moi."

Crossing the threshold into the third room, I spotted my seat: second row, right in the middle. Bloody hell, I muttered. Second row? Even worse, from either side I would have to climb over at least five people. I could start from the far side of the row, and get dirty looks from the fashion editor, features and shopping, of *Harper's Bazaar*, and the associate market editor of Italian *Vogue*. (At least they didn't have any baguettes on them, I thought with great relief.) Or I could go to the near side and earn the ire of the buyer, ladies' designer sportswear, of Neiman Marcus and a couple of stylists I didn't really know.

I weighed my options for all of twelve seconds. Far better to alienate another editor, I figured, than anyone from Neiman's, the fashion mecca of my childhood. I combed my fingers through my hair and smoothed down my jacket, straightened my back, took a step onto the makeshift runway . . . and just as I was about to attempt my most dignified shuffle down to the other side of the row, I heard the wave of gasps spread across the room, counterclockwise, and circle back to me.

And then I heard myself gasp.

Talk about making an entrance. Before I knew it—and certainly before I could do anything about it—I found myself suddenly face to left breast with a certain six-foot blonde from Latvia. Pleased to meet you, Katyarina. The season's hot new model was midstep in her peculiarly mesmerizing Monty Python gait, which her fans and sycophants described as gazelle-like. (The more reasonable might have compared her to a giraffe on acid.) And I, like a deer caught in the headlights, certainly not even a gazelle on a good day . . . whatever, I wasn't moving fast enough to get out of the way.

The gasps turned into snickers.

We veered right in unison, and then left, still perfectly aligned, as if we were doing some 1980s mirror-image dance. On the fourth parry, we collided again. Her boot's sharp stiletto heel cutting into my brand-new, beautiful slingback, we stumbled to the floor together, a tangle of splayed legs—mostly Katyarina's. The photographers couldn't believe their luck. The excited mob of arms and legs and lenses moved as one as they pounced on us. In the shock and horror of the moment my mind wandered aimlessly: *Where on earth could my left shoe be . . . I sure hope that's my own knee I'm grabbing . . . I think I did this move in yoga once . . .*

The sounds of the shutters clicking and the laughter echoing through the room deafened me, and I felt the intense heat of their flashbulbs on my face. I closed my eyes to the white lights—God, I only wished they were the ones they say you see when you're dying.

I slowly opened my eyes to a squint just in time to catch a glimpse of Katyarina's tear-stained face, the glittery fashion-show makeup puddling in muddy gobs around her eyes and then sliding down the rivulets of tears on her cheeks. She was sixteen, seventeen tops, and yet behind the tears she looked at me not angrily, just questioningly. Call me crazy, but I could have sworn she was thinking: "I know this publicity is only going to help my career, but what's in it for you?"

At least ten publicists had rushed over to pull her up off the runway. The crowd parted, and I was left alone for a split second, totally paralyzed. The embarrassment must have been written all over my face—oh, I'll know for sure when I see it in the papers tomorrow, I realized. Lordy Lordy Lordy. This was not good. Not good at all.

I feigned pride, got myself on my feet, clumsily gathered my shoes and bags, and *booked.*

Back in journalism school—the one concession to academia that I made for my father the professor after I finished college and took a job as a $24,000-a-year editorial assistant-slash-indentured servant at *The Weekly*—we were taught never to become part of a story. Like I said, we were *taught* that.

When I'd eventually have to write up this twisted story that I had practically wedded at center stage, at least I would be able to describe Katyarina's outfit in great detail. Black boiled-wool cropped jacket and matching A-line skirt, with an anklet composed of one humiliated fashion journalist. Consider it personally fact-checked.

Holed up an hour later at my room at the Ste.-Claire, which was now filled with white lilies and other flowers of condolence thoughtfully sent by my doubtlessly gloating peers, I wondered if I could ever overcome this public self-immolation. Or, for that matter, if I could ever leave this hotel room and face anyone again.

By the time I had escaped the lights and cameras at Chanel and scurried back to the hotel, my newly handy Balenciaga raised to shield my eyes as if it were the sunniest day in the Caribbean, there were already five phone messages and six e-mails from my editor, Roddy James. As annoyed as I was, I had to give him this: he had good sources.

He started out trying to be funny: "Hey, Alex, it's Roddy. You aren't leaving the magazine for TV, are you?

Because you seemed rather telegenic on Sky News . . . your face—well, it's more like the back of your head, and your left arm somehow underneath that model's right leg, and her left foot . . . My God, it was like Twister: the Couture Edition." He laughed altogether too heartily. Almost as an afterthought, he signed off with a chipper, "Call me."

By the fourth message, he sounded plaintive. "Hey, it's Roddy again. Where *are* you? And why is your cell phone off? Now, I *know* there's no witness protection plan for fashionistas. Don't do anything drastic without calling me first, won't you please?"

I didn't bother listening to the fifth one. I just erased them all and crawled into the king-size bed, still decked out in my Tuesday outfit, pulled the covers over my head, and for the first time in my thirty-one years seriously considered plastic surgery. If I could find Michael Jackson's surgeon—and if he hadn't already lost his license—I'd be positively unrecognizable. I could change my name. I could move to some place where Sky News didn't exist. Where they didn't know anything about fashion . . . Hey, maybe my parents would let me move back home to Texas.

I couldn't think of anything more depressing.

Except maybe what my life was like at this moment. Fashion Week had barely started, and there was simply no way I could withstand the stares, the whispers, the smirks. I just wasn't that brave—or stupid. Roddy would have to understand. Maybe he could get a freelancer here to finish the week . . . and I could quietly disappear for a while.

But then what? Would I ever be able to come back? As

much as I joked about having the fluffiest job at the magazine, jetting around Europe covering the fashion industry was a plum assignment. (Calling it an industry somehow gave it more weight in my mind.) I had dined with Donatella and gabbed with Gabbana. And—much to my mother's awe and pride—I had met the master himself, Monsieur Saint Laurent. My friends envied me, despite how often I told them that things just weren't as glamorous as they seemed. A sane person can take only so many hour-long waits in far-flung locales for seventeen-minute splashes of bright lights, loud music, and the occasional divinely cut suit. Squeeze thirty of those into one week, multiply by four cities, twice a year, and you've got one spent fashionista.

On the other hand . . . I got invited to sample sales that weren't listed in the Daily Candy. I was *this* close to getting a clothing allowance, for heaven's sake.

Now that wasn't something that was discussed in J school. The only free outfits my J school classmates could aspire to get on assignment were fatigues and gas masks. Of the ones who weren't stuck in Podunk on the overnight police beat, Tara Wright had written an award-winning exposé on salad bars in New York City delis. And Mark McIntyre had covered two civil wars in countries even non-Americans couldn't pick out on a map. I covered a different sort of hotspot: places like the bar at the Hôtel Costes. The closest I had gotten to a skirmish was a year ago when the French police shut down the big Armani gala at St.-Sulpice and forcefully evacuated the whole fashion pack, in all our finery, from the tents. My one war wound: a pair of Jimmy Choo snakeskin mules destroyed in the mud and confusion. But mostly I had written a heck of a lot about kimono sleeves and deconstructed seams. Pulitzer glory or fashion freebies: what's a girl to choose?

For a while, I convinced myself that I didn't really have to choose. I injected humor and intelligence into my stories, sometimes surprising even myself with what I remembered from my liberal-arts education. So what if I had gotten letters from readers wondering what the Russian Revolution had to do with the latest colors in lipstick? (Good thing Roddy edited out my references to Trotsky.) And so what if the Nietzsche reference in the feature I did last month on stilettos might have been lost on most of the readers who were just looking for a new pair of shoes? But—hah!—did I not do them a service in the end?

I was good at this rationalizing thing. But I needed to think only of one thing to snap me back to my senses. There were plenty of people out there who would kill for my position—including that frighteningly ambitious new reporter Roddy had just hired straight out of Oxford—and since I had helped them out with a little career suicide, they would be clamoring at the gates. And I just couldn't let that happen.

I poked my head out from the covers and reached for the phone.

He let it ring four times before he answered.

"Roddy James speaking."

"Hello, Roddy. It's me, Alex."

"Oh, right, Alex . . . So what's new?"

"Like you have to ask."

"Now, is that any way to talk to the magnanimous editor who is going to let you keep your job?"

"Roddy, you have no idea how horrible it was." I could no longer hold back the tears that had built up from the wretchedness of the day—losing my shoes, getting clobbered by a baguette, literally crashing a show. And now, I couldn't decide which was worse: blubbering in front of my editor, or blubbering *to* my editor. "It all happened so quickly, I was just walking in and I couldn't find my seat so I was just wandering around and then I saw my seat and it was right in the middle and I couldn't quite decide how to get into that row without pissing off a bunch—"

He cut me off. "Be quiet for a minute and listen to me. People will forget. You know how fickle fashionistas are. They'll forget you in a split second. Remember when that model, what's her name, Oona, tripped on her platform shoes and took a tumble on the runway? How long did they talk about that? A minute."

I remembered it well, actually. I was e-mailing my friends pictures of Oona's spill for weeks, updating them with every new unflattering angle I found. Damn my bad karma.

Roddy was barreling along on his lame attempt at a pep talk. It really wasn't working. I knew he didn't believe a single word he was saying, and deep down, he probably realized that I didn't either. "Sure, there are some who thrive on schadenfreude, but who needs them?" he said optimistically. "It will be a blip. You'll be able to laugh it off in no time. And knowing you, you'll be joining in when there's someone else to make fun of."

"Roddy!" I gasped. "Do you really think that of me?"

His laugh started out as a snicker, and quickly crescendoed into a full-on, eyes-watering, abs-crunching guffaw.

Sixty seconds later, when he finally was able to draw breath, he broke my stewing silence. "Alex, bottom line is that we need the story. We've got four pages in the next issue slated for your Fashion Week coverage. You've got to stick it out."

"But—"

"And, no, we're not hiring a freelancer. We want you to do it. We *need* you."

Damn that Roddy James. I could never argue when I heard those three little words come out of his mouth in that confoundedly sexy British accent of his. Before hanging up, he got me to promise that I would find *something* to write about—and in exchange, he would sign my expense report, however bloated it might become this time around. Oh, he knew where my weaknesses were . . . and I hadn't even mentioned the part my missing shoes had played in the whole ordeal.

Chapter Two

A FIVE-COURSE ROOM SERVICE DINNER—including escargots, foie gras, *and* crème brûlée—and twelve hours of pharmaceutically induced sleep didn't make me feel much better the next morning. Especially when the papers arrived with my breakfast.

Bloody hell, I thought, isn't there any real news going on in the world?

The *International Herald Tribune* had a mercifully small, grainy picture of the "shambles at Chanel" on the front page, below the fold, as a teaser for their fashion coverage inside. I flipped through the pages, my dread manifesting itself as an involuntary twitch in my right eye. When I found the story, though, I had to laugh. In any other situation, I would have been pretty ticked off that they had misspelled my name.

Regardless, there really was no way that I could show my face at the shows today. No way. I didn't care what

Roddy said about keeping a stiff upper lip and all that. I'd rather be caught dead with a mustache on my lip, thank you very much. He told me I had to find something to write about—he didn't say it had to be about the shows. Besides, hadn't I seen that Robert Altman movie where Julia Roberts and Tim Robbins played journalists who just watched the fashion shows on TV? Now, that's a brilliant idea.

Wardrobe schedule out the window, I slipped into my civvies: a black cashmere Prada turtleneck, a pair of Levi's, and my favorite deep burgundy Lainey cashmere stole, which was better than a security blanket. But I *was* in Paris, after all—and so I put on the Louboutin slingbacks I had bought the day before . . . before the nightmare, I thought melodramatically. My sense of humor was returning. That was a good sign.

I flipped through my calendar to see what was going on that day, admittedly to see what venues I should avoid to duck the fashion flock. Basically anywhere on the Right Bank was out of the question. If I wanted to be extra safe, I should probably cross off all bars and any restaurants with a Michelin star.

Discouraged, I scanned the address book in my Palm for some inspiration. Nope, she witnessed my humiliation yesterday. He would've seen it in the *IHT*. She *wrote* about it in the *IHT*. He was there; he was too. Everyone and her stylist was there.

Just when I was about to give up, there was Jacques's phone number, right after Issey and before Jean-Paul. (In the fashion world, it just wouldn't be right to organize one-name wonders by surnames.) Maybe lunch with the dashing former French teacher was just what I needed.

He was the one person in my Palm that I was pretty certain hadn't seen my fabulous show. Roddy could wait, and so could the story. It was only Wednesday, and I didn't have to file anything until the following Tuesday. Besides, Roddy was used to my down-to-the-wire deadline dashes. And, partaking in some ego-stroking, I reminded myself that he never had to edit my stories much anyway.

I was instantly buoyed by the idea, but as I dialed Jacques's number, I couldn't believe how nervous I was. My heart was bouncing like a basketball, from somewhere in my chest up to my throat and back again. What was going on here? Did I take a blow to my skull during my misadventure yesterday or what? Monsieur Jacques wasn't even my type anymore. He hadn't been in years.

I guess old habits die hard.

I cleared my throat and practiced my hellos. Or should I say hi? I've got to play it cool. He won't recognize my voice. Do I ask to speak to Monsieur Jacques? In French or English? What if he's the one answering and I don't recognize his voice? What if I panic and hang up on him?

You know how at cocktail parties you discuss with people you've just met big hypothetical questions like whether you'd want to relive your past knowing what you know now? (Or maybe that was just the premise for a failed TV sitcom.) Well, I felt like I was thirteen again, calling my first crush. Only I wasn't any wiser. Back then, Billy Terry Jr. had made rude farting noises and hung up on me, and then two weeks later asked me in P.E. class if I wanted to go into the woods and "go to first base." I slapped him and refused to talk to him again. Of course, I heard later that Billy's parents sent him to rehab in eleventh grade and he never graduated. Yeah, I always did have good taste in men.

In the middle of my daymare, I heard a male voice say, "Allo?"

"Um, hello, is this Jacques?" So much for all those complicated decision trees I had going through my mind.

"Yes?"

"Um, this is Alexandra? From your high school French class? I ran into you at the Bon Marché yesterday? You helped me find some great slingbacks?" I was fully aware of my annoying tendency to upspeak when I'm nervous. Years of practice and even ten diction classes with a Henry Higgins type in London had done nothing to cure me.

"Oh, Alexandra, darlin', so good to hear from you. And how did those shoes work out for you?"

I thought about telling him that those very shoes he picked out for me were involved in a hit-and-run with a supermodel, but reconsidered. Best to spare him the indignity.

"Oh, they worked out just perfectly," I said. "But I was wondering . . . are you free for lunch today? Short notice, I know, but I just happened to have some free time and we really didn't have a chance to catch up yesterday, since I was in such a crazy rush and all and I was probably a little rude at that?"

I also had a bad habit of not being able to stop talking even though I really, really wanted to.

"That sounds great," said Jacques. "I can take a break at two. Do you mind pickin' me up at the Bon Marché? We can get some bread at Poilâne and take a walk, maybe toward the Musée Rodin. It's a nice day."

"Well, that would be just lovely," I said. This was all too weird. I remember how Monsieur Jacques used to mesmerize us with the tales he told in French—the listening comprehension part of class, of course—of the walks he would take in Paris, through the winding streets and monumental squares. So romantic, the other girls and I would sigh. The boys in the class, meanwhile, would get bogged down in *imparfait* tense and wonder whether that's what it took to get a girl's attention. At the age of sixteen, I'd had a perfect, idealized image of every corner of the Musée Rodin, most of them occupied by me and a certain French teacher, never mind the art.

I managed to get off the phone, thankfully, without further embarrassing myself or babbling on for too long or bursting into fits of giggles. But now I had an hour to kill before my "big date," and I had to, just *had* to talk to someone.

It was only seven a.m. in New York. Too early for everyone I knew, except one investment banker who worked anything but banker's hours. Jillian was my college roommate and longtime partner in crime. Truth be told, she was more often the perpetrator and I was the aider and abettor. Like the time she convinced me to call her next-to-last boyfriend, Jake, pretending to be a pollster to find out what he really thought about infidelity. ("Not a crime if no one sees you" were his famous last words.) Or when I didn't even try to stop her from getting back at him by making him think that she was cheating on *him*.

Not that I didn't have my moments. Somehow, though, my moments had more to do with either (a) geeky boys I didn't have the heart to reject, or (b) embarrassing myself in front of my psyche-crushing unrequited loves who didn't notice anyway. Jillian's were generally melodramatic affairs with bad boys whose names would have been Ridge or Thorne had they been characters on soap operas.

When we were both living in New York after graduation, we spent most Saturday nights holed up in my tiny studio in unfashionable Midtown, pining over the boys we liked and bitching over the girls who got in our way. Before dawn—but after the buffalo wings and pizza delivery, after the three-thousandth late-night viewing of our chick-flick pantheon, *Pride and Prejudice* and *Clueless*—we'd retire, young and happy, me to my futon and Jillian to my pullout foam loveseat. The Jillian Harrison Memorial Pullout Couch, may it rest in peace. Those were the days . . . We had both made big life changes since then: She'd married a great guy, and I'd eloped to Europe. Alone.

I started up my laptop, and logged on to Instant Messenger. Sure enough, there was that yellow smiley face next to Jillian's name. I always could count on her.

AlexSi: Hey.

Jillian5: Hey back. You in Paris?

AlexSi: Like you haven't seen?

AlexSi: Uh, please tell me you haven't seen.

Jillian5: What are you talking about?

AlexSi: Um, well, I had a little run-in with a supermodel. ☹

Jillian5: You WHAT?

AlexSi: I was late for the Chanel show and I couldn't find my seat and the show had started and I didn't really see her coming.

Jillian5: YOU WHAT????

AlexSi: I kinda ran into her.

Jillian5 : YOU WHAT???? I am so Googling you this very minute.

AlexSi: You are so not my friend.

Jillian5: ☺

Jillian5: Details, I want details . . . Oh. My. God. Is that your left leg? Nice shoes, though. Ha!

AlexSi: If you're going to be that way, I'm not even going to tell you about the Big Date I have in an hour. I'm not even going to let you grill me about him.

Jillian5: You wicked girl. Forget the Internet pictures I'm going to send to all our friends. I demand that you spill all about The Man.

AlexSi: Ha. Forget it. You missed your chance.

AlexSi: Oh, all right, remember I told you ages ago about this French teacher I had in high school? The one every girl was in love with?

Jillian5: What?!?!?!

AlexSi: Yeah, you won't believe it. I ran into him while I was looking for those shoes you were admiring in that perfectly flattering photo of me and the Giraffe.

Jillian5: So he was just hanging around the shoe department trying to pick up chicks, or what?

AlexSi: Very funny. He and his wife split up and he moved here. How crazy is that? He's working at the Bon Marché. I didn't get a chance to get the rest of the story. I was late for my date with total public humiliation.

Jillian5: So what's the master plan, missy?

AlexSi: There is no plan! It's not really even a date! I don't even like him that way anymore! It's just . . . really freakin' funny. I kind of wish I were 16 again. I'd be all moony then. Not that we've made that much progress since then.

Jillian5: Speak for yourself! I'm a very respectable wife now, you know. ☺

AlexSi: Yeah, yeah, I don't know why I keep forgetting. Maybe it's all those times you keep begging me to take you with me.

Jillian5: Oh yeah. Ha. Speak of the devil—it's the old ball and chain on the phone. He probably wants to know what's for dinner. Gotta run.

AlexSi: Please. He's probably taking you to Le Cirque. I envy your blissfully ignorant life and you know it. ☺

Jillian5: Have a great time! Don't do anything I wouldn't do . . . or at least anything I wouldn't have done five years ago!

AlexSi: Yeah, right. I'll give you a full update later.

Jillian5: Oh and I promise I'll only send those pictures to our CLOSE friends. And all your ex-boyfriends. And maybe my mom. Toodles!

Jillian5 has logged out.

I really missed Jillian. She was one person I knew would always be supportive, never judgmental—not least of all because she knew we had done worse before! She was never one of those women who would disappear from your life every time she got a new boyfriend, only to resurface when they broke up. And she hasn't been that way since she got married two years ago, either. Just last summer she had met me in Milan for a girls-only shopping trip. Of her four weeks of vacation, it was one week for me, one week for her husband, one for herself, and one for her family. When I grow up, I want to be just like her: blissful and fulfilled, just like the heroine at the end of romance novels. I was that character at the *beginning* of the book: I couldn't say I was *happily* single, but at the same time I couldn't say I was actively looking. And the fashion world certainly wasn't teeming with eligible straight men. Depressing, huh?

Instant-messaging with Jillian, at least, had cut down my pre-date panic time to just twelve minutes. Oh my God, it *is* a *date*, isn't it? Now there was no chance for any last-minute changes of heart about my outfit. My strict wardrobe agenda hadn't left much room for improvisation, at any rate.

On the way out, I put on my new Chanel sunglasses. (I might have been mortified, but I hadn't been foolish enough to leave behind my goodie bag yesterday. Which was a good thing, since its contents had far surpassed my expectations.) I figured they were big enough and dark enough to shield me from any curious fashion groupies.

Before venturing into the hallway, I looked through the peephole in the door and did a careful scan of the floor. The coast was clear. I stepped out, shut the door behind me, turned toward the elevators—and ran smack into a little girl playing in the hallway. *"Pardon,"* I said to her. She stared for a moment, then scurried off, calling for her mother. "Mommy, mommy," she yelped in French, "it's that crazy woman who attacked the nice model on TV!" The precocious children of this city no longer surprised me.

In the 217 steps—I counted—it took me to get to the front door of the hotel, I had received a few odd glances from one bellhop, a chambermaid, and the elevator doorman. Maybe I was a bit paranoid, but surely I didn't mistake the meaning of the grin from the cabdriver who did a slow drive-by just inches away from my path on the sidewalk. If I'd ever wondered what was more ridiculous than being asked by a taxi driver if I was a model, it was being asked whether I could deck Naomi Campbell for him. Honestly! Yes, they took their fashion seriously in this town.

I walked past four newsstands, and I could just make out the top half of the *IHT* headline capturing my shame. Thank God my picture was below the fold. Until today, I could never have imagined thinking that. If I ever won that Pulitzer Prize, or married some European royal or industrialist, I would definitely want to be above the fold. Although, it suddenly occurred to me, I might never escape this. When you do something big—be it cure cancer or rob a bank or win some reality-TV show—the papers always seem to be able to dig up the most appallingly embarrassing photos of you to run with the story. Dammit, they practically taught that in Tabloid Journalism 101! (Not that I ever took such a class.) And if I thought my high school yearbook pictures were bad—Hello, big hair!—this could just possibly beat them on the cringe-o-meter. Mental note to self: When one becomes rich and famous, one must *destroy all negatives. Be extra nice to everyone at next high school reunion and most definitely to all paparazzi.*

But none of this could spoil my mood, which against all odds had lightened as I ducked into the Bon Marché. I could make lemonade out of the sour looks that had been thrown my way yesterday. What the hell—for one day, I could forget my professional woes and revert to sweet sixteen. I imagined how excited I would have been then if Monsieur Jacques were waiting for me and *we* were going on the most romantic date *ever*. In *Paris!*

If nothing else, it would make a funny story to share with Jillian.

I skipped up the escalator two steps at a time, but made sure to look calm and cool as I turned the corner into the shoe department. When I saw that Jacques was watching me approach, I could barely look at him. Maybe this was a bad idea. Maybe I was better off in the comfort and privacy of my hotel suite ordering room service.

I thought of the countless times I had made a second turn around the hallway to "accidentally" run into the cutest guy in tenth grade, only to panic when he, duh, suddenly was right there in front of me. What do I do? Avert my eyes? Pretend I don't see him? Get suddenly distracted by a pair of shoes in the corner? Heaven forbid, make eye contact?

How about all of the above? For a good thirty seconds I found myself fingering a pair of four-inch-high gold leopardskin boots that only Shania Twain could or would wear before I continued through those seemingly endless final forty feet, shiftily looking up, down, left, right—anywhere but straight ahead. Smiling awkwardly when I finally reached Jacques, I shyly stole a glance and mumbled hello. He looked at me kindly. I was just grateful that I didn't trip or get tangled up with a supermodel or something.

"Alex, so good to see you again!" He gave me the European kiss on both cheeks.

I must have blushed.

"Hi," I said. Just a beat too long of silence. "I hope I'm not too early?"

"Not at all. Shall we?"

I let him put his hand on my back and lead me toward the escalator. Now that I was actually here, on this "date," I realized I had no idea what I was going to talk about with Jacques. I hadn't seen him in, what, thirteen years? So, okay, we had a lot of catching up to do . . . as if we were ever on "catching up" terms when we were in high school. I mean, when *I* was in high school and he was my teacher. At the end of the afternoon, would he give me a grade for listening comprehension and pronunciation? A pop quiz, maybe?

During this little mental conversation with myself, I merely smiled at Jacques. I thought maybe he was saying something, but I was too distracted to do anything else. He must be regretting this, I thought. I kind of was.

We were almost out the door before I managed to join the conversation. I adjusted my shawl, made an attempt at a comforting smile, cleared my throat, and . . .

Oh my God, this *cannot* be happening. Out of the corner of my eye, I saw a big television screen had been set up near the Métro station across the street, and there I was on CNN, for all the world—and more important, for Jacques—to see, sprawled all over a supermodel. It was the first time I had actually seen the footage, and even I couldn't help gawking, like a rubbernecker at the scene of some grisly car wreck.

That bloody CNN, I thought. It's gone to hell since they dumped Elsa Klensch. She could always be counted on for some puffball piece on a glassblowing artisan making jewelry out of recycled Coke bottles in some tiny village outside Verona rather than this tabloidy drivel. Oh, look, you could see the unmistakable red soles of my Louboutins. Well, at least no one could accuse me of being a slouch in the shoe depart . . . *Good God, is that my thong showing?* Hah, at least I could tell my mother that I'd done better than wear clean underwear; Mom, I wore La Perla.

When I could finally pry my eyes from the carnage, I looked at Jacques, who had politely found some robins on the green to watch studiously.

"Oh, did I forget to mention that?" I said sheepishly.

My public humiliation, it turned out, broke the ice.

"Hell of a party trick," Jacques said, not skipping a beat in figuring out it was okay to joke about the ridiculousness of the situation. I glanced at his face and all I noticed was the warmth of his gentle laugh lines.

"Yeah, well, it wasn't exactly planned, now, was it? I'm hardly the performance artist."

I laughed wholeheartedly, for the first time since it happened. When I regaled Jacques with the horrible truth—even reenacting the collision with a traffic sign in place of the Giraffe—he mock-complained that I had brought shame on my new shoes, and maybe on the Bon Marché, too, considering its logo could clearly be seen on the shopping bag I was holding on TV. And, he kidded, they might just have to remove me from Eastview High's Hall of Fame: I wouldn't look right next to the professional basketball star with the five out-of-wedlock children and college cheating scandal.

Who knew that Jacques had a sense of humor? To me all those years ago, he was just an ideal—like the wholly imagined consumptive poet I longed to meet and have break my heart. I *was* pretty foolish as a teenager, it goes without saying. (I could only rationalize it as hormonal.) The more Jacques and I spoke, the more I realized I was really glad to be with someone totally removed from my life in fashion. And once I calmed down, the nervousness evaporated. Not least of all because there was absolutely zero sexual tension between the two of us. So much for the scandalous story I was going to tell Jillian. She would be so disappointed.

After picking up a loaf of bread at Poilâne and a bottle of wine and some cups around the corner, we made our way through the streets of the Left Bank. When Jacques stopped to peer into the window of a shoe store on the corner of the rue du Four—"Research," he quipped—I took a more careful look at him. Back in Texas, he used to wear his hair in that floppy Hugh Grant way before it was known as "that floppy Hugh Grant way." But now it was shorter and neater, and a little gray, as befitted a gentleman selling shoes at the Bon Marché. No middle-age paunch or farsighted squint had settled in. The elegant cut of his suit, the perfectly polished shoes: He could have stepped out of a Bergdorf's catalog. He had taken his suit jacket off and rolled up his sleeves. I noticed his all-season Texas tan—and the lack of a tan line on his left ring finger, where he used to wear a simple gold band. I tried to remember what he had told me. How long ago had he and his wife split?

We had somehow made our way not to the museum but to St.-Sulpice (which always made my stomach turn—the thought of the jackbooted police stomping on my precious Jimmy Choos at that aborted Armani show!). We sat down on the steps of the fountain, side by side, and made some small talk about my career choice. I picked at the bread as Jacques opened the bottle of chardonnay with the corkscrew on his Swiss Army knife.

"I didn't know you wanted to be a writer when you grew up," he said.

"Well, neither did I," I replied, accepting the wine he had poured into a plastic cup. "God, my editor would have a heart attack if he saw us drinking this wine like this." I thought of Roddy and his four-course liquid lunches back in London. To call him a wine connoisseur would be high praise. To call him a lush would be accurate.

Jacques continued grilling me. "Did you study journalism? How did you get into fashion?"

"I did go to journalism school, but it wasn't exactly planned. In college I didn't really know what I wanted to do, but I figured joining the school paper and getting to go to plays and movies for free couldn't be a bad thing. It turned out I was good at it. And it was fun. And next thing I knew . . ."

"So have you met Galliano? McQueen? *Gaultier*?"

I gave him a puzzled smile. He looked so eager. "I had no idea you were that into fashion."

"Oh, it's always been a great passion of mine," he said with a sigh.

"Really?" I hadn't seen that coming. I mean, I knew the man appreciated the finer things in life, but his tastes never struck me as trendy.

"When I got out of high school and hightailed it out of Houston at eighteen," he explained, "I followed a friend to Dallas in hopes of becomin' either a fashion designer or an interior decorator."

Interior decorator? Fashion designer? Starting fresh in Paris? My brain started whirling.

"But you know," he continued, totally unaware, "it just never worked out back then. I ended up marryin' young, as my parents wanted me to, and settlin' down. Teachin' high school French paid the bills and the summer vacations allowed me to travel . . ."

"Oh yes, your great travels. I remember being so enthralled by those stories! You know, when I first came to Paris I tracked down every single square and bridge you ever told us about."

He laughed. "I'm glad I made such an impression on you, young lady."

I was having trouble reconciling my memory of

Monsieur Jacques with the reality of the man sitting next to me. Could he be . . . ? I pushed aside the thought.

It was already close to three, and Jacques had to get back to work. As he rose from the steps, he brushed the breadcrumbs from his perfectly creased trousers and started fussing with some lint he found on my shawl. We said our goodbyes—American-style, with a hug—but not before he extracted a promise from me to take him to a couturier's salon one day soon. "Sure," I told him. "It would be my pleasure."

"How could I not have known?" I practically yelled into the phone at Jillian. I just had to hear her response; there would be no satisfaction in an inflectionless IM. "How did I not pick up on those clues? Even back in Texas, his nails were always buffed to a shine! He always complimented me on my hair! He—"

"My God, Alex, you sound like you've just discovered that the Pope was Jewish or something," she said, barely stifling a yawn. Jillian could really infuriate me when she refused to play along.

"Humor me, will you?" I pleaded. "I'm having a bad week, remember? This just happens to be the biggest heartthrob for all the girls in my high school. I mean, even the too-cool-for-school girls wanted to be this teacher's pet." I changed course as a thought popped into my head. "Of course, don't we all know that in almost every woman's past there is at least one boyfriend who turned out to be gay—"

"Excuse me?" Jillian said indignantly. "Speak for yourself! I take no responsibility for Steve Hillman."

"I'm not saying we *turn* them gay, for God's sake. And anyway, we all knew Steve Hillman wasn't into you in that way, or into any girls for that matter. And I think you did too. I think you just wanted to see if you could convert him or something."

Jillian gasped. "I did not!"

"But that's beside the point," I said, backing off an apparently sensitive topic. "I'm just saying that my big high school crush could very well be my first gay boyfriend." I giggled. "I always wanted one of those."

"You're priceless, you know that?" Jillian broke down and laughed. "Yes, you *could* use a guy who will shop with you and tell you honestly if you look fat and cry over boys with you . . . I'm kind of jealous of him already."

"Oh, you know I could never replace you," I said truthfully. Lest I became too earnest, I added, "Not entirely, anyway. Maybe only on Friday nights and weekends when you're nesting with that husband of yours. It's just that you're no fun now that you're married and all."

"Bitch."

"Traitor."

"Slut."

"You wish! Then I'd actually have some entertaining stories for you to live vicariously through."

"Oh yeah, I'm definitely adding all your exes to my mailing list. I looked on the Internet and found some even better pictures of your little show yesterday."

"You'd better not."

"Oh yes I will."

"Promise me you won't?"

"What do I get in return?"

I put on my sweetest voice possible and tried to butter her up in the one way I knew was surefire. "I got this great pair of sunglasses in the Chanel goodie bag . . ."

"So you're giving me your sloppy seconds because they bring back such horrid memories?"

Damn, she was good.

"Okay, okay, I'll throw in the new YSL perfume too," I said.

"Deal."

"Deal."

"Gotta run to a meeting now," Jillian said. "You know, one of those things people with real jobs have to do?"

"Ha ha. Oh, right, that's the masseuse knocking at the door now."

I hung up the phone and sprawled myself diagonally across the bed, my feet hanging off the side. Spending the afternoon with Jacques and chatting with Jillian may have taken my mind off things, but the fact of the matter was that my lowest public moment since I let myself get peer-pressured into trying out for the drill team in ninth grade was in the papers, on CNN . . . and even worse, on the *Internet*! Where it would remain in perpetuity for anyone to Google, and then maybe end up on some geek's creepy supermodel-worship website. Blast this broadband world.

Face it, I told myself, absentmindedly dangling my Louboutin slingbacks from my feet. *You are in a serious funk. You're embarrassed to be seen by anyone you knew before yesterday. You've consumed enough saturated fat and white bread in the past eighteen hours to pass for a real Frenchwoman, minus the cigarettes.* And worst of all, I suddenly realized, *you're probably persona non grata at Chanel.* I broke out in a cold sweat. *Would they drop me from their sample-sale guest list?*

There really was only one thing I could do.

I had to shop.

Retail therapy was better than any SSRI I'd ever tried. When my one serious boyfriend in college—the guy I thought I'd marry and live with in a brownstone in Boston's Back Bay with our beagle named Bagel and our 2.5 beautiful, well-behaved children—broke up with me, I marched right out to the nearest mall armed with my mom's credit card, the one she had given me for emergencies. By God, this was an emergency. I found myself at Tiffany, where I somehow sweet-talked the youngest salesman into letting me try on all the canary diamonds in the place, and then thanked him by buying the most expensive thing I had ever owned up until then: a $250 sterling silver Elsa Peretti charm bracelet. I wore it exactly twice. When the boyfriend and I got back together later that semester and then we broke up again two weeks later, I became the proud owner of a new Coach leather backpack: $329. I got over him.

Things escalated pretty quickly after that. My first error as a fact-checker at *The Weekly*—I didn't notice that the name of a Burmese peace activist, U Siligo, had been misspelled as U *Siliho*—led to my very first pair of Manolos. I remembered leaving my cubicle that day, after the managing editor (who apparently knew the poor fellow from their rowing days at Cambridge University) had ripped into the head researcher for what he saw as a glaring error, and she in turn had yelled at me for a good ten minutes that back in her day, one red mark on your file and you were out of there. I couldn't help snickering a little at the unintentional renaming (a rebranding, if you will), but at the same time I was terrified that I would be fired. So naturally my response was to head straight to that jewel box of a boutique, that haven of heels, on West 54th Street and plunk down a fat chunk of my barely five-figure salary on a pair of precious burgundy velvet kitten-heels with big brushed-gold buckles on them. Perhaps I thought my next job after being sacked would involve a much fancier lifestyle than my current one. Those shoes have moved with me from New York City closet to London closet, still resting pristinely in their box. I have, however, been known to take them out of their shoe bags for biannual visits—usually around my birthday and Christmas.

In any case, I got to keep my job, and when I was promoted (much to my surprise and no thanks to U Siligo) six months later to a writer-researcher, I bought my second pair of Manolos, this time in more practical black leather . . . with three-inch heels.

But that hardly counted; merit shopping just never seemed as fulfilling as depression shopping. For one thing, I could find a reason to reward myself just about every day: I wrote a great story. I donated my camel coat to Goodwill in the dead of winter. I found the perfect Christmas present for my mom. All valid reasons for a splurge; none particularly visceral. It was the dark moments of the soul that made the ceremonial rites of browsing and buying more meaningful.

When Jillian got engaged, and I thought I had lost my

better half, my sister in singledom, I went out and put my name on the waiting list at Hermès for a Kelly bag in that most coveted of colors, blue jean. I didn't even ask the price; I just jumped right in. I considered it my way of matching her commitment. Of course, almost three years later, she has the husband and the loft in Tribeca, and I *still* haven't gotten my bag.

With that thought of thwarted desire in mind, I felt like I had to set out on a mission. I hid myself behind the Chanel sunglasses again—Jillian would have to receive them "gently worn"—and headed out the door. Leaving the hotel, I found myself automatically heading toward the rue de Grenelle and the Prada store that beckoned with its calming pale green walls and cushioned off-white carpeting. Somehow I figured it was safer to go to Prada than to a French designer's boutique, as if an Italian design house, out of some nationalistic pride or Euroland rivalry, might have appreciated my disruption of a French fashion show, however innocent and unintentional it may have been.

I realized the flaw of my logic the moment I walked through the door of the boutique. If my very dark sunglasses kept me from actually seeing the stares, I could certainly *feel* them like lasers homing in on me. Maybe I could do what celebrities do when they don't want to get recognized (no, not avoid showering for two days). How many times had I read about stars who, if they were accosted by admirers, would pretend they were not who people thought they were, just really good-looking clones with similar tastes and lifestyles? Very good idea, I decided. I could be just another American tourist. I tossed my hair and tried to ignore my "fans."

I followed my usual strategy at this Prada boutique: I quickly cased the ground floor for the season's signature outfits—the ones I had seen in all the magazine ads and on every third fashion editor at the Milan shows—and then headed upstairs to find something less obvious. At the top of the stairs, one of the four saleswomen in the store immediately approached me. I had never seen her there before. "Hello," she said to me in English, her one word like an embrace, full of meaning and sympathy. "I think I know just what you need."

The Brit—her name was Daphne—led me through the main rooms, past the shoe department crowded with Eurostar shoppers, and into a large salonlike room in the back of the store reserved for VIPs. (Maybe that celebrity behavior really did work!) Daphne sat me down on a sleekly modern—and surprisingly comfortable—leather sofa and looked me in the eye. "I just had an inkling you might want some privacy today," she said discreetly, her smile never waning.

Even in my misery I could appreciate her kindness. And I became determined to reciprocate. "Well, I truly am thankful for your help," I said sweetly. "I would just love to find something special to buy." Note that I didn't say "wear." I just needed to buy.

Daphne took another careful look at me, mentally registering my size, and with a determined expression on her face, hustled around the corner in search of the things that were guaranteed to brighten my day. I was half-reclining on the sofa, fingering the edges of my cashmere stole, when she returned, almost hidden under a pile of skirts and tops in shades of ochre and rust, purple and brown chiffon minidresses, and one incredibly sexy gauzy white halter dress decorated around the neckline and hem with peacock-colored appliqués. "The shoes and handbags are coming," she said, adding with the subtlest wink, "and the lingerie."

She disappeared again and a minute later returned with the rest of the loot. Once the door shut behind her, I surveyed the tiny dresses with the big price tags hanging all around the room. Excellent, I said to myself. Nothing here I could possibly ever wear to the office.

I took my time trying on each article of clothing, admiring myself from every angle in the wall-to-wall mirrors and lighting that I knew had been specially designed to flatter. And yet I found myself thinking how amazing it was what being sick with worry about your viability on the sample-sale circuit—oh, and your reputation and career—can do for your figure. I mean, my legs looked longer, my cleavage fuller, my waist smaller. Like I said, simply amazing. I even snuck in a Katyarina impression, doing a slow exaggerated gallop around the room, cheeks sucked in and chest jutted out. *Not* so flattering. And then I disrobed, putting each piece back on its hanger, even taking care to replace the squares of protective fabric between the skirts and the clips. Next.

It reminded me of those bittersweet days back in New York when I was younger, poorer, and not yet blessed with the designer discount, and I used to go to Bergdorf's with Jillian and a select few other girlfriends who were brave enough to try on every single gown on the serious designer floor—Oscar de la Renta, Carolina Herrera—and buy nothing. This time, I would be brave enough to buy *everything*.

Dear Daphne knocked on the door as I stood in the

white dress, flat brown sandals strapped on my feet and a minuscule crocodile-trimmed pink frame bag hanging from my wrist. I opened the door, grinned, and practically trilled, "I'll take it. All of it."

Several thousand euros later, I walked back into my hotel room weighed down by three white Prada shopping bags, tied up neatly with white logo cotton ribbons at the top. Inside, my delicate little purchases were swathed in layers and layers of white tissue paper. There, there. I felt much better. Roddy *had* told me he'd sign my expense account no matter what, hadn't he? Oh well, all right, maybe I'll pay for the shoes myself.

By eight o'clock, after two hours of unwrapping all my purchases, inspecting each and every seam and button and hem, trying everything on three times, and cutting off all the tags—I would be feeling no buyer's remorse today—I was overcome with a lethargy not unlike the food coma that hits you thirty minutes or so after overeating at Thanksgiving dinner.

At last, I felt sated . . . if not, in fact, bloated.

But I was also feeling a little guilty about putting off work on my story for a whole day, so from my supine position on the bed, my new possessions surrounding me, I turned on the TV and flipped to the fashion channel. I propped my head up on four feather pillows. What a great invention, I thought. If only we had had Fashion TV when I was growing up in Texas, I might have avoided that whole big-hair phase. Make that big-hair *decade*. Then again, not being a blonde in Texas was bad enough for me. I wasn't a cheerleader, or homecoming queen, but I wasn't a geek either. I kept on the fringes, and for the most part they—the "cool kids," the sadists, whatever you wanted to call them—left me alone. Had I dared to break from convention, though, the bowheads would have ripped me to bits. I would have had to find refuge with the stoners and freaks. High school: the world's biggest snake pit. Far worse than the fashion scene, that's for sure.

The fashion channel was broadcasting the Givenchy show live. Held at a warehouse space near a water park just inside the Périphérique, the show was an ode to the 1980s: Michael Jackson's *Thriller* provided the soundtrack, and the models walked down a runway that was made of big black and white tiles that would alternately light up. Just like in the "Billie Jean" video, pre–skin lightening and circa nose number two. The venerable French couture house had just hired a young new designer from London, and he was bringing more than a little edge. Who knew if the house's longtime clients would buy in to the severe Joan Crawford shoulders (not to mention lips), striped cashmere leg warmers, and neon blue fur chubbies, but the press seemed to be lapping it up.

As the extravaganza ended and the room filled with the strains of "Wanna Be Startin' Somethin'," editors and stylists scrambled to praise the designer for the TV cameras. The interviewers, by force of habit, had targeted the most noticeable—which is not to say most prominent—figures in the audience, and so it came as no surprise that the first interview was with the eccentric Welsh stylist Arianna Sidebottom, who had discovered the wunderkind designer. (While her enemies gossiped that just one generation ago, Arianna, née Agnes, and her kin would have pronounced their last name the way it looked, her acolytes insisted that the standard pronunciation had always been "sid-AY-bot-OM"—*always* meaning at least from the moment she became famous.) With my eyes glued to the set—and to her peculiar headwear—I felt around for the remote on the night table and turned up the volume.

Madame Sidebottom was wearing what looked like a gray Davy Crockett hat. Yes, I marveled, there was indeed an entire stuffed raccoon on it. I didn't know what I cared about more: whether the thing smelled or how on earth the PETA activists hadn't caught up with her yet. Arianna had coordinated her headwear with her buffaloskin safari-style suit. Even as I was mesmerized by that *thing* on her head and was intent on deconstructing it, I was distracted by a blur of two people in the background. One was a young woman wearing what looked to be a Zara knockoff of this season's signature Gucci print dress—probably some fashion editor's assistant who was getting a trip to the shows in lieu of a raise, the sort of exploited minion who ended up writing naughty tell-alls. And beside her sat a guy in his early thirties. There was something about him that caught my eye. For one thing, he was really cute, and not in the waxed and self-tanned model-Adonis-pretty-boy way I had seen far too much of in my profession. More important, given his khakis, white button-down shirt, and dark blue baseball cap, he was in all probability straight.

Arianna's two-foot-high hat obstructed my view, but I could see that the pair were in the middle of a heated discussion. I scrambled to sit up in bed. I was dying to find out what was going on. A lovers' spat? A philosophical difference? Had he stepped on her new shoes? Stolen her goodie bag?

Whatever the cause, the disagreement soon developed into a full-scale scuffle. One minute Assistant Girl was leaning out of her seat to knock the baseball cap off Khaki Guy's head—its presence must have been bothering her from the moment she laid eyes on him!—and the next instant her ankles, strapped into three-inch heels, must have given way, because all of a sudden she was falling toward Khaki Guy, arms flailing. And as he grabbed her arms to brace her (or maybe he was just putting his hands up in self-defense), he too went flying out of his seat. Like an avalanche, they moved as one, spinning slowly in tight circles, knocking over chairs, and crashing into the elevated runway. The crowd had thinned, but the two dozen or so people remaining started moving toward the pair—not to help them, of course, just to watch. Soon the Fashion TV cameraman got wind of what was going on and turned his lens away from Arianna, who looked insulted. At that very moment, Khaki Guy managed to release himself from Assistant Girl's mortified death grip, but the force of the action sent him barreling back . . . right at Arianna. As Khaki Guy fell on top of her, her magnificent hat went flying—along with the long black wig it was apparently attached to. And suddenly, everything was a cloud of fake hair and chunks of fur. A couple of French security guards moved lackadaisically toward the scene, pushing people aside. "*Va-t-en, va-t-en!*" And then the camera apparently shut off, and the screen went black.

I just stared. I couldn't believe my eyes. Was Fashion

Week being sponsored by the World Wrestling Federation? But now I understood what all the fuss was about when I did a little thing like, oh, run into that model. Yeah, it was pretty bad. And pretty damn funny.

After a few seconds of dead air, the host of the fashion channel, stationed at the studio in the suburbs, came back on and breathlessly reported what had happened. The latest news was being fed into her earpiece, and she was improvising the rest. This was probably the most excitement she had ever had in her news career, if you could call hosting a fashion channel a news career. I tried hard to focus so I could follow her French. Then I turned on the closed captioning. That helped.

"Ladies and gentlemen, we have breaking news from the Givenchy autumn–winter ready-to-wear show this evening," she said solemnly. "After the presentation of a runway collection that editors deemed 'brilliant' and 'revolutionary', a fight broke out in the audience. We have exclusive footage from an amateur videographer who was in attendance at the show." She paused for an instant in order to switch to her best concerned-schoolmarm facial expression. "Please note that this footage may contain disturbing scenes," she lectured. "Use discretion if children are in the room."

My eyes widened, and I licked my lips.

The screen faded to black and then switched over to the new tape of the fracas, jumpy from the handheld camera and with sound that intermittently cut in and out. If this went on too long, I was going to need some Dramamine.

But what was a little nausea when such drama was being presented? The tape started well before the physical segment of the evening's entertainment, when the two parties were still seated peacefully side by side in the audience. Whoever held the camera must have been sitting in one of the top rows, above the pair, since I could see their backs, and below them, the models stalking down the runway. In any case I would get to hear how the argument started. I leaned in to watch.

Khaki Guy: So who's that crazy-looking woman in that big hat sitting in the front row? And why are all these photographers swarming . . . (*garbled*)

Assistant Girl (*I could tell she was rolling her eyes, even from the back*): Hello! Don't you know anything? That's Arianna Sidebottom. She's *very* important.

Damn, I thought. They're both Americans. I'm so embarrassed.

Khaki Guy: What, did she find the cure for cancer or something?

Assistant Girl (*more eye rolling*): She's discovered many important designers, like . . . (*garbled*)

Khaki Guy (*talking right over her*): Now Jonas Salk is very important. He developed the vaccine for . . . (*garbled*)

Assistant Girl (*fuming now*): You're at a *fashion show*. Get your head out . . . (*garbled*)

The show had ended and Khaki Guy and Assistant Girl remained seated, completely immersed, while the rest of the audience was on its feet. The loud applause filled the video camera's microphones, muffling the rest of the pair's debate, but it was clear from the images that the arguing had escalated. Assistant Girl continued to clap, even while turned away from the runway and yelling at him, with her forehead at a dangerous proximity to his. The editors and hangers-on had left their seats and were pushing their way through the crowds to get backstage. A woman in a yellow fur coat walked right in front of the camera, obscuring the view. She passed out of camera range, and still Khaki Guy and Assistant Girl were going at it. Enter the interviewer with Arianna, pontificating on the show: "That was simply brilliant. I've never seen anything like it. He's just gone from strength to strength . . ."

The rest of the tape, which for some reason had shifted to slow motion, resembled a *Saturday Night Live* spoof of a community-access-TV show: Assistant Girl, with a haughty look on her face, made the move toward Khaki Guy's cap. And then the dominoes of motion: First the guy and the girl were locked in their sumo-wrestling hold, and then he was floating down onto Arianna. In slo-mo, it looked almost elegant, as if they were getting ready to do some *Crouching Tiger, Hidden Dragon* moves. That image quickly evaporated, because then there went the hat, and the wig along with it, sailing across the runway like Rocky the Flying Squirrel. Arianna, shell-shocked and follicularly naked, stood paralyzed. Or maybe the tape had simply stopped on that shot for just a beat too long. It was a portrait in absurdity, and then it faded to black.

The studio host materialized again. "The young woman in the tape has disappeared," she said with a barely disguised smirk, "but after this short break, we'll have a live interview with the mystery man in the middle of this scandal. Stay tuned."

A commercial for Viagra featuring an A-list Hollywood star that would never in a million years appear on American TV came on the screen.

I turned down the volume and slumped back onto the pillows. Wow.

Exactly two thoughts ran through my mind. One, were there similar amateur tapes in existence of my collision with Katyarina? And two, could it be that the fashion pack had found a new laughingstock?

That's the great thing about this business: Intentionally or not, everyone was always showing up everyone else.

Oh yeah, I sighed, I was back in fashion.

Chapter Three

FREED FROM MY SELF-IMPOSED EXILE by something akin to a deus ex machina (as I might have described it in an article in *The Weekly*), I popped open my laptop and checked my calendar. Givenchy had been the last official show of the day. But I had overheard a couple of girls I recognized as freelance stylists for *Paint** saying on the Eurostar to Paris that off the official schedule and after hours, an unknown Peruvian-Swiss designer, Luis-Heinz Bühler, was launching his collection guerrilla-style at a hot new nightclub in Pigalle. While I had my doubts about an endorsement from that hipper-than-thou glossy—let's just say the tastes of its readers and *The Weekly*'s did not overlap—my only other choice was to stay in my hotel room and play with my new clothes. Tempting, yes, but I wasn't going to find a story that way.

Besides, I had been meaning to check out the new hotspot, even if it meant going to a dodgy neighborhood known for prostitution and drugs. It was, after all, my job to keep au courant. The two-story space had been a bordello until the late nineties, when the madam-cum-proprietor ran off to join the Moonies. After several years of legal squabbles between her two daughters, the place was sold to a pair of brothers who were said to be related to the last pretender to Napoleon's throne, and who had made a tabloid career of dating models. They came in, gutted the place, and replaced the peeling red flocked wallpaper and dirty shag carpeting . . . with brand-spanking-*new* red flocked wallpaper and shag carpeting. The dimly lit upstairs rooms were equipped with oversize canopy beds and overhead swings, and the cocktail waitresses were outfitted in bondagewear by Alexander McQueen. The brothers named the club, with an overabundance of irony, Bon Chic Bon Genre. Their biggest coup so far was getting a fashion spread shot there for the pages of *Hello!*

I couldn't imagine a better place to test the waters for my comeback. For one thing, it would be dark. And more important, the chic sharks would likely be dead drunk.

I kept the TV on in the background as I got ready to go out. The night of the Chanel hell, as I had come to call it, between the gluttony and the self-pity but before the sleeping pills kicked in, I had picked up all of my clothes off the floor and neatly organized them by day in the closet. Each day's pieces were labeled on their individual hangers and divided from the next day or evening by two empty hangers. The coordinating shoes sat on the floor just below, and the spreadsheet was taped to the closet door. That had instantly made me feel a little better.

Now I made a beeline for the Wednesday-night hanger. I pulled off my jeans and zipped myself into my designated outfit, a vintage black Azzedine Alaïa wool-and-spandex tube dress that had just about enough give to let me draw breath. I suddenly felt greater respect for women who lived through the Girdled Age. At least for me it was only for a few hours, I thought.

One glance at the footwear, though, and I was compelled to check my wardrobe schedule again. Was I on crack when I put this outfit together? I shook my head disapprovingly but nevertheless dutifully put on my gold gladiator sandals, the ones with the laces that formed a double helix around my calves all the way up to my knees. Sadly, my hotel room didn't offer the same flattering lighting as the Prada store. Hmm. I wasn't liking the sausage effect. I attempted to bend over, which caused a sound alarmingly like a rip. Then I tried to walk gracefully in the three-and-a-half-inch heels, but the dress's amorous clinch on my thighs limited each step to a mere shuffle. Just couldn't be done. I felt like Mira Sorvino in *Mighty Aphrodite*. If I could have managed to get enough air in my lungs to speak, I probably would have had the same Betty Boop voice too. The discomfort factor was bad enough . . . and then I considered the fact that even though the club was only *trying* to look like a bordello, it *was* still in Pigalle, where real ladies of the night could still be found plying their trade in the seedy narrow streets below Montmartre, in the shadow of the cathedral of Sacré Coeur. *Sacré bleu!*

Off came the Alaïa.

So much for the advance planning, I thought. Truth be told, it may have been my subconscious desire to force myself into "emergency" shopping that had led to such wardrobe-planning malfunctions. I wouldn't put it past me at all. And so—as much as it pained me to think that the purchases I had made today were anything more than frivolous—I plucked the white dress off my bed and slipped it on. That's more like it, I thought, taking three long, deep yoga breaths. How's *that* for a fashion statement: I've declared my independence from the little black dress. But I kept on the killer sandals; I hadn't forgotten what happened the last time I went looking for replacement shoes. Plus, I was already planning to carry my new pink bag, and I would *never* want to dress head-to-toe in any one designer—not even my beloved Prada.

Now, what to do about my hair? I looked at myself in the mirror and sighed. Long, straight, thick, and darker than my worst moods. When I was young, my mother's ever so proper hairdresser at the downtown Neiman's never knew what to do with my mane, and when I succumbed to the cult of big hair, she grudgingly gave me spiral perms every three months (or as soon as the fallout and frizzies became manageable again). Over the years since then, I continued to have more than my fair share of bad hair days, from the attempt at a shag that looked more like a pineapple (the first time I ever cried at a hair salon—and not the last, I should add) to the simple bob with bangs (too Anna Wintour, even without the dark sunglasses). Even Oribe and Frédéric Fekkai could do only so much; their sleek stylings would disappear in a heavy tangle the minute I got in the shower the next day. In fact, a few months ago, I ran into Frédéric in New York the day after he cut my hair and the expression on his face was so full of disappointment that I've barely been able to look him in the eye since. So until Roddy decided to give me a daily blowout budget to go with the clothing allowance, I was on my own.

While pondering my options—some of my best story ideas came to me in front of the mirror—I found myself thinking about wigs. Women with perfectly acceptable hair once wore wigs all the time. There used to be wig stores in the mall—at least where I grew up—and wig departments in the major stores. I wondered why the fashion had died out. Maybe that's the story I could write for Roddy. It would be totally off the beaten path. The headline could be "Why Wig Out?" I'd bet money that no one else would be doing it. Of course, there was probably a good reason for that. Either it was a brilliant idea or *I* was seriously wigging out. I ran my boar-bristle Mason Pearson brush through my hair a few times, then decided to just clip it up in a messy twist. Nope, no wigs for me. And no story either. Damn.

As I sat (ahh, to be able to bend at the waist and sit!) on the bed and adjusted the laces around my legs, I glanced at the TV screen. The commentators were still jabbering on about the big bust-up at Givenchy. I had apparently missed the live interview with Khaki Guy, but the clip from the amateur video was being repeated over and over again. I reached for the remote and clicked off the TV, then scribbled a note on a Post-it and stuck it on the TV screen: WATCH FOR RERUNS OF KHAKI GUY AT GIVENCHY. Surely he would be on again—maybe even on CNN, considering how much interest they had shown in *my* story.

I picked up off the nightstand the bottle of perfume that had been custom-blended for me at Creed. Almost empty. I'd have to remember to get a refill this week. I spritzed myself behind the ears, on the wrists, and behind the knees—hey, you never know!—and grabbed my black leather YSL trench coat from the closet. I looked at it skeptically, hung it back up, and quickly assessed my other options. Let's see: the short fitted brown suede jacket by Michael Kors? Nope. The double-breasted charcoal-gray wool Prada schoolgirl coat? Uh, definitely not. My bloody wardrobe chart was so specific that there really was no interchanging to be had. So the leather trench it was. I really *must* have been on crack: Combined with the gladiator sandals it screamed "dominatrix," and had I worn the Alaïa . . . Well, I decided, at least I wouldn't belt the coat. I draped it over my shoulders and stalked out.

It wasn't hard to get a taxi.

When I told the driver the address, I could see him grinning in the rearview mirror. Worse, he didn't ask me if I was a model. I could only imagine what he thought I was. And this was with the coat *un*belted!

As we sped northward through the city in blessed silence, I mentally went over different scenarios of how I could make my entrance, and how I could act toward those lovely people who had so *kindly* sent me condolence flowers and then—my imagination darkened—turned around and piled on increasingly absurd, made-up details (Her underwear was ripped! She would do *anything* to get on TV!) with every retelling of the story to every Tom, Dick, and Harry they could phone, fax, e-mail, or IM. Not that it wasn't absurd enough to begin with.

Scenario One: I walk right up to the entrance, cutting off a coven of Condé Nasties. The bouncers wave me in. The crowd parts like the Red Sea. I smile beatifically, magnanimously. Karl Lagerfeld emerges from the darkness and welcomes me back into the fold. All is forgotten . . .

Scenario Two: I get lost in the crowd and stand outside for fifteen minutes before I get herded in with the rest of the hoi polloi. I hear whispers, see the gossipers out of the corner of my eye. I ignore them. I head straight to the bar . . .

Scenario Three: I get my left big toe stuck in the laces of my right sandal and trip on my way to the front door . . .

If I wasn't nervous before, I was terrified now, my imagination entering Stephen King territory. (Think *Carrie.*) Good thing I was too paralyzed by the thoughts racing through my mind to even consider telling the driver to turn around immediately.

In any case, we had already begun inching through the cramped streets of Pigalle. From two blocks away, I saw a crowd milling at the corner of the alley leading to the club. I could easily spot the tourists who had come out of the show at the Moulin Rouge nearby—a few hundred euros poorer and still looking for something truly scandalous to write home about—and descended upon this curiosity. But had I not recognized the faces of some of my colleagues, I would have been just as stumped as the sightseers were as to who was there for the party and who was there to *work* the party.

As I got out of the taxi across the street from the club, I saw the fashion editor of a teen magazine, looking like something right out of *Pretty Woman*, standing on the sidewalk talking on her cell phone—and getting yelled at by someone who clearly *wasn't* an editor, but who *was* wearing an almost identical outfit, right down to the swath of red fishnet that peeked out between the bottom of her micro-miniskirt and the top of her thigh-high patent leather boots. Apparently the second woman was feeling territorial.

I didn't know if I should laugh or . . . well, laugh.

"Alex? Alex! *Alex!*"

As if by reflex I ducked and wrapped my coat around my shoulders a little more tightly, looking shiftily from side to side. I wasn't ready to face my audience just yet. I almost jumped when I felt a hand on my shoulder and heavy breathing on my neck.

"Alex! I've been calling your name from two blocks away!"

I whipped around and saw the smiling face of my one and only favorite publicist, Lola Eisenberg, a 5'9" blonde with Cameron Diaz's legs and Angelina Jolie's cheekbones. If I didn't know her, I would, I'm quite sure, hate her. "Oh my God, Lola, you scared me half to death."

"Feeling a little jumpy? Did you think it was the Latvian mob coming to break your knees?" She started chuckling as I tried my best to give her the evil eye.

For journalists on the fashion and celebrity beats, publicists held the keys to the kingdom. And in my experience, there were two types of gatekeepers: the ones who were never available when you needed something out of them, and the ones who were always pestering you with things you didn't want from them. Come to think of it, those were just two sides of the same coin.

Lola, on the other hand, had won me over the moment I met her. I had just started covering fashion for *The Weekly*, and I was making my rounds in Paris for the first time. Most of the publicists at the major fashion houses had responded to my request for a meeting with a puzzled "*The Weekly* . . . Isn't that a *news* magazine?" But Lola, an American raised in Paris who was working for Dior part-time while she studied art history at the Sorbonne, not only invited me to lunch but also filled me in on all the dirt—on her fellow flacks. I returned the favor as I got to know more of the fashion editors. We savored the thought that our relationship was practically subversive.

"You missed an *amazing* show this evening," she said, her eyes wide.

"I know! I would've given all my Manolos to have been there," I said. Okay, maybe three pairs—but that's hardly an insignificant gesture. "But I saw it on TV. Why else do you think I decided to make my comeback?"

"Oh, but of course. Babe, you're yesterday's news."

"Thank goodness for that!"

"By the way, I love the outfit. Is that Prada?"

We crossed the street and made our way past the tourists. As we neared the club, though, my head started spinning, my pulse racing, my breath feeling constricted. I thought I was having a panic attack. "Puh . . . puh . . . paper . . . paper bag," I gasped.

"Don't be silly," Lola replied obliviously, her eyes focused straight ahead as she turned on her camera-ready smile and continued toward the velvet-draped entrance. "There's really no need to hide your face anymore."

When I wasn't freaking out about not breathing properly, I did appreciate Lola's endearing flakiness. Really, I did.

Deep, calm yoga breaths. Breathe, Alex. Breathe. Pfffft.

I grabbed Lola's arm for support, and she put her hand on my back and gently pushed me across the threshold. It took a minute for my eyes to adjust to the darkness inside the club. It took a little less time for the TV crews and photographers to spot me.

"Alex! Alex!"

Before I knew what was happening, the cameramen had hustled Lola out of the way and had surrounded me. A microphone was thrust in front of my face. I instinctively put both hands up, pushing away the mike while covering my face at the same time—just as I had seen celebrity defendants do on courthouse steps. Whatever happened to being yesterday's news?

"Alex," said a British voice from behind the camera and lights, "what do you make of the shocking events at the Givenchy show this evening?"

"Would you have broken it up?" another disembodied voice chimed in.

"In your experience, is it more dangerous to sit in the front row?"

Another microphone. More hot lights. Flashes. I was starting to sweat. "Alex, do you zeenk zee américains, euh, must be *banned* from zee Fashion Week?"

I was speechless. I had gone from Scandal of the Week to Expert Commentator in one short day. I mean, I knew that was the common trajectory—hell, even Monica Lewinsky had gotten a gig hosting a dating show—but I had never seen it happen quite this quickly.

"She has no comment," Lola said briskly as she pushed her way back to me. "I said, no comment!" When Lola took charge like that, people listened. The mob dissipated, but not without a couple of lingering final snaps.

"I cannot believe what just hit me," I said, still stunned.

"That's what happens when you have twenty-four-hour fashion channels. That's a hell of a lot of airtime to fill," she said matter-of-factly before quickly changing the subject. "So how would you like your scotch: a double, straight up?" She summoned a waitress, who returned a minute later with our drinks. Lola's was a blood-red concoction in what looked like a double-cupped margarita glass. "It's the club's signature drink," she explained, responding to my puzzled stare. "The Double-D. Get it?" She made a lascivious gesture indicating voluptuous breasts.

"Lovely," I replied, adding with a mischievous grin, "Bottoms up."

I gulped my scotch. I could feel its warmth moving down my throat and into my stomach—which, I realized with a bit of concern, hadn't been fed since the bread-and-wine lunch with Jacques. I'd better pace myself, I thought.

"So what are you doing here tonight? Shouldn't you be getting ready for the Dior show Friday?" I was practically screaming so Lola could hear me over the thumping techno mix of the eighties hit "Obsession" that the DJ had just put on, neatly segueing from Madonna's "Justify My Love." This club was obviously adhering to a strict theme.

"That's under control," she yelled back. "I'm here doing some pro bono work."

"What?" In the din, I had resorted to trying to read her lips. "Did you say Bono's going to be here?" I perked up.

"I said, PRO BONO!"

"Ohhhh," I said, a bit dejected. "Pro bono? As in lawyers and doctors and people who have real jobs that actually help real people?"

"This *is* as real as my work gets," she said, rolling her eyes. "I'm helping this new designer. Luis-Heinz Bühler. I've been trying to call you to tell you about him ever since you got here, but you came, you tripped, you went into hiding. I swear to you, he's going to be the next big thing. Trust me on this."

"So *you're* the one behind this mystery show," I said, scoping out the packed club. "I heard about it through the fashion grapevine—that is, while passing through the smoking car on the Eurostar over."

"Then I've done my job," she said, happily noting the presence of not one but both of the socialite Sheraton sisters. "But it's not just *any* show. This is going to be *the* show of the season, even if no catfight or catastrophe breaks out. And you'll love the big surprise I've got lined up. And you'll love the clothes. This guy's simply amazing. He made this—you like?"

I had been so flustered before that I hadn't noticed what she was wearing—a shocking oversight that would never have befallen me under normal circumstances. She took a step back so I could get the head-to-toe view. She was right. It *was* amazing: Her low-cut halter dress seemed to be made of tiny strips of the finest amber-colored suede knitted on the bias that clearly cantilevered her breasts and thighs to curvaceous perfection. And yet the end result looked like gossamer and gently undulated with even the most imperceptible movement.

"I'm not wearing anything underneath, either."

"Uh, too much information," I joked, then stepped toward her for closer inspection. I touched the fabric: soft as a baby's bottom. I felt a little light-headed. Making a fashion discovery was, without a doubt, as mind-alteringly exciting as falling in love. It could be just as costly and just as heartbreaking, too, but who ever thought of that in the first throes of passion? I remembered my introduction to the young British designer

Matthew Williamson. Yes, I remembered it well. I was on vacation in London with Jillian, years before I moved there, and we were lost somewhere in Notting Hill in the middle of the day. We came across a crowd of people outside what looked like a recreation center, so we wandered in and stood with everyone else, waiting, anticipating . . . and then Kate and Naomi and Helena floated out in neon pinks and oranges and blues, flirty little outfits embroidered with whimsical little butterflies. I was a goner. He was my first, and in a perfect convergence of the moon and the stars, it was his debut show. We were, it seemed, made for each other. I searched high and low for him, returning to London the next year just to gaze longingly at his cheerful cashmere sweater at Brown's, and then back in New York, trawling eBay to find his other lovers. Of course, once his clothes showed up at Barneys, my ardor cooled considerably. I had moved on to Alber Elbaz. That's the fickleness of love for you.

"This is so unbelievable," I finally managed to say to her, my voice lowered as if to keep it our little secret. "You're going to order me one of these dresses tomorrow morning. No, tonight. No, now. You must. I don't even care if we're twins."

"You'll be at the top of my list."

"No, seriously. When do I get to meet this man, this . . . this revolutionary? I want an exclusive."

Lola's face instantly tensed up, as if she'd just gotten a double injection of Botox. "Wellll . . . that's sort of a problem."

"What? Is *Women's Wear* on to this story? Have you totally done me wrong and given it to them first?" I looked her straight in the eye, offering my best pathetic, desperate look. Sadly, it was pretty darn good from practice. "You wouldn't . . . did you?"

"It's not even that. I only wish it were that. I mean, I don't wish that I had screwed you—" She looked terribly earnest.

"Then why on earth can't I meet him?"

She grimaced. "Let's just say he's a bit shy," she blurted out. No wonder she's upset, I thought. That must be a publicist's worst nightmare: a shy client. Being Garboesque was really only viable once you'd become famous. Being unwilling or unable to self-promote from the get-go amounted to hari-kari. Or at least would drive your publicist to murder you and then commit hari-kari.

"Um, okay," I said, trying to be sympathetic—but persistent. "Come on, Lola, I swear I'll be gentle!"

"Okay, so *shy* isn't the right word. You don't understand, Alex, he's like a hermit. A real recluse. No, make that a freak. I can't even phone him. It's like cloak-and-dagger stuff. If I want to see him I have to trek to this Peruvian café all the way out in the scary twentieth—can you imagine *me* there?—give the bartender a secret password, and then I end up downing, like, three cocktails while I wait for him to give the OK, and *then* someone comes and 'delivers' me to him. Don't even get me started on the blindfolds." She shuddered at the memory. "I shit you not," she continued. "It's nuts. I think he's just spent too much time in the mountains—I mean, he *is* Peruvian-Swiss. All that oxygen deprivation can't be good for you. I know from experience! You haven't forgotten when I went to Nepal last year—my God, I was loopy. Remember when I called you on my cell phone and it was the middle of the night where you were and I started chanting . . ."

I had been nodding along throughout her rant, but I couldn't get my head around anything she was saying. All I understood was that I was becoming more and more intrigued by this character. The weirdness only made him more attractive—a better story. It was kind of how a lot of women felt about certain men. Despite Lola's frustration, I figured she felt the same way too.

I just had to meet him. *He* was going to be my big redeeming story. If only I could make Lola get a grip.

"Lola . . . Hello? Lola!" I gently shook her shoulders. I could practically see the smoke coming out of her ears. She stopped midstream and looked at me blankly. "Lola, I really, really, *really* want this story," I said. "And after that, uh, incident at Chanel, I really, really, really *need* it."

"You know I'd like to help you, Alex," she said, looking contrite. "I'll send up the flares for him or whatever, but I just can't make any promises . . ."

"Just lead me to the mountain," I said, "and I'll take it from there."

She shrugged. "I'll see what I can do."

I furrowed my brow, but stopped midfrown when my mother's voice popped into my head—and then I furiously started to rub down whatever seedlings of wrinkles might have just been planted. "How in God's name did the two of you find each other in the first place?" I asked Lola.

"Well, he does have *some* friends. Or at least one that I know—a visiting scholar at the Sorbonne, Bartolome De Betanzos. He and Luis-Heinz are from the same town in Peru, miles and miles from Lima, and they ran into each other here. Anyhow, I took a class from Bartolome last fall called 'Peruvian Iconography: From the Incan Medicine Wheel to Inka Kola.' Fascinating, truly. I'll have to tell you all about it sometime. So we started talking about Andean textiles one day after class and he mentioned he had a friend who was doing some incredible experimental stuff. And you know me—I was all over that."

"And he agreed to meet you?"

"It took three months! Bartolome really wanted Luis-Heinz to get the attention he deserved, so he asked me to help. But honestly, after seeing and feeling and wearing one of his dresses, I may have been more than a wee bit tempted to keep him all to myself." She paused, a Cheshire-cat grin slowly materializing on her face. "But then I decided I wanted to be . . . *important*. I wanted to be the next Arianna Sidebottom."

I laughed so hard I almost choked on what was left of my drink.

"Shit, what time is it?" Lola asked, looking at her bare wrist.

I checked my watch. "Almost midnight."

"Oh my God, the 'entertainment' is supposed to start in half an hour. I'd better go find the girls and make sure they're all set."

"So what's this big surprise you're promising?"

"Can't tell you. You'll just have to wait and see. But I think you'll enjoy it." She winked at me and disappeared into the crowd.

It was time for a refill. I wasn't even going to touch the dodgy-looking hors d'oeuvres that were laid out on the mostly naked, completely waxed bodies of muscle-bound men lying on top of some tables. Now *that* was taking the sex theme too far.

I walked over to the bar on the left side of the room, where I figured I'd have the best view of the show. I leaned back and propped my left elbow against the bar, my fresh drink in my right hand. What was the effect I was going for? Insouciant? Yes, I suppose . . . but mostly I was trying to take the weight off the balls of my feet, which were really killing me. Funny how it requires a bit of a masochistic streak to pull off the dominatrix look.

I was startled out of my reverie by the sudden mad exodus of camera crews and paparazzi from their girls-gone-wild watch at the back of the club, where some newer models were apparently dancing on the tables and stripping off what little clothing they had on in the first place. Getting up on my tiptoes—no small feat considering my footwear—I looked to the left and looked to the right but saw little more than a mop of dark, wavy hair peeking out from within a circle of lights and cameras. They slowly moved as one, buzzing around that one piece of flash-bait like bees vying to pollinate the only sunflower left in a freshly mowed field.

Was it some young Hollywood type hoping to score a model? Or maybe a member of his posse?

With each wobbly movement of the swarm as it made its way deeper into the club, I could see a new flash of the face in the middle—a dimpled left cheek here, a dark brow there. In one freeze-frame, as the flashes illuminated his face, my eyes caught his: sparkling and hazel, almost gray. Intense. And just as quickly, our gazes shifted away from each other. Familiar somehow, and yet . . .

If someone could have peered inside my brain at that moment, it would have looked like a scene from one of those police shows: a computer shuffling through mug shots, one in profile set next to a full-on shot, to identify a perp caught on a grainy surveillance tape. And then the stream of pictures screeched to a halt.

Match found: Khaki Guy.

But it seemed as if the computer in my brain had used up all its memory picking out a face, because I didn't think fast enough to duck, or avert my gaze, or at least make a run for the ladies' room.

In that moment that our eyes had met, some enterprising paparazzo's brain was also whirling away, putting two and two together and getting an easy five-figures.

The swarm swayed and made a sudden left toward me.

"Alex! Alex! Just one picture together!"

"Regardez-moi!"

"Let's see the disruptive duo together."

I could feel the energy rising within the pack, titillated by the thought of the money shot of the night. I spun around and leaned over the bar, pretending to be deep in conversation with the bartender, who was in fact some fifteen feet away and pouring someone else a drink. It was all I could think of doing. I shut my eyes—as if I believed, using the logic of a three-year-old, that if I couldn't see them they couldn't see me—and tried thinking positive thoughts as I waited for the inevitable.

I felt a discreet tap on my right shoulder.

Bloody hell, I said under my breath. The thought crossed my mind that I could just ignore it. But I realized that I was pretty much cornered. I couldn't make a run for it now . . . certainly not in these shoes. I took a deep inhale and an even deeper exhale and turned around, my right hand shading my eyes from the glare of the cameras, which immediately started to go off.

I squinted at the broad-shouldered figure in front of

me, and when I realized who it was, I couldn't help it. I tilted my head to one side and attempted a dazzling smile. I suspected it was more like a lopsided grin. I quickly lowered my hand. If my hair hadn't been pinned up, I might have even twirled it with my fingers.

"Hi," I said, feverishly thinking of what I should say and what I shouldn't do. Be cool. Do not make stupid attempts at looking alluring. Too late. I had unconsciously bitten my lower lip.

"Hi," he said, looking me straight in the eye. "You know, if we give them the shot they want, they might just leave us alone the rest of the night." He raised his eyebrows as if to say, "Well, how about it?"

It certainly sounded like a sensible plan. Didn't celebrities do that all the time? New moms offering the five-minute photo op outside the hospital after giving birth, so they wouldn't be stalked for weeks? Things must be so completely off-kilter, I thought, if I'm patterning my behavior after celebrities' for the third time in one day. I should wear a WWJD bracelet: What Would Julia Do?

I leaned in. "You close the deal," I whispered to him, a bit surprised by my flirtatious turn of phrase. I usually saved my best for the written word; I wasn't so good at verbalizing my inner wit.

Khaki Guy turned to the wolf pack that had been pushing him closer and closer to me by the second. My stomach did a little somersault.

"Okay, everyone, we'll pose for one shot. One shot, understand? Sixty seconds and then you'll leave the young lady alone. Got it?"

The snapping had started well before he finished making his chivalrous speech. I squirmed at first, but slowly I broke out into the tiniest grin. One minute and dozens of rolls of film later, the pack moved on to their next quarry.

"That wasn't so bad, was it?" His voice was deep and friendly, with a neutral mid-Atlantic accent of unidentifiable origin. He smiled at me and took a step backward. I appreciated his respect for personal space. "I'm Nick Snow," he said.

"Hi . . . and thanks, Nick." I stuck out my hand, firmly, formally . . . stupidly. He obviously wasn't expecting it, but he took it and held it for a split second longer than I was used to. "So you're the one everybody's been talking about tonight. I'm Alex Simons. The one everyone was talking about *last* night."

He chuckled. "Very true. And maybe we'll be the couple everyone will be talking about tomorrow." I must have blushed, or maybe just stared at him in confusion, because he quickly added, "I mean, because of the pictures of us that will be in the papers."

"Oh, right, of course," I said, trying to laugh it off. At least I wasn't upspeaking, I reassured myself. "So what are you doing here? Are you a glutton for punishment or what? Not to be presumptuous, but your tiff *was* broadcast on TV all evening, at several different angles too. You sounded pretty contemptuous of the whole fashion scene." Dumb, dumb thing to say. I looked into the distance, searching for an imaginary friend I hoped I could pretend to wave at and thereby provide my escape route. But then I noticed that half the women in the club were checking Nick out, and the other half, the fashionista half, were giving him dirty looks—that is, while they weren't busy checking him out too.

I turned my gaze back on him and discreetly reviewed

what they were all admiring: the unruly dark hair; the deep-set eyes framed by long, languid lashes; the full but not feminine lips; the dimple in the left cheek. He was no longer wearing khakis, but dark blue jeans that hugged his muscular legs, and a crisp white shirt opened at the collar to show just a trace of chest hair. He was about six feet tall. In other words, Khaki Guy—could I still call him that, now that we were on a first-name basis and he wasn't wearing khakis?—was *hot.*

"Curious more than contemptuous," he was saying when I managed to get my mind back on our conversation. "I swear I was taken out of context! Or am I not supposed to say that to a journalist?"

I gave him a playful shove, which gave me the opportunity—however brief—to feel the muscles of his shoulder and upper arm. My God, what had gotten into me? I suddenly registered how much this perma-grin was making my cheeks hurt. "So really, what are you doing here?" I said, dialing down the smile. "And what were you doing at the show in the first place?"

"One of the girls I live with knows an assistant-to-the-assistant-of-the-head-assistant or something at Givenchy, so she got me into the show," he said. "Yeah, she's *reeaaallly* happy with me right now."

One of the girls he lives with? Who was this guy, Hugh Hefner?

"Anyhow, I went to the show just for a laugh. I'd never been to one before. I'm a consultant, on a project here for six months. I work with a bunch of stuffed shirts every day. So like I said, I was curious. I'm always up for a new experience. And then I ask a simple question and . . ."

Nick's words suddenly trailed off. Only then did I feel a rather tall presence hovering nearby. I stole a quick glance to my right. Another woman. She said nothing and still she interjected herself into the conversation, simply by gazing intently at Nick and nodding along to his story. I tried to hold it to a two-party dialogue, but kept feeling compelled to turn and get a better glimpse of whoever it was looming. Out of politeness—I think—Nick paused and tilted his head at her. "Hello?" he said, raising his eyebrows. "I'm Nick. This is Alex."

She took a step forward, easing herself in between Nick and me. She was a leggy redhead—she towered over me, even with my skyscraper stilettos—and she sported gobs of makeup, teased hair, a minuscule white tube top, and a red leather skirt that in truth was more like a glorified belt. Model, I thought. Must be new this season. She continued to stare at Nick, but it was with her "I mean business" runway look—the kind that usually accompanied an angry, stomping gait—rather than with bedroom eyes. Or maybe it was just that the clumped mascara made it hard to tell the difference. Not that I was being catty and judgmental or anything. "I'm Ruthie," she said in her two-pack-a-day growl. "I saw you on TV."

"Yeah, I guess a lot of people did," he said, trying to laugh it off.

"So what do you do?" was her follow-up. Boy, she went straight for the kill.

Nick smiled and shot me a conspiratorial look.

"Well, I've just started a new activist group," he said. "People for the Ethical Treatment of Models."

I closed my eyes and put my hands to my temples in

an unsuccessful attempt at hiding a snicker. But Ruthie didn't notice, or care. She just blinked a few times. "That's so great," she said, finally. "I'm totally into the ethnical thing. I wore an African headdress for this magazine shoot once."

Nick was biting his cheek, trying hard not to laugh. I had given up on trying. "Right. Well, it was nice to meet you, Ruthie," he said, looking earnestly at her. "See you later?"

Pouting, Ruthie did a robotic end-of-the-runway spin, gave me a final once-over, and huffed off.

"You bad, bad boy," I said to Nick between fits of giggles.

"Seriously," he deadpanned. "I saw today how frighteningly thin those models are. I thought some of them might snap in two if they were ever caught in front of a wind machine set too high. And then where would the workers' comp be? We could do fundraiser concerts. Or a benefit performance of *Hairspray*. We would come up with the money to feed those poor models. And then we could break them out of the evil captivity of people like Arianna Widebottom or whatever her name is, and return them to the wild."

"Is this a big exclusive you're giving me?"

"Yeah, definitely. Now I trust you to spread the word, give the cause some much-needed publicity."

During the entire time we were talking, he kept looking straight at me and me alone. No glancing around the club for something more interesting. No craning his neck at the slightest paparazzi activity. I wasn't used to such undivided attention in this setting. In fact, it made me kind of nervous. Running in fashion circles, I had become accustomed to short attention spans. But the real reason *I* couldn't maintain eye contact with *him* was that I thought I might drown in those eyes of his. *Did I just think that?* Where were these Harlequin Romance thoughts coming from?

Thankfully for me and my dignity, the lights suddenly dimmed. "I think the show's about to start," I said. "A guerrilla fashion show for this new Peruvian-Swiss designer."

"Is there a Shining Path joke to be made here, or would that be inappropriate?" Nick said, sidling up next to me against the bar.

The crowd hushed as the thumping, raunchy sounds of the Christina Aguilera hit "Dirrty" gave way to the strains of some instrumental music—the kind of mesmerizing reeds-and-drums melodies I had often heard performed by Native American groups in the subways of New York City. Then, as a suspicious-smelling smoke started wafting through the room, the models began to emerge from the shadows all over the club. Some even came down from the ceiling, suspended by ropes. One by one, they slinked around the room in variations of Lola's exquisitely sexy dress—all made of knitted suede that lifted like a Wonderbra and floated like fairy wings, in blood-red, St.-Tropez tan, the gray of a London sky and the blue of the church domes sprinkled throughout the Greek Islands. The models glided through the room, gyrating right up to editors and revelers alike, as if in some sort of trance.

Which is how you could describe the audience, too.

"The designer—" I whispered to Nick as I tried to see over the heads of the two stylists standing in front of me. Seeing my struggle, he without a word leaned over and gave me a boost up to sit on the bar. "Thanks," I said, too dazzled by the clothes to be alarmed by the body contact. "I was going to say, his clothes are absolutely revolutionary. I mean it. Not like the fatuous 'brilliant' designation everyone gives in response to, oh, anyone who's ever stitched a seam. *This* is just, just . . ." I sighed as I stared longingly at the dresses, the dresses, the dresses. I couldn't even verbalize it anymore. I wanted one. I needed one. I wanted and needed a dozen.

And just as I was about to drift off into a sartorial reverie, Lola's surprise snapped me back to reality. Without warning the music stopped, and a hazy light from above the crowd led our eyes through the smoke and to the middle of the ceiling, where a cage, covered by purple velvet, now dangled, just out of sight. Slowly, so slowly, it began to descend. I couldn't tear my eyes away, not even to glance at Nick.

The cage hovered maybe three feet above the hushed crowd for a good five minutes before the velvet covering dropped, the sound system started thumping again, and the figure inside the cage began writhing to the music. We all must have realized what we were seeing at the same time, because in five seconds flat, the gasps and exclamations moved as one, rising in a wave above the din of the music.

"It's her! I can't believe it's her!"

"Renata! Renata!" Her name became a chant.

Before there was Cindy, Naomi, or Linda, there was Renata. And before Renata, nothing mattered. Renata, the delicate beauty seemingly carved from glowing honey amber . . . who would get into bar brawls. Renata, who would disappear for months . . . before resurfacing for the most incredible Scavullo shoot. Renata, whom hardcore Duranologists determined to be the true inspiration for the song "Rio." Renata, who finally walked away from modeling ten years ago, and—according to fashionista lore—went native somewhere in the Amazon. Either that or she lived through lipo gone wrong in Brazil and was shamed into obscurity. But from the looks of her now—stunning in a golden Luis-Heinz number—that second rumor was clearly false.

How in God's name had Lola pulled this one off?

Had my reporter's instincts kicked in as they should have, I would have been right in the middle of the crush that now surrounded the cage. And I wouldn't have been able to breathe and my shoes might well have been ruined, dammit. Instead, I remained at my perch and scanned the crowd for Lola. With my head still in a haze, I took a while to spot her, but there she was, accompanied by two of the burly bouncers. Even they had a hard time helping her push her way through the mesmerized masses toward Renata. At first Lola looked pleased as punch at the frenzy her surprise had created, but with each body that wouldn't budge from her path, she seemed to get more and more freaked out at the very same frenzy. There was no way I would be able to reach her now. But she had promised me the story, right? I would just have to collect my exclusive another day. Like tomorrow.

As I let out a long, sad sigh, I dropped my head back, and as it lazily rolled to the left I realized that Nick was still next to me, studying me intently. My neck nearly snapped as I tried to gather myself. I looked into his eyes.

"Let's get out of here," he said.

Three minutes later we were in the back of a taxi, rolling toward my hotel. I was sprawled on my side of the seat, my head resting against the window so that I could watch the streets of Pigalle get smaller and smaller until they disappeared. I had vaguely noticed some paparazzi chasing us into the streets—or maybe it was just some revelers who wanted our cab. My mind was too fogged to tell, or to care. All I could feel was the dull ache inside me—for those dresses, for this really cute guy sitting next to me—and this overwhelming haze that seemed to have a lock on my brain.

And on my judgment, I might add. Had I been cogent, I might have realized that I hadn't been this out of it since the night during my last week of college when one of my roommates decided we still had one extracurricular requirement to fulfill before we graduated: Pot 101. As it turned out, the mere *suggestion* of being stoned was just as effective as toking up, because I could not for the life of me inhale. (Insert your own Bill Clinton joke here.) Still, before long I was riding aimlessly on the subway with someone from my freshman English class whom I had never spoken to, but who happened to be at the same party that night. And now, the method of transportation may have been upgraded, but the parallels remained. Maybe if I had developed a craving for Doritos in that cab, I might have made the connection. Nice one, Lola. As if you needed banned substances when you had Renata. Then again, the thought popped into my mind that maybe we had all just inhaled Renata's secondhand smoke.

Mind you, Nick and I weren't exactly groping each other in the backseat like teenagers or anything—thank

God I was too spaced out for that—so by the time the driver stopped in front of the Hôtel Ste.-Claire, and the fog had partly lifted from my brain, there was no horrible moment of sudden embarrassment and regret, to be followed by a walk of shame.

Which is not to say it wasn't awkward. We both acted as if neither of us could recall what exactly had inspired us to jump in a cab and head for my hotel—or what we might have been thinking of doing once we got there. And maybe that was the honest truth. Or not.

"I'll just walk you to your room," he said. "I don't live too far away."

"That . . . that would be great."

We walked side by side, close but not touching, through the foyer and into a waiting lift. The elevator man recognized me and pushed 5, and we ascended in silence.

I walked slightly ahead of Nick, down the left corridor, stopping in front of my room. We stood there for a moment, smiling foolishly at each other.

"What do you suppose is behind Door Number 504?" I finally said. Oh, thank you, brain.

He laughed. "Maybe a drink? I'm suddenly parched."

Well, I couldn't not invite him in now. I fished the key out of my little pink bag and opened the door. I turned on the light in the entryway and scurried over to turn on the lamp by the sofa while he stood at the door. "Come on in," I said, spotting the empty Prada shopping bags strewn on the floor. "Sorry for the mess."

What in God's name was I doing? I'd barely met this guy, what, two hours ago, maybe, and here we were. What if he was a serial killer? Or a stalker? Or just some freak who wanted to try on all my clothes? (Yes, I was fixated on this idea.) Was that any better? Had I lost my mind? If my mother ever found out . . .

Nick took a few steps toward me and helped me take off my trench coat. My back to him, I heard him say in my ear, "What'll it be?"

I froze. "What do you mean?"

"What will you *drink*?"

"Oh, sorry," I said, nervously rubbing my fingers up and down my neck. I was starting to go through horror-movie plots in my mind. "There's a bottle of merlot on the table over there. Would you mind opening it? I just have to check my e-mail really quickly. I've been waiting to hear from my editor about my story."

As Nick made himself useful near the minibar, looking for glasses and a corkscrew, I swung open my laptop. Damn, this bloody dial-up was slow. One of the few drawbacks of staying at this old hotel . . . A dial tone, a dozen notes of digits being dialed, a hum, a buzz, and I was in. I peeked over the top of the screen. He was still searching for the corkscrew.

I logged in to my e-mail account but instead of checking the in-box for Roddy's name I created a new message and typed in Jillian's address. Priority: Urgent. I hit the caps lock key. I meant business.

JILLIAN: DID SOMETHING REALLY STUPID. I'M IN MY HOTEL ROOM WITH SOME GUY I JUST MET. IF HE TURNS OUT TO BE A PSYCHO AND YOU DON'T HEAR FROM ME BY TOMORROW, CHECK THE NEWS FOR THE GIVENCHY DUSTUP. HE'S KHAKI GUY—THE CUTE

STRAIGHT ONE. SHOULDN'T BE HARD TO SPOT. OF COURSE, IF HE'S NOT NUTS, BUT MAYBE JUST A LITTLE FREAKY, I'LL GIVE YOU ALL THE DIRTY DETAILS!!! HA HA HA!
XOXO ALEX

I clicked "Send" and looked up. Nick was standing in front of me, a glass of wine in each hand. "Oh, thanks," I said, taking a glass and adding in what I thought was a light and casual tone, "Nope, no e-mail from my editor, so I just sent him another one. He'll come looking for me if we don't talk soon!" Nice one.

"Is everything all right?" he said.

"Oh, yeah, absolutely, I'm feeling great!"

"I mean, with your editor."

"Oh." I took a long sip of the merlot. "He somehow has it in his head that the Chanel incident might have scarred me for life. It didn't help that I sort of played hooky from the shows today until you so graciously took the spotlight off me."

I motioned for him to come sit on the sofa, in front of the TV—where we simultaneously spotted the Post-it I had put there before I left. I plucked it off the screen and threw it in the trashcan.

"Khaki Guy?" he said with a smile. "I hope you'll call me by name in the future."

"I missed your interview, so I didn't know your name." I giggled nervously. "You *were* the talk of the town, you know. In my job I have to keep current!"

"Good thing you went straight to the source." He turned sideways toward me. Damn this three-seater sofa, I thought. He was at one end and I was at the other; a full cushion stretched between us like the Ice Age land bridge from Siberia to Alaska. I certainly couldn't shift from my spot now. I wasn't going to make the first move. I wasn't even sure that I wanted *any* moves to be made at all. And if he lunged at me like a fourteen-year-old boy on his first date, or did the old yawn-and-stretch maneuver to put his arm around me, well, that would be kind of cheesy and I would totally lose respect for him. The mind reeled with the complexities of the mating game.

He threw me for a loop by getting up and looking out the window. "This is a great hotel," he said, breaking the silence. And then he delivered a total non sequitur: "So do you think the French really hate us Americans?"

"After what the two of us have done in the last couple of days, I can't blame them if they do," I joked.

"Seriously, I don't get it." He walked back over to the couch and sat down again—this time on the middle cushion, close enough to almost touch. Pretty smooth, I thought, smiling to myself.

"I've loved France since I was a kid," he said with a rush of enthusiasm. "My mother spent her high school years here and so she's always been a Francophile. And she passed it on to me. I loved visiting Provence and Bordeaux with her when I was young; I loved the culture, the screw-you attitude of the Parisians, the architecture, the food . . . But then I came here to work, and I've found that my French colleagues spend more time at smoking breaks than they do at their desks, my landlady's a cranky old bat, and some of my neighbors are trying to get me deported. I'm telling you: You simply cannot be a Francophile living in France."

"Well, I posit that you can't cover fashion and still be

a fashionphile. Or work at a donut shop and still love donuts. Too much of a good thing. Plus you're just too close; you see the seedy underbelly of the business . . ."

"Not to mention your own seedy underbelly—I mean, if you worked at a donut shop."

"Exactly!" I said with enthusiasm—enough enthusiasm to give me an excuse to lean in and cop another feel of his arm. Oh my!

"But what about the fashion world is making you feel so conflicted?" he said, suddenly serious. For all of a second. "Are the models too smart for you? Like it's too hard to follow all their literary references? Their discussions of astrophysics?"

I rolled my eyes. "Yes, yes, and yes, I confess to it all. I am intellectually bullied by the models." I paused. "Honestly, do you really want to know?"

"Yes, I do," he said, looking at my face carefully. He absentmindedly brushed his left fingers across his lips. God, I really wanted to kiss him.

But I shook off the urge and pressed on. "I lead a double life," I whispered conspiratorially.

"Uh . . . huh?"

"I'm smart *and* shallow."

He exhaled dramatically. "Well, thank goodness. I thought you were going to say you were a man trapped in a woman's body or something."

"Very funny . . . but I'm being serious. When I was in high school, I was a 'smart kid'—I took hard classes and did well and left Texas to go to college. But I've also always loved fashion and clothes and movies and knowing which English pop star was married to which actress and what songs were played at their wedding. It's scholarship of a different kind." I laughed. "But covering fashion full-time, as my *day job*—well, that makes me feel like my life has taken a turn for the inconsequential and the asinine."

"At least you do still use polysyllabic words," he quipped. "Your brain hasn't completely gone to pot. Unless you count what we may or may not have inhaled tonight."

"Right. Not completely, just twenty-three twenty-fourths of it."

"But don't we all—don't we all have different sides to ourselves?" he said. "At least, the people worth knowing aren't one-dimensional. I'm not all about finding inefficiencies and telling corporate drones who've been doing their job for thirty years that I know how they can do it better."

"And your hidden side is . . . you also like to disrupt fashion shows."

"Guilty as charged," he said, bowing his head with feigned solemnity.

We talked and talked for hours, lowering our voices to whispers as the sun slowly made its ascent. He told me about his childhood in Manhattan, his mother's gourmet store in the West Village, the grand Parisian residence where he occupied an entire floor, right downstairs from a Swede, a Spaniard, and an Italian—"the girls" he had said he lived with. "Like the United Nations, only even less civil," he said. "Or to put it in terms you can relate to, maybe just like the United Colors of Benetton."

"Oooh, too downmarket," I jokingly complained.

I told him why Manolos were like an aphrodisiac. He eyed my sandals furtively. I swore him to secrecy when I shared with him my dressing chart for the week. I recounted for him how I'd fallen into my current job after the last fashion writer quit to "find herself" in Fiji: At the magazine, to quote Posh Spice, "I was posh compared to the rest of them."

We chatted about movies, how serious "Oscar" films were so overrated that it was sometimes better to just opt for the lowbrow fare—the *Animal House* knockoffs—that would surely exceed expectations. We misremembered song lyrics from the eighties. We argued about politics and SUVs. I showed off my knowledge of pop culture. He kept up. No one ever kept up with me.

We talked about everything. And then we talked some more.

When we heard the alarm clock go off in the room next door, we were still sitting on the couch as we had been at the beginning of the night, only my sandals were lying on the floor, my legs curled up underneath me. We were facing each other, our heads leaning close together, in deep conversation. Our hair may have even been intertwined.

"My God, what time is it?"

Startled, I bounced up away from Nick and looked at my watch. I gasped. "Guess."

He looked at the window, where a crack of light was seeping in through the heavy velvet curtains. "Six?"

"Try seven-thirty."

The light of day seemed to bring the awkwardness back. I could hear a cart roll by in the hallway, delivering someone else's room-service breakfast.

Nick stared at his watch in disbelief. "Oh God, I really didn't mean to keep you up all night. I really didn't think it was this late . . . early . . ." He gave me one of those puppy-dog looks that could make any living, breathing woman forgive any transgression he might ever decide to commit, including any one of the mortal sins.

"I'm just as guilty," I said, stifling a yawn with a smile. "Plus, you probably have to go straight to work now. At least I can sleep a few hours before my first show."

"Well, I hope so. Not that I'm saying you're in need of any beauty sleep, but please let me apologize again . . ."

"Don't be silly. Despite the sleep deprivation, I had a great time," I said softly. (Besides, I had some great concealer to take care of all that.) He got up, and I walked with him to the door. Was this it? Should I say something? Or should I be a Rules girl? (Not that I approved of that drivel.) I really wanted to kiss him . . . or more accurately, I really wanted him to kiss me.

"So did I," he said, stopping abruptly. I almost walked right into him. He must have been running through the options in his head too, because after a few false starts from both of us, he leaned over just slightly—to kiss me, I thought—but then retreated and for a moment held both my hands in both of his. "I'll see you again," he said simply before opening the door and disappearing down the hall.

I locked the door behind him and did a silly little dance around the room before slipping out of my dress and into bed. *I am* so *smitten*. I sighed.

And we hadn't even kissed.

Chapter Four

"WHAT THE HELL HAPPENED TO YOU last night?"

It was Lola. And her phone call preceded my alarm by about seven seconds.

"Hang on," I mumbled, rolling over in bed to shut off the clock. I groggily propped myself up with a couple of pillows. "Mmm . . . what do you mean?" I said, feigning innocence.

"What do you mean, what do I mean?" She sounded genuinely miffed. "I thought you were all hopped up about Luis-Heinz, and I wanted to know what you thought about the show, but you just disappeared. And I was planning to take you to that café in the twentieth first thing this morning, but now I'm not even sure of your interest and intentions—"

"Lola, I was desperate to find you, but after Renata dropped in, it was impossible to get to you—" I began, but she kept talking over me. Knowing full well that there was only one way to snag her attention, I paused for dramatic effect before announcing, "Okay, I met a guy."

"Spill," she said, instantly appeased. "Now."

"I will, I will, but what am I going to do about these shows . . ." I was up now, sitting at my laptop, trying to figure out what was on the day's schedule. Back-to-back shows at noon and one—and that wasn't even counting the earlier show I had already slept through. I rationalized it by telling myself that I knew I wasn't really going to write about any of them. Besides, I was on to a better story—one I'd have to talk to Lola about anyway. I could do some multitasking. Plus, there was always Fashion TV. I just hoped that Roddy's sources skipped a show here and there too.

"Screw it," I said, shaking my head at my lax new attitude. "Meet me at Café Marly in an hour."

I hung up on Lola and walked into the bathroom, where I slipped into the plush white terrycloth robe that had been warming on the heated rack. Did I have time for a proper soak? A nice bubble bath would feel really, really good. I plugged the tub and started running the water, pouring in some Annick Goutal perfumed bath salts. In the midst of checking the temperature of the bathwater with my foot and daydreaming about one Mr. Nick Snow, I remembered the e-mail I'd sent to Jillian the night before.

Aaarrrggghhh. I turned off the water and took a few steps toward my laptop. The tub was just about filled, the tiny fragrant bubbles floating up temptingly at me. I looked at the tub. I looked at my laptop. Tub. Laptop.

Tub. I didn't have to choose, really, since there was a second phone on the wall in the bathroom. I dipped my legs into the intensely warm, almost hot, water and slid in. Mmmmm. Oh, this was better than . . . I smiled guiltily. Maybe someone could change my mind sometime soon. I rested my head on the cushion placed at the top of the tub and reached for the phone. I felt like Miss Piggy—the only thing missing was a white and gold princess phone with a rotary dial.

"This is Jillian."

"It's Alex."

"Good God almighty. So now that I know you're alive, you've got a lot of 'splainin' to do, young lady. This might even call for closing my door." I heard the smooth glide of her Aeron chair and the click of the door shutting. "All right, I'm ready. Damn, I should've gotten some popcorn, but go ahead."

"A little early for that . . . by the way, what are you doing in the office so early anyway? It's, what, just about six? I forgot I was in Paris and not London—"

"Oh, you poor jet-setter. Now stop stalling and tell me everything. You promised dirty details, remember?"

"Okay, okay!" I could feel myself blushing—and the water turning tepid. I unplugged the drain for a second and turned on the hot water, hugging my knees to avoid scalding my lower extremities.

"What's that noise? Are you in a waterfall or something?"

"Umm, I'm in the bathtub."

"I won't even comment. Now go on. I'm listening."

I didn't know why I was suddenly feeling shy about telling my best friend about Nick. I was never the type to kiss and tell *everything*; it was always better to leave things to the imagination, I figured, and besides, when I was on the receiving end of the information, I didn't really want to know every single detail about what Jillian and her husband did in bed. Of course, Nick and I hadn't done anything in bed at all . . . yet.

"So . . . this guy. He was at the Givenchy show and he got in a bit of a tussle with some assistant and they knocked over this famous stylist and . . ."

"Yeah, yeah, I got that much from the Fashion TV Web site. You did tell me to look it up, so of course I watched the whole video segment. And might I just say that this man of yours is really *quite* cute?"

I giggled. "I know! Isn't he adorable?"

"Oh, this is nauseating. You're *squealing*."

"Hey!"

"Sorry, sorry," Jillian said, laughing. "Continue."

"Well, since this new *scandale* had bumped me off the headline news, I thought it was safe to go out. And my friend Lola had organized this guerrilla fashion show at this very happening nightclub in Pigalle for a new Swiss-Peruvian designer, who is totally revolutionary and oh my God, you just have to see the amazing dresses he makes. I want one in every color . . . and did I tell you that Renata the supermodel showed up?"

"You know, I still cannot get over your life. That's all I'll say for now."

I laughed. "It *is* pretty ridiculous, isn't it?" I ran the water again and added some more bath salts, quickly checking my fingers to see if I was getting too pruny. "Anyhow, that's a whole other story. You want the dirt."

"Uh, yeah, you know me. I'm here for the cheap thrills."

I told her about the paparazzi, and their demand that we pose together, and how Nick and I had started talking, and how the show began, and the mystery smoke that turned our minds into jelly, and how we ended up in a taxi headed for my hotel.

"Wait a minute, hang on one second," Jillian interrupted. "You're trying to tell me there was some illicit substance, some aerosol ecstasy, piped into the club that made you jump into a cab with a stranger? Or that the *dresses* made you really hot?"

"Crazy, I know. Maybe it was all those things. Or maybe it was just Nick . . . Did I tell you his name was Nick?"

"No, you didn't. And you haven't told me what happened at your hotel, either!"

"Right . . . Well . . ." I fumbled for words. "Well, we . . . talked."

"Alexandra Simons, I *cannot* believe that after everything we've been through together, you're going to hold out on me like this. I am deeply hurt."

"Jillian! I'm telling you the truth. Nothing happened. You know me—no action on the first date."

"Now, can you even call it a first *date*?" she mused. "Nowhere in this story so far was there ever any asking out nor accepting of said invitation."

"True."

"And since the meeting occurred at a nightclub, I would usually classify it as a hookup," she continued, clearly enjoying herself. "But that would imply some misbehavior, and we have you on record denying any such thing."

"And . . . ?" I said.

"So what we have here are unclassifiable circumstances," she concluded. "Makes it very hard to figure out the rules."

"No, no rules," I pleaded. "No games either, unless you count Olympic-level flirtation. It felt really natural. We just talked . . . and talked and talked, about anything and everything. Until seven-thirty in the morning. It was . . . amazing. *He* was amazing." I sighed. "Remember back in college, when you'd meet someone in class or somewhere and you'd just stay up all night and talk about everything? That was, like, the most stimulating thing about being in college."

"Speak for yourself," Jillian said, laughing. "I was pretty stimulated by our twin-size bunk beds, myself."

"I always did suspect that of you," I said, playing along. "But you know what I mean. You just don't find that anymore. Not as an adult. Guess no one has time for it."

"Well, not those of us with jobs that don't require hanging out in nightclubs, anyway."

"Oh, come on, Jillian," I said affectionately. "I keep telling you, it's just *not* that glamorous."

"But I like to tell my mom and everyone at work that it is. You don't realize the glory by association."

I got out of the tub, wrinkled fingers and toes first, and wrapped the bathrobe around me. I watched as the sudsy, now cool water swirled down the drain. "We just really clicked," I said. "And did I emphasize enough to you just how hot he is?"

"Yeah, yeah," Jillian said. "So . . . did you exchange numbers or something? You'll have to remind me what you single kids are doing these days."

"Umm . . . that's the part I'm not sure about. He said, 'I'll see you again.' It was a declarative. Not a question, not a 'See ya,' but 'I'll see you again.' Pretty definite, right? Or am I misreading him? Is he just being casual? You know I'm going to agonize over this, deconstruct it for days . . ."

"God knows I'm not fluent in Manspeak. I still don't know what John means half the time."

"You mean the half of the time you actually listen to him?" I joked. Jillian and her husband had a habit of mishearing—or rather, not hearing—each other. According to Jillian, it was the reason they never argued. It was sweet in a rather dysfunctional way.

I sat down in front of the vanity and started combing my hair. "So what do I do now? The ball's totally in his court. He knows where to find me. I just know his name. He's here on assignment, so he wouldn't be listed. I guess I could look up his company's number. Not that I'm a stalker. But even if I got a number, would I call? I wouldn't call today, but what about tomorrow . . ." I snapped out of my monologue and remembered Jillian was still on the line. "What's the minimum wait, two days?"

"I thought you said no rules," she said.

"Well, there are rules and there are *rules*," I said. "You know what I mean. I do have to maintain some semblance of dignity."

"God, I'm glad I'm not single anymore."

"Gee, thanks, Jillian!"

"Yes, but I'm also not giddily imagining what I'm going to wear and say and do to seduce this poor boy the next time I see him, now, am I?"

"And you think I am?" I laughed.

"Duh, of course you are," Jillian said. "But you're also a trained journalist, so I know you'll be able to find your man. I've seen reporters do that in the movies! And when you do find him, hey—you do *words.* You'll know just what to say."

"Thanks for the vote of confidence," I said. "So you think I should just jump him when I do?"

"Oh yeah, most definitely. I want some really dirty details next time."

I had spent a good half hour on the phone with Jillian, so by the time I had blow-dried my hair and put on my Thursday clothes—a pair of ecru trousers with pleated insets down the side seams from Stella McCartney's spring collection, and a black jacket cut wickedly sharp and tight from her Chloé days—I barely had enough time to apply a little concealer over the dark circles under my tired eyes, dust my face with T Leclerc powder, and smudge on some dark cherry Chanel lip stain.

Another day, another taxi. I found myself replaying in my head Nick's every word and every move—which made for a quicker ride to the Louvre, where I was meeting Lola. The taxi took me down the rue de Rivoli and turned into the small street that wound past the museum's courtyard, dropping me off where the pebbled ground gave way to something of a sidewalk. The cabbie must have noticed my three-inch Manolos (the trusty Carolyne style, in cream-colored suede).

I strode in the direction of the glass pyramid and then took a left toward the Café Marly, which was located in one of the wings of the museum, right alongside some of the world's greatest works of art. And as if those views weren't enough, the seats on the long terrace outside were prime real estate for people-watching, like a gallery for beautiful people. I often wondered how many of the regulars would consider lunching there a cultural activity.

I climbed the steps leading to the terrace and looked around for Lola, but saw no sign of her. I did hear some horribly discordant sounds being exchanged at a table in the corner. What were they *speaking*? Half expecting to see members of some lost tribe convening over croissants, I did a double take. It was none other than Laura Rivington, the latest in a line of perfectly blond and perfectly plastic former catalog models to hold the post of fashion reporter at the *Los Angeles News*. At first I thought she was talking to the waiter, but he was already halfway down the terrace. And I could see a pained look on his face as he passed by me. Laura, in fact, was deep in conversation with an up-and-coming British stylist I vaguely recognized from the last London shows. Could it be? Was that *French* they were speaking to each other? *"Je comprends,"* she was saying, only she pronounced it *"Jay con-prends."* I, on the other hand, did not at all *comprends* the need to mangle French between two purported English speakers.

I stepped into the restaurant, where Lola was waiting for me at a table right inside the door. She stood up when I approached and emphatically kissed me on both cheeks. She was wearing another one of Luis-Heinz's spectacular dresses, this one in heather gray. She released me and sat down, shooting me a look over her coffee cup that you'd give to a child who has been naughty. "Alex, you little devil," she said. "You're glowing!"

I grinned back at her. "So you want to talk about Luis-Heinz?"

"Uh-huh." She was tapping her short, perfectly manicured nails on the table. "In due time, you brazen hussy, you. First, *you* tell *me* what happened to you last night."

With exquisite timing, a waiter appeared at our table, buying me a few more minutes before the interrogation would begin. I ordered my usual *croque monsieur* and *salade verte* and a small bottle of Evian, and let Lola dawdle. Despite the fact that she was a regular there, she always had a hard time choosing what to eat. And then she'd usually end up ordering whatever I was having.

My thoughts drifted as the waiter went over the day's specials with her. Should I have been disturbed that both Jillian and Lola were so excited—titillated, even—by my meeting a guy? Had my love life been *that* dull up until now?

After a few moments of hemming and hawing, Lola copied my order, plus she pre-ordered a *moelleux au chocolat*, a soufflé-like dessert with a melting chocolate center. And she didn't even ask me if I'd share it. She must have been expecting a bad day on the Luis-Heinz front.

I decided to extract some information from Lola before I dished. "So are you just up for hearing a juicy story—and please, don't get your hopes up too high—or do you think that hell must have frozen over now that there may even be a story? And by the way, what *was* that silly smoke at the club last night?"

Lola laughed. "Alex, darling, all I can say is, it's about damn time. You've been in Paris too many times for you not to have fallen under its spell. It was bound to happen. I always *knew* it would happen. I'm just glad I had something to do with it. As for anything illicit at the club . . . let's just call it another type of spell."

"Uh-huh," I said, pursing my lips disbelievingly. "I'll get to the bottom of it all right. When I get my big story on Luis-Heinz . . . not to mention Renata. How the hell did you pull that off?"

"No romance story, no Luis-Heinz story," Lola said, shaking her head playfully.

"All right, all right." I delivered the short version of the night's events, taking care to mention multiple times how impaired my judgment must have been because of whatever had been in the air.

"Mm-hmm," she said, laughing. "Good excuse. Seriously, though, I can't wait until you see him again."

I frowned for the first time that day. "Do you think I'll see him again?" Which led to a fifteen-minute dissection of his last words to me. I fully understood that women had an inborn need to rehash every little detail of each interaction with the male of the species, and I certainly appreciated Jillian's and Lola's support and advice. But enough was enough. I was feeling exhausted, and just a tad overexposed. I would reserve any further overanalysis and wild speculation for me, myself, and I. We could do plenty of damage on our own.

"Okay, are you bored yet?" I said, only half jokingly. "Don't you think it's time to talk about *your* big catch? I mean, how on earth did you find Renata, much less get her to do your show?"

A beatific smile suffused Lola's face. She leaned back into her chair and lightly shut her eyes, as if she were bathing in a warm glow.

"Come on now," I said with a laugh. "Enough self-congratulation already. You need your friend in the press to celebrate the glory of Lola, don't you?"

Lola's eyes fluttered open. "The glory of Luis-Heinz, you should say. He's the one who got her."

"What?" I stared at her, trying to force her to crack and admit she'd been joking.

But she looked totally serious. "You heard me right. Luis-Heinz is the one who got her to come."

"How is that even remotely possible? Didn't you tell me he has no friends? But he has famous supermodel muses?"

Lola sat up and shook her head. "It's unbelievable, I know. But here's the deal. You know how everyone says Renata went native in the Amazon, either that or she had some botched lipo in Brazil?"

I nodded obediently; I knew my fashion catechism.

"Well, the truth is somewhere in between. She *was* in Brazil for some secret plastic surgery, but she didn't know anything was wrong until weeks later, when she was trekking in . . ."

"Peru," I blurted out.

"Right, Peru. And so when she started feeling feverish she was wandering around this little village, looking for clean water, and lo and behold, there was Luis-Heinz. Who of course recognized her. Even in this tiny place, he had grown up idolizing her—he even had pictures of her pinned to his wall. Now *that* is the power of fashion . . ."

"So then what happened?" I said impatiently.

"So he takes her to his parents' home, and did I mention that he was studying to be a doctor? Well, he was, so he helped her get better—"

"What was wrong with her?"

"Oh, I don't know, infection, some gross thing like that, whatever. I didn't ask for the gory details. Anyhow, while she was recuperating at their home, she saw some of Luis-Heinz's sketchpads tossed in a corner and demanded to see his dresses and told him that his genius could not be denied and that he had to quit medicine immediately. And you don't say no to Renata."

No, you didn't. That was how most of her bar brawls had started, if we were to believe the gospel according to *Women's Wear*.

"So she helped him. She gave him some money and encouraged—er, ordered—him to move to Paris and has been secretly backing him ever since, even while living out in the boonies in South America."

"Wow . . . Wow." I couldn't think of anything else to say, really. It was quite a story. Two stories in one. Two big scoops to get me out of professional purgatory.

"Of course, he never even volunteered this information to me," Lola said indignantly, her eyes narrowing. It was clearly still a sore subject. "While I was literally pulling my hair out to get him some publicity, he *never once* even hinted at this goldmine. *Never!*"

"So did Renata just show up on your doorstep one day?"

"Practically. When I was at Luis-Heinz's studio one time, this faded picture of him with Renata fell out of one of his sketchpads. Oh. My. God. You should have seen me freak. But it was well worth it, *well* worth it. I can't believe all that time Renata hadn't forced him to do a show, but I suppose she had her own weird reasons for being a recluse."

Lola raised her eyebrows knowingly. I had no idea what she was talking about, and in any other situation I would have insisted on getting the dish. But at this moment, I just needed to keep her on track. "So how *did* you book Renata?"

She groaned. "Oh God . . . If you thought that stuff I told you about going to see Luis-Heinz was ridiculous . . . There were go-betweens, secret meetings at *very* dodgy bars, fake e-mail accounts, passwords . . . But you know what got her in the end?"

What, what? My eyes widened and I waited with bated breath.

"The damn Duran Duran reunion tour. She flew in for the concert the night before last and I convinced her to stay yesterday for the show. But she's with the band now, probably on her way to Berlin or checked into a hotel somewhere as Sheik Jabooty."

At first I tried to stifle the giggles, but after a few seconds of abject failure, I burst into laughter. "That is just too perfect," I managed to say as I gasped for air between giggles. "I love this story more and more. I'm kicking myself for not throwing myself into that mosh pit last night and shoving my way to you and Luis-Heinz."

"Well . . . actually," Lola mumbled, her head hanging, "it's a good thing you didn't stick around last night . . . because he never showed up."

"How is that even remotely possible? No designer in his right mind would ever not show up to his first fashion show!"

"Right mind, yeah. As much as I tried to reason with him . . . Well, even Renata couldn't make him do it. And if *she* couldn't . . ." She looked at me sheepishly. "So are you up for a wild ride? Believe me, this is the only way he does business."

I nodded. "Oh, I believe you. A revolutionary designer? Who brought Renata out of hiding? My God, I wouldn't miss this for the world. Much less for a fashion show or two. I mean, what could possibly happen at a show that would be a bigger story than this?"

"You mean other than a journalist colliding with a model or a cute guy knocking out a very important stylist?"

I rolled my eyes and laughed. "But what are the chances that lightning could strike *thrice*?"

"All right then," Lola said, apparently happy to have someone to share her pain over Luis-Heinz's eccentricities. "I called his answering service this morning—did I mention that it just beeps, no message?" She shook her head. "I left a message saying that I wanted to meet. I don't always hear back; I just throw my message out into the ether and hope someone's listening. We'll just have to head to that café in the twentieth after lunch . . ."

Lola began digging in the deep recesses of her weathered tan Birkin bag. "Actually," she said, pulling out her cell phone, "maybe we should call his friend Bartolome. I'm not even sure he has better access to him, but at least *he* has a phone number."

I nodded at her encouragingly as she scrolled through her speed dial.

"Answering machine," she mouthed. As she left a message, I glanced around the room, trying to give her some privacy. At a table in a corner were a couple of British editors who had come straight from the Christian Lacroix show, which had taken place in one of the spaces beneath the Louvre. The House of Lacroix had long held a grudge against *The Weekly*, ever since some overeager intern at Lacroix had done a Lexis-Nexis search and found that Giorgio Armani had more hits in the magazine than Lacroix. Or at least that's what Roddy had told me, by way of explaining why I never got a front-row seat at Lacroix. In any case, I doubted that anyone would have missed me at that show.

While Lola checked her voicemail at the office, I took my own cell phone out of my new Vuitton ellipse bag. No missed calls. Well, he doesn't *have* this number, I told myself somewhat defensively. Then I rang the hotel and asked if there had been any messages or deliveries for me. The desk clerk put me on hold for a minute—Maurice Chevalier warbled "Thank Heaven for Little Girls" while I waited—and came back to tell me that a large pot of orchids from Chanel was waiting for me in my room. "Oh," I said halfheartedly, then thanked her and hung up. Wait: Chanel was making nice and I was disappointed? Had I completely lost sight of my professional priorities?

This boy was definitely trouble.

After splitting the dessert—no matter how bad things got, Lola would never consume so many calories on her own; then again, she had never collided with a model on a runway—we set out in a cab for the Machu Picchu café. "Not in the Michelin guide," she said, "but it's not hard to find. Just follow the Doors groupies from Père Lachaise and take a right when it seems like you've left civilization behind."

"Great," I muttered.

"Alex, the journey is half the fun," Lola said, pretending to lecture me. "Besides, you can write all about it in your article: My Quest for Luis-Heinz."

"And what his dresses can do for your heinie," I chimed in, causing Lola to cackle uncontrollably. "Hey," I said, trying to be serious, "so did your show make the papers this morning? I haven't had a chance to look."

"Well, first of all, your sweetie dominated yesterday's coverage—nice action shot in the *Catwalk Caterwaul,*" she said, pulling the new Fashion Week 'zine out of her bag and handing it over to me. I tore at it greedily. In my giddiness I had forgotten that Nick and I had met essentially because he had made a bigger scene than I had. What a pair—that is, if we *were* a pair. Which we weren't. Yet.

"And anyway, we started too late for their deadlines," Lola continued.

"Or maybe their writers just couldn't think straight after they inhaled," I said without even looking up from the front page.

There they were in all their glory. Nick and Arianna Sidebottom were photographed midmotion, with her wig and hat farther along in the trajectory. Oooh, I thought, not pretty. I could barely see Nick's face, though. Had I not just spent hours looking at it last night and many more hours thinking about it this morning, I might not have recognized him. Well, good. Maybe it would all blow over and his outburst would be forgotten by the fashion flock and we could . . .

Oh shit.

My eyes shifted from the photograph to the two-inch headline next to it: "Exclusive! Givenchy's Gladiator Tells All!"

I looked up at Lola. "Why on earth didn't you tell me about this before?"

"About what?"

I flashed the cover at her.

"Oh wow. I didn't even read that," she said apologetically. "I was just looking for a mention of Luis-Heinz. Sorry, I was a bit single-minded."

I was too busy reading to respond.

> Nick Snow may not look like a rabble-rouser, and he may not throw paint at fur, but don't let his charm deceive you. After yesterday's brilliant Givenchy show, he became involved in a tussle with a young woman believed to be a junior editor from *Teen Vogue* but who remains unidentified. (Please contact us at the *Catwalk Caterwaul* if you have any leads.) In the fracas, he stumbled into Arianna Sidebottom, causing unimaginable grief to the influential stylist, who has been in seclusion ever since. Snow, 33, on the other hand, remained on the scene, and while he expressed concern about Sidebottom's injuries, he made no apologies about what he had to say. In an exclusive interview, the American in Paris revealed to the *Catwalk Caterwaul* his true feelings about the fashion world, and the people who populate it.
>
> "What's so great about a woman with a dead animal on her head whose sole contribution to society is supposedly 'discovering' people?" he said. "How about discovering a cure for cancer? Would that person be celebrated and followed around by paparazzi?"

I couldn't bear to read any more. He was right, of course. But fashion is what it is. Hadn't we discussed that? "Lola," I said, looking at her worriedly, "do you think I'm sleeping with the enemy, er, so to speak . . .

Would I be sleeping with the enemy . . . Damn, I need to find a different metaphor. But you know what I mean. Do you disapprove?"

Lola stared at me. "Two words for you," she said. "Parachute pants. You know what I'm saying? No one will remember him the minute the shows end."

She was right. I hoped. I really had to stop thinking about it, him, us.

Just as Lola had promised, as the Jim Morrison pilgrims faded into the distance the cab turned right onto a rather sketchy block. I suddenly did have something else to worry about. Like our safety.

"So you've been here before, Lola?" I asked, hoping for some reassurance.

"Yeah, once, with Bartolome."

"And you know what you're doing, don't you?"

Silence.

"I *am* going to get my dresses, right?"

"Even if they have to come from my own closet." She gave me a weak smile. "Alex, think of this as an adventure!"

An adventure? *The Weekly* hadn't doled out combat pay along with my press card. My idea of an adventure was the time Jillian joined me in Rome a few months after I first moved to London. I had heard that Prada operated an outlet store in the middle of the Italian countryside, so with very vague directions in hand—essentially the name of the nearest town—we woke up in the wee hours to board a fast train to Florence, where we changed to a rickety old local train that chugged its way deep into the Tuscan hills, destination unknown. We passed by a factory here, a village there . . . and then not much of anything at all. Several stops in the middle of nowhere later, we disembarked in Montevarchi, which looked like it was populated by about ten people. I was supposed to be the guide ("We're in Europe—your turf," Jillian had said. "I promise I'll get us around the Hamptons next summer"), and all I had was a description in a weathered Italian guidebook. I spotted a dapper old man standing by a white taxi in the empty parking lot and figured I could just show him the page and ask him how to get there in my pidgin Italian. So Jillian and I nervously made our way over to him. But before I could even make eye contact or open my mouth to greet him, he took one look at us with our Burberry raincoats and Vuitton bags and said, quite simply, "Prada?"

Now *that* was an adventure more my speed. But now I could only try to be optimistic. I reminded myself that *this* adventure could also end with great clothes.

A sharp left turn jolted me back to the present. The taxi stopped abruptly in front of a tiny storefront on a narrow side street. The windows were blacked out by heavy curtains; the only indication that there was any sort of place of business inside was a small sign on the door, one of those plastic ones featuring two clocks with movable hands to indicate the opening and closing hours. "We're here," Lola said. She slid over toward me and followed me out the door and onto the curb. The minute she slammed the door behind us, the taxi was off like a prom dress. "Damn," I muttered. "Do you think we should have asked him to wait for us?"

"Come *on*," she said, putting her arm around my shoulders and nudging me toward the door. "Trust me. Luis-Heinz is just a little weird, but it works. Besides, think of you in one of his dresses . . . on a date . . ." She gave me an exaggerated wink. She had me there.

We never would have guessed it, but inside, the café was bustling with diners. No one even looked up when we walked in. There were six round tables crowded into the space, holding large dishes of ceviche and rotisserie-grilled chicken and rice and fried yucca and half-empty drinks, water condensing in tiny pools around the glasses. The thirty or so people were seated so close to one another that they all seemed to be part of the same group, merrily chatting and smoking and drinking together. The aromas wafting from the kitchen made my mouth water. And this was after the chocolate dessert (well, half of it).

"This isn't so bad," I whispered to Lola.

"Never as bad as you imagine," she whispered back. "Now for the tricky part."

I followed her as she squeezed her way through the restaurant, between chairs and tables and diners, and over to the bar in the back. The bartender had watched us the whole way in, but now he merely looked blankly at us.

Lola leaned against the bar and got his attention. I scooted over next to her. "Is this a good vintage for the Inka Kola?" she said, looking him straight in the eye. She was more stern than I had ever imagined she could be in a situation like this. Not that I had ever imagined a situation like this before. Not even in my wildest "Alex Simons, investigative reporter" fantasies.

The bartender nodded at her. "I find out for you," he said curtly, and disappeared into the kitchen.

I gave her a sideways glance. "What is it with you and the Inka Kola?"

"Peru's national drink." She shrugged.

"And I can't believe you weren't joking about the secret password," I whispered. "I feel like Nancy Drew. Or maybe the Bobbsey Twins. If they were both girls and one was short and one was tall. And if they dressed really well."

"Just wait," she said, entirely too seriously. "It gets better."

"You realize this is all going in the story, right?"

She sighed. "Well, could you at least call him eccentric, rather than an out-and-out wacko? Eccentricity doesn't keep you from big wholesale orders at Saks."

"I think it *helps* you get the big Saks orders." I laughed. "Can you just imagine the trunk shows?"

The bartender emerged from the kitchen without acknowledging us and went back to work, opening a liter bottle of yellowish liquid. He poured some out into two highball glasses, added crushed ice, sugar, and what looked like egg whites, stirred, and slid the glasses down the bar to us.

"Pisco sour," Lola said. "Peru's other national drink. Drink up." She lifted her glass at the bartender and gulped it down. I looked at mine, sniffed it . . . and what the hell, I downed it. Not bad.

It was a good thing I found it palatable, because Lola and I ended up tossing back four rounds, which the bartender just kept sliding down to us every twenty minutes or so. After the fourth glass, I was about to keel over—despite the fragrant aroma and sweet taste, the grape brandy packed quite a punch—and so we moved over to a table in the corner that had just been cleared. The lunch crowd was thinning. It was four o'clock. This was getting to be like waiting for Godot . . . Smyth-Jones—yes, really, Godot Smyth-Jones, the latest design discovery to come out of London this season. His show, held in a former waste-processing facility in the Docklands, ran three hours behind schedule. (At least the smells at the café were much more acceptable.) If intentional, it was a risky but clever tactic. After spending so much time waiting, we were bound to love the collection. It was like waking up early and going out of your way to a sample sale: you just felt compelled to buy *something*.

"So do you think we passed muster?" I asked Lola.

She hesitated. "I've only done this once before, you realize. I really don't know what all the different outcomes might be."

"Those dresses had better be transferred from your closet to mine by the weekend!"

"Don't you want to talk about that Nick guy or something?" she said. "You were in a *much* better mood when we were doing that."

The door opened, letting in a sliver of a breeze. I looked over and saw a slight young man wearing Helmut Lang jeans, a black cashmere sweater, and wraparound Dolce & Gabbana sunglasses. He stood out as much as we did.

"This is it," Lola said. "Are you ready?" I nodded.

Helmut Boy walked up to us, looking a bit exasperated. "I wasn't expecting two of you guys," he said in a strong accent—Chicago's northern suburbs, in my estimation, with just a splash of . . . drama. What was going on here?

"I only have one bandana, so one of you guys is gonna have to just promise to close your eyes really tight."

Lola looked over at me and raised her eyebrows. "I'll take the blindfold."

"Okay, but not until we get to the Vespa," he said. "I don't want the people here to think we're weird or anything."

We followed him dutifully out of the café and around

the corner, where a red Vespa had been left idling perpendicularly between two parallel-parked cars. I hoped this wasn't an indication of how Helmut Boy drove. And I really hoped Helmut had helmets.

"Okay, you put the blindfold on the tall girl," he said to me. "You'll just have to hang on tight to her."

Helmut Boy hopped onto the scooter and looked back at us. We were still standing in the middle of the street, scoping out the logistics. He snapped at us impatiently. "Come *on*, girls!"

I tied the bandana loosely around Lola's eyes and guided her to the Vespa's seat. I slid in behind her—thank God she was a stick—and we both hung on for dear life. Helmut Boy backed out of the parking slot and we careened down the street. "No peeking!" he yelled back at me. "I can see you in the rearview mirror!"

"Trust me, I will not peek if it means you'll keep your eyes on the traffic instead of looking in the mirror," I replied.

But peek I did. As we veered in and out of traffic—or maybe just veered from the unwieldy weight distribution on the scooter—I rested my cheek against Lola's back and opened my eyes just a crack. Of course I had no clue where we were, but I did see people in passing cars staring at us, their mouths agape, then curled up in hysterical laughter. First Katyarina, now this. I was really tired of being a freak show.

Five queasy minutes later, Helmut Boy sped into another do-it-yourself parking space in the middle of a sidewalk in front of a big, seventies-era cement block building. I quickly shut my eyes as he killed the engine and hopped off. "Okay, girls, let's go." He helped us dismount and shepherded us to the gate, where he punched in some numbers until a buzzer sounded, unlocking it. We went through another code-alarmed entry and then filed into a tiny elevator, the kind with the door you had to fold closed behind you. I could hear the pulley creaking as it moved us slowly up the building. Four floors up, the elevator stopped with a lurch, and the door slowly slid open. Helmut Boy pushed us out and to the right. I was still walking when he called me back. "You can open your eyes now. It's the apartment on the left."

I blinked a few times and scurried back down the hallway. The yellow floral wallpaper was peeling in the corners, and even in the dim lighting—one of the uncovered lightbulbs on the ceiling was burned out—I could make out some curious beehive-shaped stains on the gray carpeting. I found Lola and untied her blindfold.

"Nervous?" she said.

I gave her an excited grin. "Jesus, my heart is pounding!" I looked around. Helmut Boy had made himself scarce.

"Well, this is it," Lola said, then knocked on the door in two groups of three.

Nothing.

She waited twenty seconds, then knocked again. "Luis-Heinz?"

This time I heard someone padding toward the door. *"Qui est-ce?"* a muffled male voice said, seemingly from ten feet behind the door.

"C'est Lola," Lola yelled at the disembodied voice. She turned to me. "That's weird. Luis-Heinz doesn't speak French."

"What? You never told me that! What *does* he speak?" I said in a frantic whisper.

"Spanish, Romansch, and Esperanto."

"Esper-what? Is that like Franglais?"

"No, no. It's this arcane language, invented by some utopian who wanted to make it the universal language. Luis-Heinz's parents didn't speak each other's language, so they learned Esperanto. At least I think that's what he was trying to tell me."

I stared at her blankly.

"What can I say? They were hippies in the sixties."

"I won't even start to worry about how on earth we're supposed to communicate with him," I said, my whisper sounding increasingly agitated. "First things first. Now what?"

She knocked again. *"C'est Lo-la,"* she said slowly. *"L'agent de presse."*

The voice's body padded closer to the door and then stopped short. I heard him slide the cover of the peephole away for a split second and then release it.

"Merde," he mumbled.

Then came the sounds of his hands fumbling with a series of deadbolt locks before the door finally began to creak open, slowly, one millimeter at a time.

I stepped back and took a deep breath. *Merde* indeed.

I swore in the name of the holy trinity—Coco, Karl, and Yves—it was Jacques.

Chapter Five

GOD KNOWS WHAT WAS GOING ON in that pisco-and-Vespa-addled brain of mine, but my immediate thought was that Helmut Boy had left us on the wrong doorstep . . . where Jacques just so happened to live.

"Well, fancy meeting you here!" I said, trying to cover up my confusion with a muddled little smile. "What a funny coincidence. I guess we must have knocked on the wrong door. So this is where you live? Wow, that's some trek to work . . ."

"Alex . . . Alex," he said, gently but insistently, yanking me by the elbow. "I'm not sure why you're here, but I can guess that you're in the right place. Now come *on!*"

I stopped in my tracks, midthreshold. Jacques's words hit me like a Wile E. Coyote anvil. Weighed down and bewildered, I couldn't be budged. As crossed as my own wires were, I certainly wasn't telegraphing my thoughts to Lola, who blithely walked right into me and would have stumbled from her stilettoed perch if Jacques hadn't grabbed hold of her too. "Lola," he called over my shoulder, "I've been hoping you'd make contact."

Lola stopped and tilted her head, searching Jacques's face for any familiar features. "Did we . . . did we meet at the club last night?" she said pensively. "Sorry, it was kind of a blur. Ohhhh . . . did you buy me a drink?" She paused. "You know," she added delicately, "just because I accepted it didn't mean I was interested . . ."

Jacques shook his head and kept trying to get us inside. I had to stifle a giggle; it amazed me how easily Lola would put things into context. That is to say, her own. As I started to explain to Lola that he was my high school French teacher—and perhaps more meaningfully, the guy who had helped me find those great shoes she had seen, heels up, in the papers—he hustled us into the apartment, relocking the three deadbolts behind us. I was about to joke that he needn't worry; we'd lost the baddies in the low-speed Vespa chase. Only when I glanced over at him did I notice that anxiety had deadened the sparkle in his eyes and drained the tan from his face. I decided to let him take the lead.

He motioned for us to sit down on the folding chairs that represented the total furnishing in the curtainless, rectangular studio. Scraps of fabric and yarn stubbornly clinging to the faded Persian carpet were the only signs that a fashion designer had worked there—that is, until you looked up and saw the hundreds of clippings and Polaroids that had been neatly tacked all over one of the ecru walls, from the ceiling to the floor. I was mesmerized. I wanted to walk over there and study the images, one by one, but before my mind could wander further, Jacques started to talk.

"I'm sorry for the rigmarole with the Vespa and all," he said. "That was my nephew Will. He's doin' his semester abroad from Northwestern. Smart boy, just a li'l overly anxious about followin' Luis-Heinz's rules. And after what's happened, I'm thinkin' we can't be too cautious."

"After *what* happened?" I asked. "I saw Luis-Heinz's creations, and I'm dying to meet him."

Jacques looked distraught. "I haven't seen him or talked to him in almost two days," he said, followed by a long exhale. "Yesterday morning he was fine, he was talkin' like he had finally let go of his worry about the show."

"I'm so glad to hear that!" Lola exclaimed, her face beaming. "Maybe next time he'll actually show—" I shot her a "not now" look and shook my head. She started staring at her hands in her lap.

"He was real conflicted, you know, what with likin' his privacy," Jacques continued. "But he wanted to give women this gift that he'd come up with. Then I went to work, and I saw you, Alex, and I was fixin' to tell him all about you . . . but then he just never came home. This isn't right. Luis-Heinz and I have never been apart this long. Never. All his things are still here. It's not like he up and left me . . . no, that's just not a possibility. Something bad has happened. I just know it."

Jacques's eyes were wide, glassy—they told me everything that he couldn't, wouldn't, and ultimately didn't need to, put into words. The last pieces of the puzzle fell into place.

"Lola, have you heard from him at all?" Jacques asked.

"No, not since he sent the dresses over to me last

week," she said. "The show was such an incredible success that I wanted to congratulate him, and Alex was going to write—" Out of the corner of my eye, I could see that Lola was fidgeting in her hard vinyl-covered seat. "I'm sorry about your story," she said under her breath.

"Never mind that," I told her. "Jacques," I said, reaching for his hand and grasping it as tightly as I could, "I'll do everything I can to help you find Luis-Heinz. I promise."

At that very moment I would have given my last ounce of Crème de la Mer to recover those lost lectures on investigative reporting back in journalism school. Oh, all right, so they weren't exactly lost; I slept through them. I was going to classes *and* working full-time, okay? And yet there I was, promising Jacques that I'd hunt down his boyfriend. Nowhere in my Palm—stuffed as it was with every fashion flack and showroom mole you'd ever need—was there an entry for "Missing Persons, How to Find."

I tried my best.

"Jacques, did he tell you that he was going somewhere yesterday?"

"No, he didn't," Jacques said, squinting as if he were trying to make out an image, a memory in his head. "He doesn't leave the apartment much, anyway. Just went to the boulangerie every afternoon . . ."

I pressed on with my rudimentary line of questioning, mostly informed by years of watching the likes of *Magnum, P.I.*

"Did he seem different yesterday? Agitated or nervous?"

"No more than he usually was, I mean, *is*. 'Specially with the show comin' up an' all."

"Right," I said pensively. "Anyone call him?"

Jacques shook his head. "No, I don't . . . Wait, I did hear the phone ring just after I closed the door behind me, but I was late for work, so I didn't stop. I heard Luis-Heinz pick up the phone, and . . ."

"And?" Lola piped up. Suddenly she was at the edge of her seat. She had been so quiet that I had almost forgotten she was there.

"And I heard him say somethin' in Spanish, so I knew it wasn't for me, and I kept walkin' out . . . Why, why did I do that? Why didn't I stay?"

"Jacques," I said, grasping his hands in mine, "you had no way of knowing . . . but this is a good start. We'll find out who called him and follow the trail from there."

His head hanging, Jacques nodded silently. I thought I heard a sob—but I realized it hadn't come from him. I looked up and saw Lola, tears streaming down her cheeks. I gave her a quick concerned glance and turned my attention back to Jacques. Knowing I wouldn't be getting much else out of him, I changed the subject. "The truth is, I came here to do a story about Luis-Heinz for *The Weekly*, even before I knew you were . . . involved," I said to him.

For the first time that afternoon, Jacques seemed to perk up. "I knew people were goin' to find out how brilliant he is! I am jus' so thrilled!"

"So what do you think about giving me an exclusive interview, and I'll finish the story when Luis-Heinz comes back?" I picked up on the slightest hint of hope in Jacques's voice, so I gave him an encouraging smile and added with a giggle, "No fibbing—he's going to fact-check everything you say!"

We spent the rest of the afternoon talking about Luis-Heinz—well, listening to Jacques talk about Luis-Heinz, anyway. I turned my tape recorder on and let Jacques's soft drawl spin the tale of love and loss. And Lola, who had actually met the man, was struggling to make sense of an entirely different side of the designer she had simply deemed an eccentric genius.

"I had just gotten to Paris when we met," Jacques began. "My darlin' wife—"

I saw Lola's left eyebrow go up, so I shot her an "I'll explain later" look.

"Alex, you *did* realize it was a marriage of convenience, didn't you?" he continued. "Our families couldn't accept a gay man and a woman who loved her independence . . . Well, my darlin' wife and I felt like it was high time we started making things convenient for us instead of for our families. We had just both turned forty, and we decided to have a midlife celebration instead of a midlife crisis. So she went her way—moved up to New York to make her name in the art world—and I went mine."

He leaned forward in his chair and absentmindedly brushed his hair from his forehead. A faint smile crossed his face. "It was the hottest May on record—unbearable," he said. "And this comin' from a native Texan. But Alex, you know what wimps we are at heart; even our garages are air-conditioned back home! Anyway, I had this romantic notion that I'd just get to Paris and retrace my steps from the first time I went there as a nineteen-year-old. I found the tiny hotel I had stayed in, almost all the way up to the top of Montmartre. And to my astonishment, nothin' had changed: The wallpaper was as tacky and floral as ever, and the wooden floors still croaked like a horned frog. It kinda warmed my heart. Not as much as the heat in my fourth-floor room, mind you! The air was so stiflin' that I spent most of my first week just walkin' around, tryin' to find shade or an overworked fan in an unfashionable café where I could spend an afternoon over little more than an *orange pressé.*"

Lola and I sat motionless and spellbound, as the shadows began to creep across the room with the sunset. I felt more like a second-grader at story time than a journalist trying to get a scoop. I had to stop myself from raising my hand and asking, "And then what happened, Monsieur Jacques?"

"It was at that Peruvian café that we met," Jacques continued. "I decided I'd go to Père Lachaise—don't laugh, it wasn't for Jim Morrison! For Balzac and Colette! Anyhow, I wandered into the café and there he was, readin' a magazine in Esperanto."

Lola stifled a giggle. "See, I didn't make it up!" she whispered to me.

Jacques nodded. "Yep, of all the things in the world, L-H and I met over Esperanto. I'd learned a little of it when I was in college, studyin' linguistics. L-H had learned it from his parents. That was the only language they could communicate in, since his mama was from Peru and his papa was Swiss. They could choose from Spanish, German, Italian, French, Romansch—not to mention English—but they chose Esperanto. A language invented to be the universal language. But that's what they say about love, right?"

Lola and I both sighed.

"So L-H and I followed in his parents' footsteps and communicated through Esperanto. My Spanish isn't any better, I have to say, and y'all know he doesn't speak French. He doesn't get out much, you know. He just works day and night on his textiles, his designs. I knew how revolutionary they were, but for the longest time he insisted he was just doin' it for himself. I was so proud when he finally agreed to let you show them, Lola, so that the world would finally see . . ."

Lola suddenly looked stricken. "This wouldn't have happened if I hadn't put on that show," she said slowly. "It's my fault, isn't it? What have I done?"

"Darlin', I didn't mean to make you think it was because of the show . . ."

Lola was blinking back tears. "I can't help thinking, though . . . The same day, he disappears. Was he better off being just our little secret?"

Things were spinning a bit out of control. Jacques started consoling Lola. And feeling helpless, I found myself telling Jacques that maybe it made sense for him to call the police.

"No," he said quietly, firmly. "No, I don't want to do that."

I looked up at him quizzically. He'd seemed to weigh his words carefully. "We're not exactly livin' here legally," he finally said. "And I told you, L-H values his privacy. But I trust you girls. You'll help me, won't you?"

That was the end of that. Jacques appeared to be spent, and Lola and I took that as our cue to leave. As we got up, I once again told Jacques that I'd do everything I could to find Luis-Heinz, and that we would stay in touch.

Lola and I rode the elevator in silence, broken only by the occasional sigh. As we stood in front of the building—suddenly remembering where we were and wondering how we were going to get back to civilization—a white cab careened to a halt at the curb across the street. The grandfatherly driver stuck his head out of the window and insistently beckoned for us to get in. A would-be knight in shining armor, he spent the first two minutes chastising us for standing around alone in such a neighborhood before rolling into how lucky we were he'd come to our rescue. I smiled appreciatively and let him ramble on.

In the backseat, Lola and I kept quiet for a good five minutes before I finally ventured a comment. "You know . . . I don't think I'm cut out to be a girl detective."

"Oh my God! I was hoping you'd say something like that," Lola replied. "I was starting to wonder if your article was going to be headlined 'Nancy Drew and The Case of the Disappeared Designer.' "

"Now that we're back in the light of day . . . Do you really think we have reason to worry about Luis-Heinz? Or do you think he's just gone AWOL for a while?"

"Honestly, I think it's just Luis-Heinz being Luis-Heinz," Lola mused. "I can imagine him walking through that door now—that is, if he has followed orders and worn his bandana over his eyes while on the Vespa."

I had to laugh. What had come over us? We were, after all, a runaway French teacher, a fashion reporter, and a publicist—if we walked into a bar we'd be the beginning of a joke. Who were we to play Charlie's Angels?

"Jacques, bless his heart, is probably just overreacting," I rationalized. "It's only been a day and a half. Maybe he misunderstood something Luis-Heinz said in Esperanto. Not to be totally callous about it, but I'm sure Jacques will call me tomorrow and let me know that everything's just dandy. And then I'll get my story . . . But who do you think that phone call was from yesterday morning?"

"Uh, someone selling long-distance service to Spanish speakers?" Lola said, grinning. "I don't know, sometimes when he doesn't understand what someone says in French or English, he just speaks Spanish. Really."

"Really?"

"Oh yeah. Or heck, it could have been Bartolome—who, speaking of which, will probably have news when he calls me back," Lola said, with a long stretch and yawn, looking as snug as a kitten curled up by the fireplace. "So what are you going to do now?"

"Umm," I said evasively. "I guess I should go back to the hotel and check my messages. Catch up on some work stuff . . ."

"Uh-huh. And would tracking down a certain dashing American count as 'work stuff'? Would that be 'The Case of the Infatuated Fashionista'?"

"I really have no idea what you're talking about!" I said, lying through my teeth. I hated it when I was as transparent as a not-ready-for-mass-market runway dress.

Chapter Six

THE CAB DRIVER DROPPED LOLA OFF at her apartment in the terribly chic Marais and continued west to my hotel. The sun was setting on another day of Fashion Week, and what did I have to show for it? Public humiliation (there really was no better kind). A Prada hangover. Too many skipped shows to count. A missing designer, and hence no story (or no story yet, anyway).

And, I thought as the cab stopped in front of the Ste.-Claire and I paid the driver and asked for a receipt, one really big expense report. At least I was saving Roddy a few pennies by not demanding a private car and driver like my predecessor Laurel had. "But *all* the other fashion editors are doing it," she had pouted and he had grudgingly capitulated. Of course, it lasted for all of one week; Roddy blew his top when he found out that Laurel's expenses for seven days in Paris could have kept *The Weekly*'s recently shuttered Tbilisi bureau running for another two months. Laurel didn't think she'd ever get over being "cut off" by Roddy, but as it turned out she didn't have to. When I told Nick that she had gone to find herself in Fiji, what I really meant was that she had found her sugar daddy (appropriately, the heir to a sugarcane fortune) and he had taken her to Fiji.

In any case, I learned Laurel's lesson for her: If you're not happy with the set limit, at least know what the acceptable margin of error was. Roddy was a lot like the customs officers at JFK. They weren't going to bust you for going, say, $100 over your $800 duty-free limit. At the same time, they'd be highly suspicious if you declared a really low amount. And the other thing to remember: They can sense your fear. After countless episodes of night-terror-level sweating and hand-wringing every step of the way, from the moment I received the customs declaration forms on the plane, to the long walk from the gate, through immigration, and then to customs, only to be waved through after a perfunctory search and an ominous warning, I realized something. I must have looked more suspicious than a Rastafarian reeking of incense and ravenously munching on Cheetos.

Now, I've learned to be calm, cool—and no fines collected. Not that I would ever, *ever* underdeclare what I'm bringing in! (And if I ever shopped too much abroad, surely I was only trying to help the world economy.)

With that philanthropic thought in mind, I made my way to my room, where, just as I had been told, a pot of orchids from Chanel was waiting for me. I picked up the envelope that was on the table next to the flowers, expecting to read some warm, but not *too* warm, sentiment from the head of PR that laid the groundwork for a future reconciliation at a time and place to be determined by the powers that be (i.e., her).

But that's not what it was. The flowers may have been from Chanel, but the note came from an even better source.

Thursday, 2:35 p.m.

Alex: Had lunch with a client in the neighborhood so stopped by to say hello. (I nearly dozed off right into my soup. You're a terrible influence.) But you're not here. Well, obviously . . . Shockingly, the elevator man let me up here to leave you this note; is there no security here? I *do* look very honest, I suppose. Oh, and I guess he saw me this morning and assumed . . . Anyway, I did say that I'll see you again, and you did seem to acquiesce. So how about tonight? I have your number; the nice maid went through your things and got it for me. Just kidding. I do know how to look up a hotel in the phone book. I've got a dinner, a work thing that I can't bag. But I'll call your room after, maybe around ten. Nick.

P.S. I hope I'm not being too presumptuous. You could instruct the operator to block my calls, and I'll know to slink into some corner in a fetal position.

I read the note at least five times before I even thought to put down my Vuitton bag or take off my shoes. What time was it? Six-thirty. I pranced over to the bed, Nick's note still clasped in my hands, and flopped down on my stomach. I inspected the envelope: hotel stationery. But the card, white and watermarked, was from Smythson of Bond Street—nice touch. Curious. Did he walk around with his own stationery? Or had he written this before he came over? Okay, so maybe it wasn't so weird to have stationery with you. Maybe he carried it in his briefcase. Consultants carried briefcases, didn't they? What did consultants do, anyway? *Consult*, I mused, was one of those verbs that could be interpreted either way. Whom did they consult? Or did others consult them?

But much more important, what on earth was I going to wear? I got up and walked over to look at myself in the full-length mirror. I could tell from ten paces that I desperately needed to touch up my makeup. Of course, when I got closer to the mirror I was reminded that I hadn't put on enough this morning to qualify for a touch-up. And after the Vespa ride, I needed to start all over with my hair. Now, the outfit was quite flattering, if a bit rumpled. The black jacket gave me as close to an hourglass figure as I could ever muster, short of wearing one of those boned corsets, and, well, Stella did know how to cut a pair of trousers. I stood on my tiptoes. And when I put on the heels I had taken off, I would almost look willowy . . . if I leaned back and squinted at the mirror at a funny angle.

I now had three hours and seventeen minutes before he was supposed to call—that is, if his "maybe around ten" meant what *my* "maybe around ten" would mean. (And that was at least eleven in fashionista time.) Far too much time on my hands, and yet not nearly enough to get ready completely from scratch: long bath, shaving, waxing, conditioning, manicure . . . Maybe. Damn, this *was* awfully short notice. And awfully "maybe."

As I stood there, gazing into the mirror and scanning my face for any stress-induced zits, it occurred to me in a flash of panic: How did I know this outfit would be appropriate for where we were going?

Dammit, men could be *so* incredibly inconsiderate. He had given me no clue as to where we would go or what we would do. I had seen him at a club; did he want to go *out*-out? Or would he want to go more casual, after a long day of work? I frowned. I felt the barely perceptible hot flash, the sure sign of a zit starting to rise up just below the surface of my left cheek, right by my nose. Stress.

There was really only one solution. I would have to pick out both a dress-down outfit and a knock-him-dead one, and when he called I'd subtly finagle some information from him and then, in the time it took him to get here, I'd be able to change into the appropriate clothes. I amazed myself with my own resourcefulness sometimes.

My current garb was still in the running, though I really needed to have it pressed. No time to call housekeeping. I'd have to steam the clothes the old-fashioned way. I slipped out of the pants and jacket and wrapped myself in the hotel bathrobe. Then I hung up the clothes on the back of the door, turned on the shower at the highest possible temperature, and shut the door behind me.

But now for the potentially torturous part. I suppose I should have been glad I owned a finite number of suitcases and so I had only a tiny fraction of my wardrobe with me. Too much choice had long been the bane of my existence.

What had Nick seen me in? The Prada dress and the gladiator sandals. So I should continue the working theme of sexy yes, dominatrix no. Well, all righty then. If we were just going to hang out, I could always wear a pair of jeans—the new dark denim Sevens that made me look like I actually had a bubble butt (yes, that is the technical term). I pulled them out of the closet. Check. Ooh, they'd look fabulous with the strappy camel and white Jimmy Choo slides with the three-and-a-half-inch heels. I examined my pedicure, which had escaped any chipping after almost a week. Excellent. I was glad I had decided to bring the Choos at the last minute. Always good to pack an extra pair of shoes. (Of course, it would have been better to have packed the planned pair of shoes as well . . . I had finally admitted to myself that the Eurostar shoe fetishist I had been cursing was just a sick fantasy to deflect blame from the real culprit: me.) I worked ahead to the weekend section of the closet. I passed on the Michael Kors sleeveless black turtleneck; too dull. No on the Lotta embroidered tunic; too trendy. (As if any man would ever make such a judgment.) Found it! Almost hidden in the back was the black superfine cashmere Lainey tank with a deep V-neck accentuated with two braids of silk that swung over the shoulders. Perfect.

This was going a lot better than I had expected. Gently carrying the delicate sweater on my left arm, I jauntily twirled its braids as I walked over to lay the clothes down on the bed. Just as I was about to go back to the closet, the phone rang. Too early for Nick, I thought. I picked up the cordless on the end table.

"He-llo!" I said cheerfully. Too cheerfully, it turned out.

"Alex, it's Roddy."

My face fell. Was it too late to hang up? Damn. I cleared my throat and tried to put on a more serious voice. "Oh, hello, Roddy. How are you?"

"Well, I'm fine, Alex. Thanks for asking . . . Now, I

would know how *you* were if only you had responded to my many e-mails."

"Umm . . . Well . . ."

"Alex, what's going on? I haven't heard from you in two days. How big is your room-service bill by now?"

"Roddy! I haven't been holed up in the hotel this whole time, you know." I tried to sound indignant. "I'm . . . I'm . . . I've been chasing a story."

"Uh-huh?"

"It's this new designer. He's revolutionary, truly. His first show was last night—simply amazing." I got more enthusiastic just thinking about it again. "His designs will change the way women dress. I mean it!"

Roddy made some appreciative sounds, or, knowing him, the sounds he *thought* he should make to seem interested. "Really, Alex, what have you got cooking?" he said finally. "Do I need to send in reinforcements?"

"No, of course not!" I gulped. I thought Roddy trusted me; hadn't I always delivered? Of course, I had never crashed and burned so publicly before. I didn't blame him for thinking the worst . . . Only then did I remember the one detail he would truly appreciate—duh! "Um, and Renata came out of nowhere to be in his show!"

"Okay, now you're talking."

I patted myself on the back—and went in for the kill. "And Roddy," I said, trying to sound nonchalant but I'm sure my glee got the better of me, "this designer—he's disappeared. Gone, just like that. Vanished into thin air."

"Really!"

"Everyone's talking about this guy, but no one's got the story," I continued, biting my lip and hoping I wasn't lying. "But I'm on it. I'm working on an exclusive with his publicist . . . and I've got an in with an unbelievable source very close to him." I felt guilty somehow, almost as if I were exploiting Jacques merely by saying any of this, even though he had made it clear that he wanted L-H to get the publicity. But I really did need to make Roddy stop worrying about getting a story for the magazine.

"Well, that sounds terrific, Alex. I'll leave you to it, then."

"Thanks, Roddy. Sorry I haven't called. It's . . . It's been really hectic." That much was true.

"I would think so," he said. "Just keep me posted."

"Promise," I mumbled. "Talk to you soon."

I hung up the phone, fell onto the bed, and rubbed my head with the inside of my palms. "I am such a failure waiting to happen," I moaned, pounding my arms and legs against the mattress, like a four-year-old throwing a tantrum. I shut my eyes for a minute, then shook my head and propped myself up on my elbows. "Well, I guess I could at least enjoy my last night of freedom . . ."

As I got up from the bed, I looked forlornly at the sweater I had selected just minutes before; somehow Roddy had made me second-guess even my choice of attire. Standing in front of the closet again, I scanned the dozen pairs of shoes on the floor. I reflected for a moment that to most people, that would seem rather excessive. But if you thought about it, I really didn't overpack. I had purchased two of those pairs in the past two days. (Wait, that didn't sound very sensible either.)

I often found it helpful to pick the footwear and work upward from there. The choice was between the leopard-print Dolce & Gabbanas or the Choos. (Trying to make them work with another outfit somehow made me feel better, as if I were the queen of practicality.) After much internal debate, I decided upon a simple black knee-length sheath that I had gotten years ago at a Dolce sample sale. The fit was amazing, and the low scoop neckline pushed it over the edge into eveningwear. There was a reason I always threw it on my wardrobe calendar as the dateless wonder. Tonight, for once, it—and I—would be the *dating* wonder. I felt my face flush at the thought.

Impressed at myself for having my choices made with more than two hours to go, I figured I could spare some time for a bath. I walked into the bathroom and checked my hanging clothes—still wrinkled—then turned off the shower and prepared the bath, testing the water until it was just the right temperature before putting the plug into the drain. Now that I felt like I was back to my efficient, multitasking self—for a good half hour at least!—I decided to take a couple of minutes to catch up on the shows while the tub filled. After Roddy's call, I did feel a need to ease my conscience.

I shut the bathroom door behind me to keep the steam working on my outfit, then slumped down onto the sofa, stretched and yawned, and lazily reached for the remote. I had forgotten how little sleep I'd gotten last night.

It must have been a slow day at the shows; the fashion channel was featuring that rarest of creatures at the Paris ready-to-wear, the up-and-coming French designer. Brits, Americans, Brazilians, Belgians, Israelis had all made a splash in Paris in recent years, but for the life of me I couldn't recall the last Gallic newcomer who had been more than a blip. And as the runway show began to fill the screen, I decided that this Balthus Maquereau wasn't the one who was going to stop the downward trend. The show, which had apparently taken place in an abandoned warehouse, followed some sort of enchanted-forest theme. Craggy fake trees had been placed strategically around the catwalk, which allowed the models to indulge their pantomime skills as they wandered down, stopping here and there to hide behind a tree. The girls, sporting long blond braided extensions and apple-red cheeks, started out modeling variations on a Snow White dress, the one you remember from your Golden Book anthology: blue bodice, pseudo Tudor ruff, yellow skirt, puffy red sleeves. My eyelids fluttered, and as I snickered at the ridiculousness of it all, I yawned some more.

Before long I segued from Snow White to Sleeping Beauty, and I was the one running in a forest, stopping now and again to hide behind a towering pine tree. It all seemed so real. I was breathing hard and, pressed against the tree, I could feel the sticky pine sap on my hands. I looked up and could barely see the dark sky between the unruly boughs. I kept moving. I heard some rustling. Was it me? I stopped, shuddering when the sounds of indeterminate origin continued. It was as if I were in the middle of a horror movie, lost in the woods with nothing more than a flashlight—or perhaps in my case, a Gucci bag—for protection. The sounds seemed to come from my left, so I headed right, but suddenly I couldn't move. I looked down . . . and saw that my new black Louboutin slingbacks were caught in a vine and covered in mud. What *was* it with me and my shoe woes, I muttered under my breath as I bent down and untangled myself. From that vantage point, I could see a clearing in the distance. I started running . . . and running . . . and running . . . but I didn't seem to get any closer. Finally, I reached the clearing. I gasped. There was Arianna Sidebottom, drifting along a babbling brook. And across the water was Nick, dressed in breeches and a flowing white shirt. I called out to him but he didn't hear me, because the brook had somehow morphed into a waterfall, and the cascade of water was causing a din, pounding inside my head. Then Nick saw me and jumped into the water, clothes and all . . . and my God, it was straight out of *Pride and Prejudice*—or maybe Bridget Jones's interpretation of *Pride and Prejudice*. Was that Nick or was that Colin Firth? All that water . . .

What was that noise?

I woke with a start, practically jumping off the sofa, if not right out of my skin. I exhaled deeply and shook my head and shoulders, but the sound persisted. I'm not in a dream, I told myself. That's not a waterfall next door . . . Oh my God! Maybe not a waterfall, but it was definitely water. I leaped across the room and toward the bathroom, where wet steam was seeping through the crack at the bottom of the closed French doors. Oh bloody hell. My body tightened, as if I were bracing for a deluge. I swung the door open and walked into a sauna. The wrinkles would be out of my clothes all right.

I slid across the flooded bathroom floor and shut off the water. I felt a pain in my stomach just thinking about what would have happened if the flood had reached my closet. I almost cried at the thought. Soaking wet and trying not to slip, I took all ten towels off the racks and threw them onto the floor, trying to sop up the water. It *was* a big bathroom. I just stood there, in the middle of the room, surrounded by islands of thick white terrycloth. Good thing the mirrors were steamed up. I didn't want to think about how I must have looked.

Until I heard the knock on the door, that is.

Holy freakin' shit. What time was it? I checked my watch: 10:06. Oh God! How did this happen? I frantically rubbed one of the mirrors with the sleeve of my robe. I could barely make out the face looking back at me; all I could see was the mess of damp, tangled hair hanging off what I assumed was my head. Oh help me, God.

Another string of knocks.

I was paralyzed. And in my bathrobe.

"Uh, hang on just a second!" I finally managed to yell out.

"Okay. It's just me, Nick."

My heart bounced up to my throat. Well, who else could it have been, right? But the sound of his voice not only confirmed my worst fear but also, of course, kind of got me hot and bothered. Oh, but did I mention, I was in my bathrobe?

I didn't know what else to do but just stand there and cringe at myself and mutter dark words. What the hell was I going to do? How quickly could I get *anything* on? How was I going to explain this mess?

Thank goodness some survival instinct must have kicked in, because before I knew it I was halfway toward my bed, pulling my hair back into a damp ponytail, throwing on the jeans and cashmere top—screw it, I didn't have time to find my push-up bra—and then jogging back toward the door, with a quick detour to the closet to slip on the Jimmy Choos before slowing down to a dignified stroll. I took three deep yoga breaths, smoothed my hair as best I could, tested out a few different smiles, and opened the door.

And there he stood in all his glory. Nick's black suit

and open-collared, crisp white shirt—he held his undone Hermès tie in his left hand—may not have been quite as heart-poundingly sexy as the Mr. Darcy breeches and white shirt of my dream—don't forget, those were *wet*—but pretty darn close.

"Am I too early?" he said with a sly smile. (Or maybe I was just projecting about the sly part.) He was leaning against the doorframe.

"Uhh, well, um, I don't think so. Do you? What time is it?" I sputtered. I mentally kicked myself and self-consciously smoothed down my hair again. And then, finally: "Oh! How rude of me. Come in."

The steam was starting to spread out of the bathroom and into the rest of the suite, I could tell. I wondered if he noticed. I wondered if I had remembered to close the bathroom door. I wondered if he had started a conversation without me.

". . . and then I realized that I had forgotten to bring your phone number so I just headed over here," he was saying.

I nodded. "Oh, I'm glad you did," I said, not quite certain I was glad he did. "So, um, why don't you have a seat? Just give me a minute."

But before I could make my great escape to the bathroom, I discovered that I indeed hadn't closed the door. And Nick was craning his neck, trying to figure out what on earth was going on in the room behind me.

He gave me another dazzling smile. After several years of meeting mostly British and French men, I had to give credit where credit was due: good old American dentistry.

"Really, did I catch you at a bad time?" he said, sounding concerned.

"What makes you think that?" I said, feeling like a deer caught in the headlights.

"Well, uh, I'm no expert on these things, but your hair has been dripping a trail across the floor."

As if by reflex, my hands went immediately to my head, which was, admittedly, somewhere between damp and drenched. And just as instinctively, my right hand then leaped up to cover my mouth as I laughed, half from embarrassment and half from relief.

"I couldn't fool you, could I?" I got out between fits of giggles.

He stood up and faced me. "Well, either that or you're really trying to send me a message to buzz off, but you're too nice to say it."

I looked down coyly. "Yeah, I would rather drown you in my wet hair than tell you to leave. Much easier that way." I grinned. "Just a little household accident, I'm afraid." I explained to him how I had been drawn in by the Snow White show—but glossed over the exact contents of my dream.

Nick looked past me, toward the bathroom. "Should we be doing something about this?"

"Well, um, it *is* a bit of a mess in there. I'd feel pretty bad to leave it for the maid tomorrow."

"Let's see," he said, casually taking my hand in his and leading me toward the erstwhile steam room. Which meant that instead of worrying about what a clumsy idiot he must have thought I was, I was analyzing the size and texture of his hand—big enough to enclose mine, soft to the touch but masculine. Hands were important to me. They could tell me a lot about a guy, and I wasn't talking about (a) the whole size thing, or (b) palm reading. Call me traditional, but I liked to know if my man ever did any manual labor. Or seemed like he might be handy. Or at least wouldn't mind taking out the trash.

When we stopped at the threshold to view the disaster area, he released my hand and put his on my back, on the bare skin just past my neck. I felt this frisson up and down my spine. He leaned over, his head close to mine, to whisper something to me. "Alex, what *are* we going to do with you?"

Oh, anything we please, I thought. I smiled sheepishly up at him. "I was just . . . I was just steaming my clothes . . . while drawing a bath . . . and falling asleep in front of the TV . . ." I gave him my most innocent, eyelash-batting look.

Next thing I knew, he was taking off his jacket and shoes and socks, and rolling up his pants legs and sleeves. He gestured at me. I raised an eyebrow and responded with a "Who, me?" look. "Snap to it," he said, mock-sternly.

Wow, house-trained and everything. My mom, whose own man—that is, my dad—couldn't even boil water, would *so* approve.

I kicked off my Jimmy Choos, rolled up my jeans, and waded in alongside him. "Where do we start?"

The towels had already absorbed all they could, and an ominously dark shoreline seemed to be spreading into the carpeting in the adjacent room.

I picked up a towel and started to wring it over the tub.

"Hey, make sure the drain's not plugged," he said. I shot him a dirty look.

Little by little, we made progress, engaging in small talk while we worked. He told me that he had been roped into a dinner with the CEO of his consulting firm, who was in Paris for some meetings. After five courses and four bottles of wine at Taillevent—one of Roddy's favorite three-star restaurants—Mrs. CEO, evidently intoxicated, started to get a little frisky, playing footsie with Nick. To Nick's great relief, his boss gracefully called it a night before anything truly embarrassing could happen.

"Quite a ladies' man, aren't you?" I teased him.

"Well, among a certain set of sixtysomething housewives in Greenwich, Connecticut, I am quite the cat's pajamas."

"You're lucky you didn't get fired."

"Well, the flip side is I might just get a raise."

"Playing footsie at a business dinner and mopping the floor on a date—" I clammed up when I realized I had said the D word.

Nick looked at me. "It's still early," he said.

I tried to look busy, staring at my corner of the floor to hide my high-beam grin.

Within half an hour, what had been a pond was down to a few puddles. And that was when I felt the splash of water on my back. I turned around. "What the—?" Another splash. My left side was soaked. I pretended to seethe. "Oh, you want to play that game?" I said, grabbing a wet towel and edging closer to him.

"What do you mean?" he said, showing me the most angelic face. And then I noticed he had one hand behind him. I threw the towel at his head and made a run for it. I was laughing so hard I could barely break into a jog. I didn't make it far before my feet left the floor. Nick picked me up like a rag doll and plopped me on my back on the sofa. He leaned over me, tantalizingly close, smiling, not saying anything, just . . . waiting. His hair was wet and mussed up.

I found myself staring at a drop of water that was forming at the end of a clump of his hair. I watched as the droplet fattened, and burst, and started to fall, as if in slow motion. I raised my cheek to catch it. I blinked as it dropped at the corner of my right eye. Nick bent down toward me, until I could feel his hair grazing my forehead, and then his lips, gently pressed against mine.

And just like that, the slo-mo screeched back into real time. I sensed movement around me as my eyelids fluttered open. I looked up, and there was Nick sitting on his heels next to the sofa, his pants legs still rolled halfway up his calves. So of course I started to giggle. Perhaps it was some reflexive response, caused by neurotransmitters sent from that part of the brain in charge of girlish awkwardness (which in my case was surely more worn than the parts that control, say, learning foreign languages or hand–eye coordination). Or maybe I was just really flustered and completely at a loss when it came to men in general, never mind extremely attractive men who have just kissed me. Damn, I hated it when I was too good at that whole self-reflection thing.

Nick looked a bit stricken, but I wasn't sure by what. Embarrassment? Guilt? God forbid, disgust? If I did say so myself, I really didn't think it was the last one. Hey, it was good for *me*.

Finally he leaned toward me. "Weren't we going to go somewhere?" he said, and flashed one of those smiles that should have made me forget any dark thoughts I might have been entertaining. But still I gazed absentmindedly at his bare calves—causing him to self-consciously start to roll down his pants. He seemed glad to have something to do.

My face must have seemed blank to him, but beneath the surface I was desperately telling my brain to stop overthinking things, to stop replaying that kiss. But what was *that* all about? said my rebellious brain. Shut up, I insisted. Just smile and nod. Look at that irresistible dimple. But don't stare. Don't want him to think you're weird. And for God's sake, say *something*!

It was like I was having an out-of-body experience. Next thing I knew, I was on my feet. Then I heard a voice—it must have been mine. "Where on earth did I leave my shoes?" I padded over to the bathroom door. The slides were lying on the carpet, where I had flung them. I picked them up and brought them back to the sofa, where Nick had taken the "dis" out of disheveled. Except for his hair, that is, which was still a little damp and tousled. As if—and I found myself much too titillated at the thought—he'd just gotten out of the shower and toweled off . . . Memo to mind: Please exit the gutter. Suffice it to say it was dead sexy.

"So where should we go?" I said, my gaze stopping a few seconds too long on his face, despite what I was telling myself not to do. My feet safely Chooed, I sat on the sofa, my hands demurely folded on my lap. I was determined to go for the sweet and innocent look.

"How about somewhere quiet?" Nick said, standing up and offering me his hand. He pulled me up with just enough extra force that I was drawn close to him. I leaned back a fraction of an inch and felt his arm bracing me. He looked down at me. "So we can talk." Better yet, I thought, somewhere dark, so he wouldn't be able to see how I was staring at him. My God, I was a silly girl.

Chapter Seven

WRAPPED IN MY CASHMERE STOLE, I followed Nick out of the hotel. But instead of heading for the taxi stand, he led me to a late-model black Mercedes idling at the curb maybe fifty feet away. The driver hopped out instantly and opened the door for us. "One of the perks when your boss is in town," Nick explained as he followed me into the backseat. "Of course, if it were a limo, I'd be far too embarrassed to use it as my ride."

"But if you brought me an orchid corsage and wore a baby blue tux . . ."

"Oh yeah, in that case it would be totally cool. Just like my senior prom."

"My hair's not anywhere near big enough to relive that night." I giggled.

Nick raised his eyebrows. "Hold that thought," he said before leaning forward and giving the driver, Sébastien, an address in Montmartre that I didn't recognize.

As the car glided into the light traffic, Nick turned ninety degrees in his seat and commenced his hair inquisition. He pretended to study my still-damp hair, which was twisted into a knot and tied back—about as low-maintenance as it had ever been. "Now, I don't know mousses from gels," he said, "but I cannot imagine how your hair could ever have been *big*. And trust me, I remember the eighties. I went to a Bon Jovi concert in 1988! I had friends who had girlfriends from New Jersey, where the eighties lasted well into the nineties!"

I could barely hear his words over the gales of laughter—mine. I just shook my head; I couldn't get any words out, either. Nick took the opportunity to keep riffing: "This one time—I must have been in eleventh grade—I went on a double date with my friend Timothy Raines. He was dating a girl from Jersey City. I'm sure you, ahem, might have known girls who were into bad boys. Well, we Manhattanites thought that Jersey girls were bad, in the good way. So his girlfriend set me up with one of her friends. They came into the city and met up with us on St. Mark's Place, as you did when you were seventeen and thought you were cool. Who knows, you might even get mistaken for an NYU student."

"Oh, yeah." I was still giggling, but was now managing one-syllable words in moderation.

"So Timothy and I were standing in front of that vegetarian restaurant, Dojo's, looking around for his girlfriend Jenny and her friend," he continued. "We finally think we see Jenny rounding the corner, but we're not sure, because it seems like she's got this swarm of gnats around her head. And then our gazes shift twelve inches to the left and ten inches up, and there's this really tall girl walking next to her. I swear I thought she was an Amazon or something. Timothy certainly hadn't told me that my date had a pituitary disorder."

My stomach was hurting so much from laughing that I was reduced to making a face at him that was meant to telegraph, "Watch where you go with this because it may be too close for comfort."

"And as they're approaching us, I notice that Jenny looks like she's been crying," Nick said. "Timothy's totally oblivious, because he's just staring at her hair. And to be honest, so am I. Up close, it didn't look like a swarm of gnats anymore. It was like *The Bride of Frankenstein*, like she had stuck her finger in an electric socket and her hair was made of straw in the first place . . ."

"Oh God, stop!" I was practically in tears. "Stop, please—"

Of course, we both knew I didn't mean it. "So apparently Jenny and her friend had been to the hairdresser to get ready for our big double date in the big city, and Jenny had had a bad reaction to whatever treatment she had gotten. Like bad couldn't even begin to describe it. Her scalp was *red*. And the hair—well, it smelled like it was burning. Of course, her friend's hair had worked out just as she wanted it—and it had made her a foot taller! I think that was the shortest date I've ever been on . . . well, tallest girl, shortest date."

At this point, I was doubled over. I was trying to hit him with my Vuitton bag, but I was so weak from laughing that I could barely even lift it (and this was after my whole downsizing kick, which came about when I complained to my doctor that my back was hurting and he eyed my overstuffed Vuitton Speedy 30—yes, the big one—suspiciously).

"Oh my God, you are *evil,*" I finally got out.

He chuckled a tad too gleefully. "Maybe you've just got some burning confession to make."

I narrowed my eyes at him and pretended to give him the cold shoulder. I waited two beats. "Maybe . . ."

"Oh, come on, you can trust me," he said, trying to look earnest.

"Uh-uh," I said.

Nick leaned in. "Just between the two of us. You can whisper it to me."

"Isn't that what Connie Chung said to Newt Gingrich's mother as the cameras rolled? In front of millions of TV viewers? Rhymes with witch?" I rolled my eyes. "You know, you really can't trust journalists!"

He suddenly backed off. "I was only joking," he said, sounding honestly concerned.

"I know, silly," I said, playfully poking his left shoulder. "I'll tell you my deep, dark secret." I lowered my voice dramatically. "Two words: hairspray addiction."

He started to laugh again. "You needn't say any more," he said mock-solemnly. "I know twelve-step programs are meant to be anonymous."

"Oh, yes, it got that bad. My parents threatened to hospitalize me, where they would wean me off the stuff with a methadone-based nonaerosol. They were concerned about the environment, really."

"Of course, you must have been fully aware of what was going on in the stratosphere, since you were so much taller then."

"Exactly! In fact, I was recruited to play basketball at UT."

"Really."

"Really . . . okay, not really." I crossed my legs and propped my elbow on my thigh. I smiled and rested my chin in my left hand, my fingers covering my mouth. He mirrored my move and smiled back at me. I raised my left eyebrow. He raised his right one. We smiled some more. My jaw was starting to hurt.

Nick and I were still locked in a moony gaze when the car rolled to a stop, the door opened, and the night air rushed in. Sébastien helped me out, while Nick got out the other side and walked over to join me. We were so close to Sacré Coeur that I had to crane my neck to see its pristine white dome, glistening in the darkness.

You could toss a pebble anywhere in Paris and hit a romantic spot. I just hadn't tried that until now. I saw some flashes of light in the near distance; in another context I might have assumed they were paparazzi cameras. Tonight I imagined they were falling stars. And that made me feel warm inside.

Nick led me by the hand into Aux Négociants, a tiny wine bar that was as dimly lit as a dungeon, minus the smoky torches. When I stumbled in the darkness—those old wood floors were deadly on stilettos—Nick was there to keep me upright. I got my wish; he would have needed night-vision goggles to see me blushing. I really didn't understand how I could be so klutzy. Tall women who were all legs could be excused for being gawky, getting tangled up. Nicole Kidman, whose legs were probably as long as my total height, said in interviews that as a girl she felt like a wild horse with long, skinny legs she didn't quite know what to do with. (I stopped to consider that I was yet again comparing myself to a celebrity and sighed.) I should have been the model of grace with my lower center of gravity and all that.

We finally made it to a small round table in the back corner, where we were seated in creaking wooden chairs. There were only a dozen people in the whole place—and still it seemed cramped. The table was lit by what must have once been a single white candle; as if through years of erosion, the streaks of dripping wax had transformed it into something akin to a craggy tree stump. I reached out to feel the warm wax, which was squishy to the touch. I left a fingerprint.

I looked up at Nick, who was illuminated by the candle. The shadows around his face danced as the flame, coming perilously close to the pool of wax below it, flickered. I absentmindedly nodded when Nick suggested a 1983 Burgundy.

"I'm sure it was a fine year," I said, launching into nervous chatter. "At least it was for music. *Seven and the Ragged Tiger* was the first record I bought, since my older sister had already called dibs on Culture Club. Then my friends and I fought over the members of Duran Duran. I was a Roger girl myself, but probably because someone else had claimed Simon and John. Back then we thought Nick Rhodes and Boy George were the epitome of male sex appeal—makeup, billowing sleeves, and all."

"Yeah, well, that was perhaps a bit too much lip gloss and hairspray for my taste . . . Oh, sorry."

I laughed. "Does it always have to come back to the big hair?"

"That does seem to be a recurring theme . . ."

"I've come to terms with it," I deadpanned. "I no longer have those anxiety dreams about going to school wearing nothing but lots and lots of hairspray. Or going to my locker and not finding my homework, just empty cans of hairspray . . ."

"Alex," he said with mock solemnity, "have you thought about starting a support group?"

"What?"

"You could be doing a real service. Imagine all those fashionistas who once had big hair . . . They need to deal with their shame, just like you did."

"Right. Maybe I could share space with your organization for the ethical treatment of models."

"Absolutely. I would be more than happy to help a fellow charity."

The self-deprecating jokes, combined at the same time with his casual disdain for just about everything, were all part of Nick's appeal—but I had to wonder if he ever took *anything* seriously. And, at that moment, it suddenly popped into my head: What about that interview he gave to the *Catwalk Caterwaul?*

"Yeah, what about that interview you gave to the *Catwalk Caterwaul?*" I heard myself saying. That brain–vocal cords filter wasn't working so well either.

"Wha—? Huh?" His mouth was starting to form a smile, but his brow was furrowed, as if trying to rack his brain for a likely story. Or maybe I was just being overly suspicious and he really didn't know what I was talking about. "Oh wait," he said slowly, the grin spreading across his face. "I did talk to some fashion reporter after the Givenchy show, but since I honestly couldn't believe that there was actually a publication called the *Catwalk Caterwaul*, I didn't think anything of it. So it's real?"

My eyes involuntarily shifted from side to side. No turning back now. "Yeah, it's real," I mumbled. "I read it this afternoon."

Nick chuckled. "That's the funniest name I've ever heard," he said. "So what did I say? Did they make me out to be a villain?"

"No, you didn't look like a villain," I said. No, you always look pretty great, I thought. "You basically just went off about how fashionistas are self-important fools whose contributions to society are nothing compared to medical researchers and Nobel laureates."

"And?"

"Oh, Nick!" I exclaimed, half exasperated at his attitude, but only half, because deep down I knew he was right on just about any level except the one on which the fashion world existed, and by extension, the one on which I existed at least eight hours a day. "Of course you're right. But remember where you were—at a fashion show! It's just entertainment. I mean, do you really hate what I do? Because—"

Nick reached over and put his hand over mine and shook his head. "Alex, I really didn't mean to offend you," he said. "Smart and shallow. I remember. I think we could all use some of both."

Good answer. I smiled shyly at him, and luckily the awkward silence was broken by the waiter, who approached the table and launched an almost balletic performance of presenting the bottle, uncorking, decanting, and serving it. When he finished and waited for us to taste the wine and deliver a verdict, we were almost afraid to pick up our glasses. I gestured to Nick. "You do the honors," I whispered. He gestured back. "Ladies first . . . oh, all right." He raised his glass, enthusiastically breathed in the wine, swirled it around, and took a sip. "*Superbe,*" he said. The waiter gave us an ever so curt bow and disappeared. I breathed a sigh of relief.

"I'm such a philistine," I confessed. "I don't have a clue about wine. You're talking to someone who picks wine bottles by how nice the labels are."

"Hate to tell you this, but Armani doesn't make wine," he teased. I pretended to glare at him. "Sorry, that was too easy," he said, flashing just a hint of his puppy-dog look. "But I'm no connoisseur either. I only know the basics my father taught me . . . So I'm wondering if our waiter lost respect for me because I didn't spit it out, express disgust, and send it back."

"I always thought that, too!" I exclaimed. "Like it's uncouth not to be a wine snob. You *must* complain."

"Of course, there's always the risk that they're offended by your taking offense, and then they might do something gross to your food."

I laughed. "That's why I never read those exposés about the restaurant business, or the health inspection reports about grocery stores or, for that matter, what really goes into hot dogs. You have a pretty good idea already. You'd just rather pretend not to know."

"What *are* hot dogs made of?"

"If you really must know, my grandma used to tell me it's the last parts to go over the fence."

"Lovely imagery. On that note, let's drink to something that'll make you squeal like a pig," he said, raising his glass to mine as I giggled some more. "Here's to eighties hair bands."

By the time we had consumed the *Seven and the Ragged Tiger* vintage, and toasted the year of *Rio*, we were the only ones left in the bar. Having swept the floors and blown out the other candles, the waiters were placing the chairs on top of the tables around us. As they hovered, still we lingered in the darkness; the candle had been reduced to a messy puddle, and I was left tracing the rim of my empty glass with my index finger.

"I guess we should let these people go home," I said finally, without looking up.

"Yeah, that's probably a good idea," Nick said, glancing at the check that had been placed on our table half an hour before. He pulled some bills out of his wallet and slid them under his glass before leaning back in his chair. "Shall we?"

Only when I stood up did I realize just how woozy I was. As I leaned over to pick up my Vuitton bag, I felt like my head was spinning, the room was spinning, Nick's face was spinning—it was like that ride at Six Flags, where the force of the spinning pressed you up against the wall. And then the floor dropped. I must have been twelve the last time I went on that ride with my aunt. She cried; I laughed like a hyena. I wondered if it would make me cry too, now that I was an adult.

A more immediate concern was whether I'd make it back to my hotel. Nick must have picked up on my condition—well, it was pretty obvious since it took me two minutes to grab my bag—because he hustled over to me and braced my arm. "I've got you," he said. I sighed, much too enthusiastically. *In vino veritas,* right?

We walked out into the night air, which did me some good. The Mercedes was still parked nearby, but the thought of getting into a car in my condition made me feel even more nauseated, if that was possible. Sébastien seemed to appear out of nowhere, and in a flash was holding the door open for me. I looked up at Nick and just shook my head, in all probability looking rather pathetic. "Um, could we walk a bit?"

"Of course." He turned to Sébastien and asked him to wait for us at a spot at the bottom of Montmartre.

As the car slowly drove away, Nick wrapped me in his left arm in one fell swoop, and looked intently at my face. "I've planned this romantic walk so carefully," he whispered, "so please don't spoil the mood by throwing up on me."

"Mmm," I said, mustering a smile. "I can't make any promises." I reached back and undid the barrette holding up my hair—anything to make this headache go away. I ran my fingers through my hair and tried to give myself a scalp massage. "Well, that's a little better."

Nick took my hand in his and led me toward Sacré Coeur. I remembered from my first tourist trip to Paris that the view from the steps of the cathedral was monumental—you could see the rooftops of the city stretched out before you—which made the area a big make-out scene for tourists and teenagers alike. And also, for some reason, a big grazing ground for dope dealers. Sure enough, despite the late hour, there on the steps was one entwined couple, oblivious to the strung-out kid looking to score in an altogether different way.

"Let's just walk a bit more before I make you go down the hill," Nick said. "I'm afraid we can't see much of the view in the darkness."

"That's okay. I'm kind of seeing double anyway."

"Good to know."

We ambled around the cathedral and through the place du Tertre, which was almost unrecognizable without the paint-by-numbers artists who offered their services to tourists during the day. Even as my head cleared and I became a bit steadier, I still let Nick lead the way. "Hey, Jack," I said finally, "Jill's ready to go down the hill."

"No tumbling, please," he said, squeezing my hand.

We doubled back toward Sacré Coeur and followed the railing down to the steps that lined the side of the hill. I momentarily had a bad feeling about the treacherous heels I was wearing, but let it pass. The steepness of the hill was enough to make me forget about the shoe problem. I closed my eyes and grasped Nick's hand a little tighter. Slowly, I reopened my eyes and tried to take a peek downward. Not good. I shut them again.

I vaguely noticed that Nick was saying something. "Are you going to be all right?"

"Yeah, I think so." I didn't sound very convincing. Not to myself, anyway.

"We'll go slowly. And hang on to me."

I gladly complied: one foot down a step; the other foot down to the same step; pause; repeat. Nick patiently led the way, like the costumed court officers who so memorably walked backward in front of the Queen of England when she opened Parliament. Not that I had any delusions of grandeur.

"This isn't so bad," I said, after managing five steps.

"And you haven't thrown up on me, either."

"Thoughtful of me, isn't it?"

I should have known better than to try to walk and banter at the same time. Just as I was getting confident, I tripped on a pebble and stumbled down a couple of steps before Nick scrambled to catch me.

"Are you all right?" he said, helping me take a seat.

"Oh my God, I was hoping you didn't notice." I grinned through my blush. "How embarrassing!" I looked at my feet. I wasn't hurt—physically, anyway. The psychic pain came when I saw that the heel of my left shoe was mangled. "I really liked these shoes!" I said with an exaggerated pout. (Well, I made it *seem* exaggerated for Nick's benefit, in any case; deep down, a part of me *was* truly sad.) "But what I would like more is to get to the car. And even I don't carry a spare pair of shoes in my handbag."

"Well, I can't let you walk down barefoot," Nick said. "I'll carry you."

"You'll what?"

"Come on, let's go."

"Sorry? I can't let you do that. I—I—"

"Hey, if my romantic walk didn't quite work out, at least I can tell all the guys that I picked you up."

I tilted my head and gave him a smirk that said, "I give up." "This is all very Scarlett O'Hara," I said. "Only I'm not wearing a velvet curtain."

Nick swept me up, my shoulders resting on one of his arms and my legs dangling over the other. I wrapped my left arm around his neck and clutched my bag and shoes in my right hand. "Well," he said, "when we tell the story, we can do all the embellishing we want. To some, wearing a curtain would sound kind of kinky. Of course, to your fashionista friends it may be a horrible faux pas."

"Are you sure you can talk and carry at the same time?" I said a dozen steps later. "You know, I won't be offended if you need to take a break."

"Please—this is nothing," he replied. "Don't I look like I work out? In fact, I'm training for the wife-carrying world championship in Finland."

"I thought it was wife-tossing."

"It may have been, but they seem to have become more civilized. I imagine wife-tossing might have engendered a boycott or two or twenty."

"I guess so. Makes for a better story, though." I added casually, "So, you have a wife you haven't told me about?"

"Just my boss's wife, remember?"

Nice dodge, I thought. If it was in fact a dodge. Why was I being so suspicious? Was this man not *carrying* me down a hill?

"Anyway, it doesn't have to be your wife, just any woman over seventeen. And if you win, one of the prizes is the woman's weight in beer."

"Oh, great," I said. "Imagine how much longer you'd have to carry me around if I'd had that much beer to drink."

"It's really charming, how you're such a lightweight."

"Cheap date," I said, smiling sweetly.

"Well, not including the chiropractor's bill . . ."

"How do you *know* all this trivia, anyway? It's one thing to know about wife-tossing, carrying, whatever, but you've got the small-print rules and prizes down pat."

He shrugged—well, as much as he could, with my

arms and legs and Vuitton bag and shoes dangling off him. "Jack of all trades, master of none," he said. "Dilettante extraordinaire. I just absorb useless information. I would have been a great *Jeopardy!* contestant."

"You could still be one."

"Nah, don't think so," he said.

"Camera-shy, are you?" I teased him. "A little bronzer and blush and you'd be fine. Just ask Ben Affleck, who relaxed and learned to love being J. Lo'd."

"And look how that ended," he said. He shook his head, fighting back a smile. "It's not that at all," he said. "I think I would've kicked butt on *Teen Jeopardy!*, or even the college tournament. Lots of pop culture questions, and the contestants are all nerdy types who could run the tables on physics but wouldn't know Puff Daddy from Papa Smurf. But in the big kids' *Jeopardy!*, I wouldn't remember enough of my real education. Or they'd have a fashion category and I'd have to use you as a lifeline."

"Wrong show," I said. "But I appreciate the thought nevertheless."

"Too many game shows, reality shows to keep track of," he said. He paused for a moment. "Especially reality TV," he added. "Do you watch?"

"Oh God, don't get me started," I said, rolling my eyes. "I've only seen the British ones, and I don't really get the appeal. And I've heard that the American shows are *so* much trashier. Of course, the Brits look down their noses at American TV and *they're* the ones who created an opera about Jerry Springer! It's so utterly humiliating. What's the one where a bunch of women compete for a guy who's dumb as a rock but they think he's a millionaire? Or the one where a bunch of guys compete over a woman, just because it's a contest and they're being filmed? Honestly, would people really do anything just to be on TV?"

"Uh, yeah, I guess you could say that," Nick said. "Hey, we're almost there."

"Is it safe to look down?"

"Definitely."

I turned my head and saw the bottom of the hill—and the black Mercedes parked across the street. "What's Sébastien going to think?" I said, feigning embarrassment. "Is he going to snitch to your boss's wife?"

"Well, only if I give him something to really talk about." Nick stopped on the last step and gently let me down, swinging my bare feet on top of his shoes. Teetering, I grabbed hold of him around his waist. "Don't worry, I won't let your feet touch the ground," he whispered, cupping my face with both hands. He leaned down, and as his face reached mine, I shut my eyes and just let go. It was one of those deep, longing kisses that stole the breath right out of your body and the sense right out of your brain, that left you hanging, hoping, hungering for more.

Ground? What ground?

Somehow, what seemed to be an eternity later, Nick and I made it down the final step and across the street and into the waiting car. Sébastien, ever discreet, shut the door behind us, and once Nick told him our destination, he kept his eyes on the road. Nick and I, like chastened teenagers, stayed in our respective corners of the backseat, sneaking glances at each other, only our hands daring to touch. It was a long drive to the Ste.-Claire.

"Am I allowed to ask you what you're doing tomorrow?" he whispered.

"Am I allowed to tell you?" I whispered back.

"I want to see you again."

"I don't think there are any rules against that . . ."

"Good."

"Glad that's all out in the open."

I smiled—a lot—as we drove through the darkened boulevards of Paris and past the opulent old opera house, which seemed to sparkle under the glow of the almost full moon. Suddenly everything looked different to me, full of life and opportunity and magic. Heck, with my new critical heart condition, I might have thought that Euro Disney looked romantic.

"Damn, I almost forgot," Nick said, temporarily breaking the spell. "I might be late again tomorrow. Have to help the boss entertain the clients, you know . . ."

"Oh, of course," I said casually, trying to hide the train of thought that was careening off the rails in my head. "I'm sure there's some work stuff I have to do too . . ."

"We can meet up after?" he asked.

"Sure . . . and I promise I won't make you mop up my bathroom floor again, so it won't be *that* late a night."

"You *are* a most generous hostess," he said.

With impeccable timing, the car came to a stop in front of the hotel. Nick got out and walked around to open my door for me. "I think," I said, inspecting the red carpet that led into the lobby, "I can safely walk barefoot here—no tetanus shot needed."

"But if I carried you in, they might upgrade you to the honeymoon suite."

I blushed. "Mmm . . . that's okay. But you can walk me to my room if you'd like."

We retraced our steps of the night before, but with considerably less shyness. We might have even made eyes at each other behind the elevator man's back. During that long march down the hallway to my room, my mind—the wooziness replaced by giddiness—was in overdrive, trying to figure out what to say while anxiously anticipating a repeat performance of that kiss on the steps. Heaven help me, I thought. Heaven help *him*.

So there we stood in front of my door. I was swinging my shoes and bag with my left hand—nervous tic. Nick had taken his jacket off, and was hanging it over his shoulder on his index finger. He leaned sideways against the wall.

"So I'll see you tomorrow night," he said.

"Tomorrow night it is," I responded slowly, trying to buy more time—more time until I got to do what I had been wanting to do for a good half hour. There was really no explaining my logic.

I smiled. He smiled. I leaned my head and shoulder against the wall and looked up at him. I swung my bag and shoes some more.

After a minute of this, he finally said with a smile, his eyebrows arched, "Are you trying to make me crazy?"

"No," I said sweetly.

He lunged. I lunged. I dropped my bag and shoes and stood on my tiptoes (and for a hundredth of a second took note of the true practical purpose of wearing heels) and returned his kiss. I felt his warm hand on the small of my back, just beneath my sweater. The heat spread through me. And I broke away.

"I—I—I should get some sleep," I stammered. "I should sleep. You should sleep. I'll see you tomorrow."

Nick looked a little perplexed, but he smiled and ran his fingers through my hair a second longer before releasing me. "See you tomorrow," he said, and walked down the hall toward the elevator.

I hadn't really lost my mind—just my nerve. There was something uncontrollable about the warm—well, hot, really—feeling I got when he kissed me. Sort of like taking a nosedive in an airplane between two mountain peaks, and then soaring back up in the nick of time. Or like jumping into the ocean when you can't swim. Perhaps that was the best analogy. I didn't have the skills and I didn't have the life vest either.

The second I let myself into my room, I went straight to my jewelry box on the nightstand by the bed. Underneath the Me + Ro necklaces (I always hoped that the inspirational words of Sanskrit carved on the pieces would somehow rub off on me), the pearls my grandmother gave me when I turned eighteen, and my college class ring (which I never wore but still carried with me all the time—more portable than my diploma, I suppose) was a letter, the stationery faded with age and wear and tears. When I received it two years ago, I must have held it and read it and reread it a hundred times. And every now and again, I still went back to it. Call me masochistic.

The letter was from my college boyfriend, the one who

started me on my retail therapy. But it wasn't a Dear Alex letter; it was the letter after that, years after that, when he told me he had been so wrong. Crazy, right? Shouldn't that have made me feel vindicated somehow? Or made me feel avenged, that he had been pining for me all those years, long after I had gotten over *him* (with the help of a few key purchases)?

Well, no.

Mostly it reminded me of how much love could hurt. It told me not to jump so fast. And at this moment, I knew it was a reminder I desperately needed.

Chapter Eight

I DIDN'T REMEMBER EVER GETTING INTO BED that night, but somehow, when the phone woke me—again—the next morning, there I was, sprawled on top of the sheets in my flannel men's pajama top. My jewelry box was open on the other side of the bed, and when I rolled over and reached for the phone, I discovered that I had slept on my class ring. I had an imprint of my college's insignia on my left cheek, for God's sake, just beneath that burgeoning zit.

"Dammit," I said aloud before picking up the phone. "Hello?"

"Alex it's Lola I got a really weird message from Bartolome and I called Jacques and he's all frantic and I am really starting to worry what are we going to do Alex?" And then finally an exhale.

"Lola?" I said groggily. "Could you repeat that, but pause for punctuation this time, please? What time is it, anyway?"

"Oh I don't know quarter to seven or something like that so well what are we going to do?" Her voice seemed to get louder with every word.

"Um, are you breathing, please? What did you say about Bartolome?"

"Bartolome, yes. He left a message on my cell in the middle of the night, really weird, like he waited till he knew I wasn't going to be answering my phone to leave a message. Just like some ex-boyfriends I've known . . ."

Despite the worry in Lola's voice, I had to giggle.

"Anyhow, he just said he was calling me back, and he said something vague about hearing from Luis-Heinz and not to worry. But I worry. Because I called Jacques thinking he must have heard from Luis-Heinz if Bartolome had, but no. He hasn't. He still hasn't."

"Did you talk to Bartolome?"

"No, I tried to call the number that registered on my phone—which isn't his regular number—and it was disconnected."

"Is he usually as elusive as Luis-Heinz?" I asked. I was starting to wonder about these Peruvians.

"No, he's not," Lola said. "He was usually the reliable one, so this is really weird. But I invited him to the show today, so I'm hoping we can talk to him there." Her voice seemed to trail off; then I could hear her giving some muffled instructions to a minion in the background. "Sorry, but speaking of which—Jesus, it's almost seven. I'd better get going. The stylists are restless. See you at the show."

I hung up the phone and rolled over in bed. I wonder what's going on with Bartolome, I thought. Then: Man, am I tired . . . if I can just get a few more hours . . .

The minute my head hit the pillow, the phone rang again. Grrrr . . . Without moving anything but my left arm, I picked up the phone, held it close to my hair-tangled face, and sighed dramatically. "Geez, Lola, what now?"

"Alex, where *are* you?" said a faint voice, muddied by the bad connection.

"Huh?" It took all of three seconds to figure out who it was. And at that moment of recognition I also remembered something really, really important that I wasn't supposed to forget.

It was my mom. And she was coming to Paris for the weekend.

"Mom! Oh my *God*! Where are *you*?"

"I'm at the airport . . . Alex, weren't you going to pick me up?"

"Uh . . . uh . . ." My mom, coming from a place where people drove to get to their cars, couldn't absorb the fact that in places like New York, London, and Paris—namely, places where her daughter had spent most of her postcollege years—people did things like take cabs. "Mom, I'm sorry, I thought I told you it would be hard for me to *take a cab* and pick you up, with work and all. Can you take a cab here?" Damn, for once I could have used that car and driver.

"Well, all right, I guess I might as well." She sighed. "I just wanted to make sure you weren't stuck in traffic or something. I have the hotel address."

"Good thing you speak French fluently, huh, Mom?" I figured flattering her language skills, such as they were after thirty years of nonusage, would help.

"Yes, you're right, dear."

I smiled. "Mom, so I'll see you soon. I'm in room 504."

"I'll see you soon," she responded. "I can't wait to take a hot shower! What a horrible flight . . ."

"Okay, Mommy, bye now!"

Crap. Holy crap. How could I have forgotten? How could I have forgotten that MY MOTHER was coming to town? Oh Jesus. What was I going to do? My room was a mess, and good heavens, I had a date that night! I stopped to listen to myself. Had I just regressed fifteen years? Was my homework finished, my plate cleared? Good thing it wasn't a school night.

The suite had an adjoining second bedroom, which had its own entrance. But we would share a bathroom, and it occurred to me that there wasn't a clean towel in sight. I immediately phoned housekeeping—what time was it, seven?—and asked for a quick cleanup. My mom would be here within an hour, in all likelihood, so my own hot shower would have to wait.

I hadn't seen her in six months, and this was supposed to be a girls' weekend. Lola had arranged a front-row seat at today's Dior show next to mine, and we had planned to spend some quality time shopping together on Saturday. We even had an appointment for the couture at Chanel. As far as my dad knew, we were only going to be window-shopping there. But my mom had other ideas. "You can't take it with you," she would tell me cheerfully, especially now that she was happily retired from her job as an investment banker (early, she'd be sure to tell anyone she met) and managing her own investments. "But it sure would be nice to be buried in couture."

And she deserved every bit of it. This was, after all,

the woman who dropped out of business school when she got married at age twenty-four and had my sister and me in quick succession. When we started school, she went back to work as a banker. She wasn't one of those Kool-Aid moms I saw in TV commercials, but she did cook dinner every night and clean the house and take care of three babies: my sister, me . . . and my domestically challenged dad. With all those responsibilities at home, her track to managing director just took a little longer than most.

As I got older, I came to realize just how remarkable she was. She loved her family, and she loved her life, and if she ever felt the slightest twinge of regret about having to juggle so many demands, she certainly never told us. Not directly, anyway. When I was six or seven she started replacing my favorite fairy tales at bedtime with her own Choose Your Own Adventure stories about girls who finished their educations, traveled the world, kept their own bachelorette pads, and generally lived the footloose and fancy-free life—in other words, more fairy tales.

Mom: So, Alex, you've just graduated from an Ivy League college with highest honors. You can either spend the summer with your good-for-nothing boyfriend back home or you can accept an internship at an art gallery in Rome. What do you do?

Me: Umm, Mommy, do I go to Rome?

Mom: Let's see what Alex is going to wear in Rome!

How much did I love this woman, who taught me everything I needed to know, my disastrous romantic track record notwithstanding? (And thanks to years of therapy, I knew that I couldn't blame her completely for that, either.) The woman who was going to let me live vicariously through her when she became a couture customer, after all these years of her living vicariously through me?

Which is why it stressed me out to ponder how I was going to juggle my mom, my work, the shopping, *and* Nick. I hadn't been this overbooked since senior year of high school. Or as zit-prone, I thought as I gingerly felt the telltale bump on my cheek.

I wrapped myself in my bathrobe when I heard the knock at the door. I let the maid in, practically prostrating myself at her feet, I was so grateful, and sat down at my laptop. I opened the calendar, and there it was in twenty-four-point bold italics. ***Friday: Mom arrives!!!***

The Dior extravaganza was scheduled for eleven, and after that there were a couple of small shows that I could conceivably miss. Fashion Week was winding down, after all, and my story lay elsewhere. I really could use a sit-down with Lola about Luis-Heinz. Maybe I could kill two birds with one stone and send my mom to the shows while I met with Lola. Brilliant idea! Mom would simply adore it. And we could meet up for dinner and then . . . maybe she would be so jetlagged, she would call it an early night. Then I could see Nick. Good thing he was working late. As for Saturday—I'd deal with Saturday later.

I was getting pretty good at this multitasking and troubleshooting. I could have been a military mastermind. Well, okay, maybe an event planner, a wedding planner. I scoffed at my earlier panic. I figured I wouldn't be me if

I didn't go through the freaked-out, nervous-Nelly stage, but still. Why did I ever doubt myself? I had it all worked out. This would be a cinch. Right.

To make it all official-like, I sent Lola an e-mail with my proposed plan of action, then I shot Jillian an e-mail saying that we absolutely definitely *must* talk later today. The clock on my computer said seven-thirty. I felt like I had already accomplished so much this morning. When the maid finished fluffing the towels and cleaning the remainder of the mess I had made the night before, I bade her farewell with a ridiculously large tip, locked the door, and raced to the bathroom. I figured I could fit in a quick shower, after all, before my mother arrived. She would be so surprised to see me up and ready to go this early in the morning; she had spent seventeen years (the first year of three a.m. feedings notwithstanding) of her life having to rouse me from my slumber well before my body was ready to get up.

But on this day, despite the little sleep I had gotten—or perhaps because of the lack of sleep, and the reason why—I was raring to go. Stepping out of the shower and toweling my hair, I hummed my way through Duran Duran's greatest hits, and halfway through "Is There Something I Should Know?" got distracted by the snicker-inducing thought that maybe I was a Nick girl now. I hadn't been this giddy since the moment I received my very first invitation to a Chanel sample sale. Or maybe the moment a few days later, when I actually walked into that hotel ballroom and got an eyeful of all the miraculous bargains that were to be had there.

Still wrapped in a towel, I walked over to the closet and pulled out my Friday clothes. While packing, I had searched long and hard and chosen carefully, keeping in mind that my mother was going to be with me. It was, quite possibly, the one demure outfit that had come off the Dior runway in the past four seasons: a black silk jersey top with a low V-neck that was covered up by lacing, and the slimmest black tuxedo pants. The black Manolos that I had forgotten to bring were slated with the outfit, so under other circumstances I would have substituted the new Louboutin slingbacks. But after what happened the last time I did that . . . I decided not to chance it. Since my Choos were wrecked, I'd have to wear the leopard-print Dolce & Gabbana heels. Mom would have to live with them.

I quickly got dressed and, with my wet hair still wrapped in a towel, returned to the bathroom to put on some makeup. The minute I sat down in front of the mirror, there was a knock on the door. I skipped over to the door and got ready for a big hug.

"Hi, Mom!"

"Hi, honey," she said with her slight twang. "What an awful cab ride. I know my French is rusty and all, but I swear he asked me if I was a model!"

I kissed her on both cheeks and hugged her tight. I truly was glad to see her.

The porter followed her into the room with two huge wheeled suitcases. (No one needed to wonder where I got my packing or shopping habits.)

"Ah, excusez-moi," I said, *"ma mère va rester dans la chambre adjacente."*

I led him through the bathroom and into the bedroom next door, and he followed, wheeling the suitcases along. I could only imagine how heavy they were.

My mom happily walked alongside me, carrying her Vuitton train case. "I had no idea you got us a suite, honey," she said, clearly pleased. "This is just too much!"

"I wanted your first trip to Paris to be the best ever," I said, hooking her arm in mine and giving her a squeeze. "We're fixin' to have the best time, just you and me." My Texan accent was slipping back into my brain. It just couldn't be helped.

When the porter deposited my mother's luggage in front of her closet, she gave him a twenty-euro note and sent him on his way. They must have been *really* heavy. She did a quick survey of the room and plopped herself on the bed. "I'm just beat," she said. "But when's the show, Alex? I have to get ready."

"Not until eleven, Mom, which really means noon," I explained—to deaf ears, apparently, as she jumped off the bed and made a beeline for her bags. "So you have plenty of time. Why don't you take a hot bath and we can have brunch before we go? Did you sleep on the plane?"

"Mmm-hmm," she said absentmindedly. She was already busy rifling through her suitcases. She pulled out a wrinkled silk blouse—the one I'd gotten her at the Armani sample sale last year. "Is there an iron here or do I need to steam this in the bathroom?"

"I'll iron it," I quickly replied. "I'll definitely iron it."

It was quarter of eleven by the time my mother had unpacked and primped and had her first real croissant and café au lait. And then she was ready to go. Despite what I had told her about fashionista time ("Oh, that's so cute y'all call it that!"), she wanted to be there promptly, so she could soak it all in. She had been so excited about the whole day—especially the part where she was going to fill in for me at the afternoon shows—that she had to call home to tell my dad all about it. His time? Oh, three-thirty in the morning.

Unused to the luxury of not having to scramble for a taxi and race across town, I took a leisurely stroll out of the hotel with my mother. And naturally, there was no one in line at the taxi stand—and five cabs waiting for a fare. We hopped into the first one, and I told the driver to take the scenic route to the Louvre.

"Mom, did I give you your invitation?"

No response. My mother had her face pressed against the window, transfixed by her new surroundings. She hadn't heard a word I'd said. I gave her a hug and a kiss on the cheek, and we sat in silence as the taxi wound its way through the streets of the Left Bank, past the Sorbonne, the Panthéon, the Jardin du Luxembourg, the Hôtel des Invalides, and the Eiffel Tower, then across the Seine and down the Champs-Elysées toward the Louvre.

The taxi dropped us off at one of the entrances on the rue de Rivoli, and we skipped down the escalator, two steps at a time, to the concourse level. Just around the corner from the shops that filled this Parisian version of the underground mall—Courrèges instead of the Gap, a few doors down from the much more chic European equivalent of the Tie Rack—was the auditorium where the show was to be held. It was just past eleven, so the crowd had reached critical mass. Behind a velvet rope was a corps of publicists, clipboards and walkie-talkies in hand; on the other side were the huddled masses yearning to breathe free perfume, but who would inevitably remain locked out, wretched refuse. I recognized some of the usual suspects in the latter category who formed something akin to a shadow fashion pack, hoping their number would be called one day. They could be found in every fashion capital anywhere there was free food and drink, and for that reason they were sometimes indistinguishable from journalists.

My mom and I passed serenely through the crowd—apparently, my ignominy was short-lived—and were cleared by the gatekeepers. We followed the trickle of attendees through some heavy velvet curtains and into the hall, which enveloped us in some dim mood lighting . . . and one big sand trap. There was sand everywhere, scattered all over the floor and dusting the white chairs; in fact, even days later, I would find tiny granules in my shoes, my bag, my suitcase. As bare-bones as the decor was, it was hard to tell whether the theme was beach party or desert caravan.

Instead of the usual setup of a catwalk down the middle and rows of stadium seating on three sides of the room, chairs were placed in groups all around the room, like one massive labyrinth. From any spot on the floor there was no telling the rhyme or reason of the seating order, but even in this chaotic configuration, there was clearly the front row and not-the-front row.

Still starry-eyed, my mother wanted to walk around the entire room, purportedly to find our seats. Which was fine by me. That's what everyone always did anyway; there was no point in being the first person sitting when the game was Critical Stares, not Musical Chairs. Besides, there was no way Lola would be able to hear her cell phone down here, so I'd just have to keep an eye out for the tall, leggy blonde—surely she'd be the only one, right?

As we milled about, my mother would tug on my arm and provide a running voice-over, as if she were narrating some Discovery Channel documentary, every time she saw someone she recognized from the pages of *W*. "There's the rubber-plantation heiress who just left her husband for a matador—such a scandal," she whispered. "And that's the viscount who made the mistake of marrying into dot-com money," she clucked, shaking her head sympathetically. "Ooh, and there's that New York socialite who's had as many ex-husbands as facelifts."

"Which number should we be more shocked about?" I asked, truly curious.

By half past eleven, the room had filled up. We found our front-row seats—and, more important, the goodie bags beneath them. My mom oohed and aahed over the freebie wraparound sunglasses. I thought the gilt touches and oversize frames were a bit over the top. Then again, *she* still lived in Texas.

Her attention was soon diverted by our neighbors: Across from us sat the rubber-plantation heiress, so my mother couldn't resist sneaking her new digital camera out of her red leather Dior D'Trick bag (the "something new" element of her Dior outfit, to go with her vintage Gianfranco Ferré–era suit). I was shocked that she could have fit even a wallet in that handbag, much less a camera, but then again my mom's purse always did seem to be magically bottomless, prepared for every one of my needs. Kleenex? Check. Nail clippers? Sure. Moisturizer? Yup. Granola bar? Here you go, honey.

"That's simply the most adorable camera," said a voice coming from the seat next to my mother. We both swiveled our heads in that direction.

"Thanks," my mom said casually, before doing a double take and realizing who it was sitting next to her. "Oh," was all she could say. "Oh."

It was, after all, Liza Rowland, the legendary silver-haired editrix who had left her regal mark on every major fashion magazine in the past twenty-five years. We were both struck speechless to be in the presence of such a fashion luminary.

I had to do something. "Hello, Ms. Rowland," I said, reaching around my mother's frozen figure and offering my right hand. "I don't know if you remember me, but we met last year at that big Armani fiasco—you helped me find my shoe. I'm Alex Simons, from *The Weekly*. And this is my mother, Mrs. Simons . . . umm, Pauline Simons."

Liza shook our hands warmly. "Of course I remember you, Alex," she said. Though I was sure she didn't, she sounded convincing, and I appreciated that. My mom did too. "And how lovely that you've brought your mother along."

"It's her first trip to Paris . . . right, Mom?" I said, nudging her to say something to her hero.

"Oh yes, and I'm just lovin' it," she said, finally.

"Where's that accent from?" asked Liza.

When my mom proceeded to trace her roots, they discovered that Liza had grown up in the town over from the one where my mother was raised in East Texas—and in fact they had had friends (and even a boyfriend, though thankfully not my dad) in common. Who knew? I always imagined that someone with Liza's bearing must have been eighth-generation Connecticut born and bred. Of course, no one would ever guess where I was from unless they saw my high school yearbook pictures. And if said pictures came with a voice recording circa 1991.

As I sat there pondering the hidden pasts of fashionistas, I was quickly becoming as extraneous as hips at a modeling go-see. Every so often a roving photographer came by to snap Liza, and she would pull her new best friend into the frame. My mom would do a quick hair toss and grin from ear to ear.

Checking my watch—twelve-fifteen already!—I looked around for any sign of Lola. She was so excited for my mother's initiation into the fashion cult that I was sure she'd stop by. Things must be pretty crazed backstage. Then I scanned the seats around me, trying to figure out if any of the men could be Bartolome. Hmm, I wondered, what exactly would a Peruvian professor look like? As I mentally eliminated the guy with the dreads and hemp outfit and, after some internal debate, the immaculately groomed middle-aged man in the mauve three-piece suit sitting across from me, the lights started flashing, and the speakers reverberated with the wailing sounds of gale-force winds. As the models began to move through the aisles, the wind machines wheezed into action. Sand, wind, dresses made from tarps and worn with Wellingtons: Could this be . . . hurricane chic? As the sand started kicking up, one by one the audience members scrambled for their goodie bags and slapped on the sunglasses. Some parts of the show plan were clearly better thought out than others, because before long, programs and pages from notepads were swirling across the room, and fashionistas were too busy trying to keep their hair in place to watch the runway. Seven minutes in—halfway through the show—the wind machines were finally turned down a notch, which downgraded conditions to merely tropical-storm level.

By the time the lights came up and the wind died down, everyone had a new beehive hairdo, and Liza and my mom had bonded like sorority sisters. I stood up and for a while tried to shake the sand from my clothes, my hair, my everything. I finally decided I just needed to be hosed down. I looked at my mom, who was showing Liza the unavoidably grainy pictures she had taken on her camera's LCD screen. "They're rather impressionistic," she joked. "Almost pointillism."

I kneeled next to the Texas twins and put my hands on my mom's knees. "So . . . this was quite an introduction to Fashion Week," I said. "I hope you had fun in any case."

"Honey, it was fabulous! The girls back home are *nevuh* gonna believe this." She looked at Liza and giggled. "And they're *nevuh* gonna believe I met you here."

"I can hardly believe it either!" Liza said, brushing some sand from her shoulder. "Alex, may I borrow your mother for the afternoon? She told me you had some work to do anyway."

"Yeah, Alex, I can get out of your hair for the afternoon—well, actually, I don't know how you'll get *anything* out of that mess on top of your head right now." The Girls laughed some more.

"Well, Mom, I think you're in good hands. Go have fun. We'll have our day together tomorrow, right? Oh, let me give you my tickets—"

"Oh, never mind that," Liza said. "Leave that to me. Let me just make one phone call, and we'll be off."

While Liza stepped away to use her cell phone, I turned to face my mom and put my arms around her. We did a group squeal. "Are you having fun?" I squealed. "Oh my God yes!" she squealed back.

"So I'm going to find Lola now," I said, trying to run my fingers through my tangled hair. "I'll see you back at the hotel, Mom . . . But wait a sec, do you have a brush I could borrow?"

The second I stepped backstage my heart sank. How was I supposed to find Lola when the place was swarming with tall blondes with windswept, sand-knotted hair? And how was she supposed to be able to spot me, flying below said tall blondes? I did a quick turn around the area, stopping once or twice to say hi to the fashionistas who had been sniping about me just a few days before. No matter. The collective memory was short in this business, which explained why certain unflattering styles—say, microminis and big shoulders—kept making comebacks.

Among the jaded fashion crowd paying their requisite respects, I could easily spot the newbies, mostly heterosexual males whose publicist friends had given them the gift of a lifetime by allowing them into the inner sanctum of modeldom. They were the ones with their jaws hanging agape as the models unabashedly stood around in their unmentionables. Stare too long, though, and they'd be glared down. Had the voyeurs been lucky enough to be backstage during the mayhem of the show, they could have watched at their leisure while the clothes went flying off and on at the speed of light, the girls too busy to notice who might have been watching. The first time I went backstage during a show, I too found it hard not to stare—but only because models, contrary to popular belief and their job title, were in fact more like freaks of nature than proportional ideals. They weren't considered human clothes hangers for nothing. I discovered that it was possible to be extremely tall *and* extremely scrawny at the same time. (Mind you, this was in the depths of the heroin-chic era.) In truth, it kind of frightened me. And oddly enough, it made me want to go out and have a burger.

Inching my way between the racks of clothes and packs of hangers-on, I finally saw Lola, curled up in a corner away from the action. She seemed completely engrossed talking on her cell phone, her free hand alternately gesturing dramatically and trying to untangle her hair. I lingered at a distance until she was done. She finally snapped the phone closed and let out a frustrated stream of expletives.

"Hey, watch your language, Miss Thing," I said, waving my hand in front of her face. "You're lucky my mom's not with me."

"Alex, hey," she said, still frowning. Almost subconsciously, she switched into publicist mode. "Oh, where is your mother then? How was her flight? Did she enjoy the show? Were your seats okay?"

"They were great," I said. "Better than any of us could've imagined, in fact. Seems that she grew up the next town over from Liza Rowland, of all people. They're like bosom buddies now. Liza's escorting her to the rest of the shows today."

"Wow. What a small world," Lola said, still sounding distracted.

"So what's the bad news you have for me?"

"Oh, right, yeah," Lola said as she absentmindedly dislodged sand from her bra—hang around backstage long enough and your inhibitions would disappear too. "I'm not sure what to make of it, actually."

I raised my eyebrows.

"Well, it was really strange," Lola began slowly. "I told you I invited Bartolome to the show, right? I didn't have time to look for him beforehand, so as the girls were making their final turn on the catwalk, I went over to find him. He was talking to this woman—God, she looked familiar, but I just couldn't place her . . ."

"Someone else who knows Luis-Heinz?"

"No . . ." she said distractedly, still racking her brain. "Oh my God, I just remembered. It's what's-her-name . . . What *is* her name?? The girl from Arkansas who won that *Mode* magazine modeling competition three years ago . . . Real cute, but with the weird name?"

"Oh crap, what's her name? Shanice . . . Shannie . . ."

"Shaunee!" we shouted out in unison.

"Oh my God, that is so gratifying," I said as Lola nodded enthusiastically. I loved it when I plucked a celebrity name or movie credit or sixth-degree-of-separation out of the air and matched it with a *Jeopardy!* answer or a face in a crowd, on a bus, on a TV sitcom. Somehow, each pop culture connect-the-dots made me feel a little better about all the proper education, say the trigonometry and physics, that had been slowly seeping out of my brain all these years. Well, at least they made for better cocktail party conversation than Bernoulli's principle. Whatever that was.

"... I know, and I haven't seen her in a long while," Lola was saying. "Whatever happened to her career, anyway?" After a good thirty seconds pondering that unsolved mystery, she finally continued. "Where was I? I know Bartolome totally saw me, we made eye contact and everything, but you know what? He just turned right around and ran off, dragging Shaunee along with him. I mean, really *ran off*. Turned back a couple of times to sneak a look at me, as if he wanted to make sure I wasn't following him. So I tried calling him just now and he didn't pick up. Guess he saw my number pop up and ..."

"Umm, are you starting to get just a little paranoid here?" I said, one eyebrow raised.

"No, definitely not. I mean, yeah, Luis-Heinz has some weird quirks and all, but this is really unlike Bartolome." Lola was pacing the floor now. "What if," she said pensively, "what if there's a love triangle here?"

"Huh? What are you talking about?"

"Like, what if Jacques and Luis-Heinz had a lovers' spat and Bartolome was the man in the middle?"

"Uh ... are you serious?"

"Well, why else would Bartolome not return my calls and act all furtive when he saw me?" She nodded emphatically. "See what I mean? It makes perfect sense. I think we have another mission to accomplish. We need to get Jacques and Luis-Heinz back together ... not just for fashion ..." She sighed. "But for *love*."

I wasn't quite sure how Lola had gotten from Point A to Point Z like that, but who was I to stand in her way? Giddy as I was at my own romantic prospects, I wasn't about to deny someone else's happiness. What the hell, I thought. Lola certainly had her heart in the right place.

Hadn't we both been deeply moved by what Jacques had told us about Luis-Heinz? Wasn't I glad to see him happy after all those years pretending to be something he wasn't? Wasn't looooove just so faaaaabulous?

"All right," I said, grinning. "Let's do it. Let's get Operation Cupid under way."

"Yay!" Lola exclaimed. "I thought you'd go for it! I'm so glad you're all gaga over that guy!"

She had me there. I just decided to ignore the comment. "But we still don't have any ideas on how to find him," I said.

"Oh yeah," Lola said, looking suddenly dejected. "I really don't think we're going to get anywhere with Bartolome. I mean, especially if he's trying to break them up . . ."

Even with my limited knowledge of the principal players, I didn't think that was the case, but I figured there was no point trying to burst Lola's bubble. She was right about his mysterious behavior, anyway. We couldn't rely on Bartolome for information.

"But," she continued, "maybe we can find some of Luis-Heinz's family? Maybe they've talked to him? When I first started working with him and I was trying to get a bio together, I managed to extract some information from him about his father's family in Switzerland. Can you imagine? It was like . . . like waiting for a bad haircut to grow out." Lola's face darkened at the memory.

I could empathize. I had had my share of deadly interviews in my career, like the time I had to write a three-page profile of the new face of a French perfume house that happened to be near and dear to Roddy's heart for some surely embarrassing reason. (Better that than some blatantly ad-sales-related reason.) In any case, I was dispatched to the model's hometown of Hjedding, Denmark, which I quickly realized was the European equivalent of the sleepiest farmland in, say, Wisconsin. There I spent a day—and since it was summer, it was a *long* day—with the fresh-faced, nineteen-year-old Mette Acthon and her five very proud, very protective, very Paul Bunyan–like brothers. Their English was perfect, of course; it was just that on this flying visit home, all Mette could talk about—to me or to her brothers—was how everything was *cool, yah*. Walking the runways for Armani? *Cool, yah.* Meeting Donatella Versace? *Cool, yah.* Growing up on a farm? *Cool, yah.* Living away from that farm? *Mmm . . . cool, yah.*

I could be excused, then, for bemoaning my lack of usable quotes or color or anecdotes for a good week before finally writing my allotted one thousand words in the form of a fairy tale. Happy ending and everything.

But before we could achieve a happy ending for Jacques and Luis-Heinz, Lola and I had to figure out where we were going to have to look. All he had told Lola was that his father's family was famous for its yodelers, and that growing up, he used to go to a festival they organized in the village of Aarau. "See what I mean?" she said, still frustrated. "And how was I supposed to work with that?"

Before I could give her a thoughtful answer, my cell phone rang. I checked the caller ID, but I didn't recognize the number.

"Alex Simons speaking."

"Honey, it's me." I could barely make out my mother's words over the loud hip-hop music playing in the background.

"Oh, hi, Mom," I said. "Where *are* you?"

"Oh, I just wanted to let you know that I might be late," she said. She must not have heard my question over the noise. "I'm with, uh, what's his name again, Diddly? Oh, sorry, I mean Diddy!"

"Diddy? As in P. Diddy?" I shot Lola a bewildered look.

"Yeah, P. Diddy," she said, giggling. "Liza and I ran into P. Diddy and we're joinin' his posse." More giggles, followed by the sound of champagne corks popping.

"Umm, all right, P. Mommy," I said, finding it hard not to be infected by her giggles. "You go have fun. I won't wait up!"

I hung up and turned back to Lola. "My mother is out of control. Champagne in the afternoon. What's next? Oh God, is she becoming a fashion groupie? Remember that guy my friend Veronica knows? The one who's paid to be that German designer's friend? *That* could be my mother!"

"Darling, worse things could happen," Lola said. "At least she'll look good."

"But what am I supposed to tell my dad? We'll have to go after her next, after Luis-Heinz."

Lola folded her arms in front of her chest. "Yes, well, let's get to the matter at hand: When are we going to Switzerland?"

"Umm, I can't yet . . ."

"It's that boy again, isn't it?"

"Uh! Please! Give me some credit! I was thinking about my mom," I said, knowing full well that my face was exhibiting a telltale blush. "I can't go until after she leaves. I'm taking her to her first Chanel fitting, remember?"

"Of course," Lola said, a dreamy look crossing her face. "How fabulous will that be?"

And as much as I tried, I couldn't keep from blurting out my Nick news. "And I do have a date tonight too . . ."

"I knew it!" Lola exclaimed. "I knew it, I knew it, I knew it. That's really shameless, hiding behind your mom like that."

"I *know*!" I said. "I am *so* bad." I giggled (it was really uncontrollable at this point). "We had a *fantastic* time last night. And . . . he asked to see me tonight, too." It occurred to me—for a second, before I brushed it off in my exhilaration—that this gloating might be really annoying. But what were friends for, after all?

"So is your mom going to meet him while she's here?" Lola asked.

That's what friends were for: asking the tough questions.

"Oh my God, it's far too early to be parading him in front of my *mother*, isn't it?" I gasped. "But how can I avoid it? She's staying with me. Oh good Lord, what am I going to do?"

"Um, hope she stays out all night with P. Diddy?"

While I giggled like a blushing schoolgirl, Lola joined in with her own high-pitched snicker, which I suddenly noticed I could hear quite clearly. The crowd had thinned considerably, leaving us alone with two guards and a few models who were packing up their new freebies from the show. The rest of the fashion crowd had moved on to the next runway.

"I guess we should get out of here," Lola said. "Someone else is taking the clothes back to the showroom, but I have to get ready for all the appointments tomorrow.

But don't worry, I haven't forgotten that I'm taking you and your mom to lunch."

We made plans to meet at Dior the next day, but we figured we wouldn't be able to launch Operation Cupid until Monday, when our schedules would be clear (except for a rendezvous or two with Nick, I silently hoped). Lola hugged me goodbye on the sidewalk and wished me luck that night. It was only two o'clock, and inspired by my newfound appreciation for the city of romance, I decided to walk back to my hotel, heels and all. I ducked back under the passageway and into the courtyard of the Louvre, and strolled toward the river. I dug around in my bag for my cell phone and speed-dialed Jillian.

"Hey, it's me," I said.

"Alex! I've been waiting for my daily update. Where are you?"

"Um, standing on the Pont des Arts . . . I'm walking back to the hotel."

"Walking? In your heels? Standing on a bridge? Are you . . . *in love?"*

"Oh Christ. Is that your expert diagnosis? I've tried, really—I've tried to resist."

"This is *Jillian* you're talking to. And I'm going to tell you, as your best friend, that it's okay to have a little fun!"

"I am . . ."

"Uh-huh. And I'm sure you're also second-guessing yourself every minute, too. And I want you to stop it!"

"Wow, where's this tough love coming from?" I asked playfully.

"From someone who knows," she said, quite authoritatively. "Now I gotta run to a meeting. But I want to catch up later. I'll call you, okay?"

I hung up with a smile on my face. Jillian knew me better than anyone else in the world, so she had to be right. What *was* the harm in having a little fun? It wasn't like I was practicing signing my name with Snow at the end of it or anything. Damn, I muttered to myself, now that I think about it . . .

An hour later, I was at the door of my suite, having released my aching feet from my heels the minute I hit the carpeting at the hotel. A tiny blister had formed on the side of my big toe, so I limped into the room and headed over to the bed. Halfway there, out of the corner of my eye, I spied a big vase of red roses on the table, so I stopped in my tracks and limped right back. I took a big whiff of the bouquet, sighed, and picked up the card at its side. Better not be from Chanel, I laughed to myself. It wasn't, of course. Just four sweet little words: "See you tonight. Nick."

I breathed in the scent of the roses again and flung myself on the sofa, propping my aching feet up. From that vantage point, I could watch TV and still gaze over at the flowers. I sighed contentedly. This might call for some extra fashion-induced suffering tonight—I might just have to wear that super-sexy, super-suffocating Alaïa.

After a quick scan of the TV channels—during the shows, all the stations were practically all fashion, all the time—I went to the bathroom to soak my feet. I had to make them look presentable for tonight. What the hell was I thinking, walking the streets of Paris in three-inch heels? Today, at least, there was time for touching up my pedicure, if not for going to get one in the hotel's salon.

Keeping my toes daintily splayed, I shuffled over to my laptop; I figured I could get some work done while the polish dried. I picked up my tape recorder and started transcribing the interview with Jacques. With every word I typed, I became more and more emotional. Before long, tears were streaming down my face. As I reached for a tissue to blow my nose, I reckoned that in my current state a TV commercial about diapers might make me cry. (Babies! Awwww . . .)

Given the pace at which I was sniffling, blowing, and typing, I still wasn't finished with the interview when I heard the key turning in the lock. I looked at my watch: six o'clock.

"Mom, is that you?" I called out, still staring at the screen of my laptop as I typed. "Are you alone?"

"Of course I am, honey," she said as she practically pranced into the sitting room, her new Dior sunglasses perched atop her head and a bottle of Cristal in her hand. "P. Diddy sends his best regards," she said, placing the bottle on the desk in front of me with a dramatic flourish. "Oh my Gawd, it was so wild! You shoulda seen the spread he had at his suite. The whole floor, actually! Everything was blindingly white, even all the food. Liza and I were the only ones not wearin' white . . . Honey, what does *hoochie* mean?"

That instantly got my attention. I raised my head from the screen and looked my mom in the eye. The tables were turned. Was this not something I might have asked her when I was seven? "Umm . . . it's, uh, kinda like, uh, *skanky*."

"Oh! Well, that makes sense then," she said primly, slipping her shoes off and reclining in a chair across from me.

"I'm surprised you're back so early," I said, saving my document and closing the laptop.

"Honey, I'm here to see *you*. I thought we were havin' dinner together."

"You'd had enough of the Puff, huh?" I grinned at her.

"Plenty enough to tell all my friends," she said. Her eyes scanned the room and landed on the vase on the table. "Why, who sent you those gorgeous roses?"

I could see she was getting up to go inspect them. My reflexes sharpened by my sudden panic, I shot out of my chair and—somehow maintaining a casual air—scooped up the note while pretending to rearrange some of the stems. "Oh, they *are* lovely, aren't they," I said, pausing to sniff one of the roses. I added in a mumble, "Just a nice gesture from some publicist."

Now, why would anyone lie to her mother about something like that? A reasonable question—without a reasonable answer. The minute the words came out of my mouth, I was already wondering why I felt compelled to hide Nick—or even the idea of Nick—from my mother. I was, after all, thirty-one years old, and though I almost never talked to my mom about my love life (what there was to tell, anyway), I could safely assume that she safely assumed that I had one. It just seemed to me that neither of us particularly wanted to fill in the details. In any case, I thought she was always more interested in hearing about my datelines, not my dates.

Speaking of which, I hadn't figured out how I was supposed to go on my date with my mom here as my roommate. My mind was racing, trying to come up with an excuse to slip out. Damn, why didn't I have Nick's phone number, so we could arrange to meet elsewhere? He's going to turn up at our door, and Mom . . .

"Honey, do you mind if we have an early dinner? I'm just pooped."

Oh, thank you, Mommy.

"Sure," I said. "It's a little touristy, but I figure you can't go to Paris and not eat at Café de Flore. It's a ten-minute walk from here. We'll save the really nice dinner for tomorrow, after our couture appointment!" Just saying those two beautiful little words—and seeing my mother's reaction to them—made all the other complications in my life drift away. For now.

It was seven-fifteen by the time we were seated at the storied café on a prime corner of the boulevard St.-Germain, whose former habitués, beautiful minds like Jean-Paul Sartre, had lately been replaced by beautiful people wearing Jean-Paul Gaultier. The weather had turned chilly, so we took a small table indoors. Compared to her earlier adventure, Café de Flore should have seemed prosaic. But still my mother soaked it all in: the original Art Deco moldings and lamps and mirrors, the chain-smokers, the haughty waiter who barely acknowledged us when we were ready to order. This *was* a Parisian experience.

"Je voudrais le confit canard, s'il vous plaît," my mother said. *"Et un express."*

"Décaféiné," I interjected. I was thinking of my ten o'clock rendezvous. I ordered an omelet—surely that would be fast.

The waiter brusquely turned on his heel and returned a

few minutes later with a basket of sliced bread and butter, followed by my mother's espresso and my bottle of Evian, with the tiny drinks receipt slid underneath. I involuntarily stared at the espresso. *It had better be decaf*, I thought.

"So what should I wear tomorrow? I brought my cream Chanel suit, from the spring 1998 collection. Do you think that'll do, Alex? I mean, it's just ready-to-wear and all . . ."

". . . and we're going to the couture!" we yelped in unison.

"Oh, Mom, this is so exciting," I said, and I really meant it. "This is going to be the best!"

"I've been waitin' for the longest time to do this, and Lord knows how long I've been savin' for it!" she said. In truth, a couple of years of not having to pay my college tuition anymore probably did the trick. She just never felt comfortable dropping thirty grand on a suit until she had gotten her retirement in order.

My mom smiled sweetly at me from across the table. "I'm so glad you're here with me. It's the best mother–daughter bonding experience I can think of."

"Me too, Mom."

"Okay, so I was thinkin' of what I should order." Suddenly all business, my mother opened her handbag and pulled out a sheaf of color printouts from a fashion Web site. She shuffled through the pages and passed me the third one. The sixth outfit, a fluted knee-length coat of red-flecked cream tweed that was edged with chiffon, was circled in red marker. "I just love this little suit, but do you think it's too young for me? God knows what young girls are doin' buyin' couture . . ."

I stared at the picture and sucked in some air. "It's

amazing," I said, gently petting the picture with my fingers, as if I could feel the fabric.

But my mom was already on to her next selection—the second of twenty, it turned out. As we discussed the pros and cons of each outfit, I stole a glance at my watch. Already quarter past eight. And where was our food?

Wrapped up in her life-altering decision about what to order at Chanel, my mother didn't notice my fidgeting. I tried to focus on the conversation—which was largely my mom's thinking out loud anyway—and when the food finally came, I talked and ate at the same time, hoping she'd succumb to my peer pressure.

"I didn't realize how famished I was," I said, scooping a big piece of omelet into my mouth. "Mmm, delicious. So how about outfit number twelve?"

By the time my mother finally put her fork down, unable to finish the duck salad, I was already frantically waving my American Express card at the waiter. Luckily my mom was too busy still poring over her printouts, happily debating the merits of look number eight versus look number twenty, to notice my breach of etiquette.

We got back to the hotel in eight minutes flat—I suggested we walk briskly since, despite the cloudless night, I fibbed that I had heard that it was going to rain—and once inside our room, I excused myself to go to the bathroom. There, I zipped myself into the Alaïa that I had hung up earlier (not to steam, certainly) and wrapped my bathrobe around it. I rubbed my eyes and practiced yawning as I walked back out to the sitting room.

"Haven't we both had an eventful day," I said cheerfully, letting out a yawn. "And we're going to have a big day tomorrow, too."

"I know!" my mom said. "I don't know how I'm going to be able to sleep."

I involuntarily let out a gasp, which I tried to cover up with a stifled yawn. "Mmm, I think I'm gonna be out like a light," I said, "and you're probably more tired than you think." I nodded for emphasis.

My mom was flipping through the magazines on the coffee table. I glanced around the room, searching for inspiration. Nothing. I stared at her and concentrated hard, silently willing her to move. To my intense surprise—would I be bending spoons next?—she yawned and got up. It was nine-fifteen. I walked over to her to give her a big hug, and at the same time subtly nudge her toward the bathroom door.

"I'll tuck you in," I said with a laugh.

"Oh, honey, I have to clean my face and brush my teeth and find my moisturizer in my train case . . ."

The panic manifested itself, as it was wont to do, as a twitch in my right eye. "Oh!" I said, a light going off in my head. "You can use my Crème de la Mer. It's right on the vanity there." Nicely averted. Now if only I had a sleeping pill to slip her . . . *Did I just think that?* I banished the evil thought from my head, but kicked myself for not planning ahead.

Luckily for me, my mom wasn't a dawdler by nature. In fifteen minutes, she was cleansed and moisturized and ready for bed. I walked her over to her bedroom, kissed her good night, and threw in another yawn for good measure.

"Sweet dreams, Mom," I said, retreating through the bathroom door.

I checked my watch. Twenty to ten. I took a look at

myself in the mirror and gasped. I had forgotten all about the sandstorm I'd been through. In a panic, I hung my head over the sink and shook it until I felt a migraine coming on. I looked back up. Not much improvement. Christ. Not the wet-hair look *again*. I turned on the water and did my best to rinse out the sand. I picked up the hairdryer, then put it back down when I realized it would wake up my mother. I grabbed a towel and started patting, then gave up and just tied my hair back. I really hoped that Nick was running late. Bloody hell. I hadn't yet figured out how I was going to intercept him before he made it up to the room. I'd have to hang out in the lobby and come up with a reason later . . . so I'd better hurry.

I dabbed on some concealer—not that it did much for that zit that was now in full bloom on my left cheek—and powdered my face. Some eyeliner and lipstick, and that would have to do. I raced back to my bedroom and put on some thick cotton socks and slowly tiptoed through the bathroom to the door to my mother's bedroom. Grimacing, I prayed that the hinges were well oiled as I tried my best to push the door open a millimeter at a time. It didn't make a sound—and in the dark all I could hear coming from her room was her heavy, cadenced breathing. Phew.

I shut the door again and slipped back into my room, where I threw off my bathrobe and socks. I picked up the Dolce & Gabbana heels from the floor and spritzed myself with some perfume. I took a deep breath. T minus five.

This sneaking around was all new to me; I certainly never did it as a teenager. Back in high school, I was as good a kid as any parent could hope for. No breaking curfew, no drinking, no smoking. I guess I was saving it for my thirties.

On an exaggerated tiptoe, I jauntily made for the door. Wait! Abort, abort! I realized I hadn't changed purses, so I had to double back to the bedroom, where I emptied my Vuitton bag and picked out my ID, credit card, some euros, a compact, and a lipstick and stuffed them into my new little pink Prada bag. I headed back to the door and ever so gently turned the knob, opened the door a crack, and slipped out, slowly shutting it behind me with the quietest click of the lock I could muster. Standing safely outside the room, I patted my hair, tugged my dress down, and crept my way to the elevator.

I was ready for takeoff.

Chapter Nine

I HIT THE ELEVATOR'S CALL BUTTON ONCE. Hearing no movement, I punched it again. Still nothing. I leaned on it like a car horn in rush-hour traffic. That is to say, ineffectually.

If this was going to be my one instance of being an ugly-American tourist, so be it. Where was that elevator? I tapped my right foot. I tapped my right fingers on my left arm. I tugged at my dress and wiggled and thrust my décolletage into place. I picked at my manicure. And just as the sound of the elevator car started coming closer, I scanned both sides of the hallway. Certain that I was alone, I took advantage of what I figured would be my last opportunity of the evening to get some temporary relief from what had to be right up there with strapping on bunion-inducing, nosebleed-high heels in the Things Women Do to Make Themselves Look Sexy, Not That Most Men Would Ever Notice category. I hiked up the right side of my dress and pulled my Cosabella thong out of the wedgie position.

I was quick.

The elevator was quicker.

As the door slid open, my right hand was somewhere on the back of my right thigh, my body bent back as if I were about to dodge bullets à la Keanu Reeves in *The Matrix*. And there, with perfect timing as always, was Nick, stepping off the elevator.

I jerked back to vertical, hands on hips. As I stood there, trying out a smile, I noticed that in my startled rush I hadn't quite gotten my dress smoothed down. The bottom of the right side of the dress was folded up, doubly binding my thigh. No wonder I couldn't feel a darn thing.

"Uh, Nick!" Out of the corner of my eye, I saw the el evator man wink at me as the doors slid closed discreetly and he retreated down to the lobby. I scrambled to roll down the dress, and then couldn't stop patting it, smoothing it down, just to be safe.

"Hi, Alex," Nick said, not even trying to be subtle as he checked me out. I looked down at my feet and felt my face flush. He leaned over, kissing me lightly on the lips as he swung his arm around my shoulder. "Have you been lying in ambush all this time?"

With his arm still wrapped around me, he motioned toward the hallway to my suite. I felt my head slowly shake an almost imperceptible no. Then I planted my stilettos. I hadn't exactly thought this one out. Was I going to tell him that my *mommy* was asleep in there? Uh, no. But I couldn't exactly tell him it was a mess or something. Not again. Then he might think I was a walking disaster.

"I thought we'd spend some time alone, far from the

madding crowd," he said, giving me a smile that looked innocent but screamed naughty. My body almost revolted against my brain. What's the harm, I thought. Mom's fast asleep . . . Brain took charge.

"Um, how about going to your place then?" I raised my face toward his and shot back an equally meaningful grin.

For the first time since we'd met—not that it had been that long—Nick looked nervous. Call me paranoid, but his smile seemed to freeze for a second too long, and his eyes blinked, blankly, just a few too many times. And then the moment passed. He chuckled. "So you want to see how neat I really am?" he said, giving me a playful squeeze.

Sure, I *was* curious whether his housekeeping erred on the side of obsessive-compulsive or on the side of empty pizza boxes and stinky socks. But in that split second, when I couldn't tell just what thought processes were going on behind those ever-changing, hazel-gray-green eyes of his, I was a lot more anxious about what he might be hiding back at home. Was he mentally checking whether there was any evidence on public display of a girlfriend . . . a wife . . . or, as Jacques suddenly popped into my head, a boyfriend? I wasn't entirely sure why I was being so distrustful, so suspicious. Maybe because, in a weird and wacky way—i.e., despite the unexpected entrances, the flooded bathtub, the broken heel, my new chaperone tucked into the bed next door—things really seemed too good to be true.

Then again, maybe it was just me.

"You know, it's not fair," Nick was saying while I brooded (unnecessarily, I thought to myself when I rejoined the conversation). "*You* have housekeeping at your hotel, turndown service, even. I have to clean up after myself, you know."

"And look what good that did me." I grinned. "Are you going to get back at me by making me clean *your* floor?"

"What a great idea, and thanks for offering!"

Nick hit the elevator button, which seemed to work for him a lot better than it had for me. The elevator zipped up to our floor in two seconds flat. Embarrassed by the earlier peep show, I avoided eye contact with the elevator man as he ferried us down to the lobby. Outside, Sébastien was ready for us, standing by the Mercedes across the street from the hotel. He held the door open for me as I slid into the backseat. Instead of joining me immediately, though, Nick stopped at the door and leaned against it, nearly shutting it. He bent his head close to Sébastien's and seemed to be talking; I couldn't really see or hear. Sébastien, poker-faced, just nodded. Damn his cool demeanor. I wanted to know what was going on.

The conversation took less than thirty seconds, and when Nick climbed into the car, he said that he was just organizing a little surprise for me. I decided to give him the benefit of the doubt . . . but I wasn't necessarily going to give him an easy time.

"Wait a minute," I said, "didn't you tell me you lived near my hotel the night we met? Within walking distance, if I recall. That was why you got out of the cab with me."

"Well, umm, errr . . ." He grinned sheepishly. "Did I mention that I come from a long line of marathoners?"

"Uh-huh. Starting out with a white lie . . ."

"Hey, give a guy a break . . . Besides, what was that banned substance we were inhaling that night?"

I just sat there, arms folded, trying to keep the giggles from breaking up the stern look I had on my face.

"Well, technically, the Eiffel Tower *is* just one arrondissement over from where you're staying," he said.

"Is that where we're going?"

"Just a pit stop. Then my place is right around the corner."

I unfolded my arms and edged closer to him. "You . . . are such a guy."

"You won't hold it against me, will you?"

"I'll try not to."

He reached out for my hand and laced his fingers through mine. He looked me straight in the eye, suddenly serious. "I—" He stopped and started again. "I—" More hesitation.

I looked back at him, eyebrows raised, head tilted questioningly.

And just like that, his smile returned. "I—I hope you don't think going to the Eiffel Tower is terribly cheesy."

"Well, I can't say I haven't been there before," I said, adding with a giggle, "but I've never been there with a *boy* before."

"Uh-oh," he said. "Now I'm nervous. I've got expectations to live up to!"

"I'll be easy." My brain caught up with my mouth a split second after those words came out. My face must have instantly shifted fifteen shades to beet red. "Easy—easy on you," I sputtered. "I meant, I'll be easy on you. That's what I meant to say . . . Umm, are we there yet?"

I turned my head awkwardly and started staring out the window. I could already see a smattering of lights that beckoned from the Eiffel Tower. Thank God. If I concentrated, maybe I could keep my Dolce & Gabbanas safely out of my mouth.

Sébastien pulled up alongside the curb adjacent to the Champ de Mars, the grassy field leading up to the Eiffel Tower. He opened the door and helped me out while Nick went out the other side. As Sébastien held on to my arm to make sure I wouldn't stumble—I guess he'd seen enough of my smooth moves last night—I noticed that his brow was furrowed. But I couldn't read the expression on his face. I wasn't sure if he was bothered that my lipstick was amiss or if he was actually trying to look sympathetic. And sympathetic to what, I didn't know.

So I shrugged it off and rejoined Nick, who had walked around the front of the car to meet me. It was getting late, and only if we hurried would we be able to catch the last elevator ride to the top and steal a few minutes of the panoramic view.

As I turned my head to look for Nick, I saw two dark SUVs pulling up behind us. At first I assumed there were tourists inside, first-timers in Paris trying to squeeze in every sight in their six days, seven nights. But then I noticed the blacked-out windows, and as their engines purred in unison and their low-beam lights illuminated the street before me, I instantly imagined—what else?—two celebrities, in the first blush of secret love, huddled with their respective beefy bodyguards in their respective cars, traveling separately to evade the paparazzi, only to be spotted on their tryst by me, Alex Simons, fashion reporter. Why the subterfuge? Were they costars in a romantic comedy that was continuing off the set? Were they otherwise engaged or married or cohabiting? Star-crossed like J. Lo and Puffy . . . or just list-crossed—she A-list, he borderline C?

My fantasy scenario soon evolved in my mind into the big scoop I could deliver to Roddy. Of course, I had never been trained in the mysteries of celebrity reporting-cum-stalking: (a) "doorstepping," a quaint colloquialism I learned from a friend who had cut his teeth at an Australian tabloid, which essentially meant hanging out in front of a celebrity-in-turmoil's house for hours in hopes of getting a glimpse of him or her taking out the garbage—which, naturally, segued into (b) digging through said garbage, and (c) hiding in the bushes with a long-lens camera. But I could just wing it, if a juicy bit of gossip happened to land in my lap . . .

Before I could unmask the mystery couple, Nick had his arm around me and was shuffling us toward the massive tower, which at this close range cast a huge shadow over everything, even in the dark. After a quick glance back at the SUVs—no sign of life, celebrity or otherwise—I turned my attention to the living, breathing man at my side, who was tugging at me to get a move on.

"Hey, you, if we don't hustle, we're gonna have to take the stairs," he said.

I covered my mouth and let out an exaggerated gasp. "Oh no, not the *stairs!*"

"Desperate times, desperate measures," he said.

As we approached the base of the tower, we fell into step with the tourists and couples milling about. Even at this hour there were souvenir vendors hawking everything Eiffel, from glow-in-the-dark stickers to miniature replicas to postcard reproductions of photographs that seemed to have been taken sometime in the 1960s and mimeographed a thousand times since. We bypassed them all and made our way to the ticket booth, where ten euros bought you the view from the top of the world, and followed the small crowd into the line for the lift.

"Can't you use your press pass or something to cut the line?" Nick joked.

"You know, that only works in the movies," I said. "And I don't even really *have* a press pass. Or a hat that says 'Press' on the brim, either."

"Well, what good is that, then? Where are the perks?"

"These days," I said, laughing at the absurdity of the truth, "you don't need a press pass to get you places. You just need a camera crew following you: instant fame and access."

Nick didn't respond. He had suddenly started craning his neck toward the front of the line. "By the looks of it," he said, "we'll just make the next group going up."

I nodded and glanced back at the dozen people who had suddenly materialized behind us in the line. It was always reassuring to see people behind me when I was waiting; it was like realizing I hadn't been at the tail end of a fad. "Are they all going to make it?" I mused. "Seems unfair to sell them tickets and then shut the door in their faces, doesn't it?"

A few minutes later, Nick and I and fifteen other people were crowded into the elevator, watching in sympathy as the three unlucky leftovers began to walk away, and get tinier and tinier as we went up and up.

I was leaning back against Nick, who was standing along the side of the elevator, and still I was in close enough proximity to three other women that I could identify their perfumes: two Chanels and one YSL.

We rode up in silence, except for the three American backpackers in the opposite corner, who, as I could barely make out, were discussing the pros and cons of their hostel. I could feel Nick's breath on my neck, his nose grazing the hair behind my left ear.

"I have something to tell you," he whispered suddenly.

I tilted my head five degrees toward him. "That you're claustrophobic?"

"Mmm . . . no. Really, something important."

The elevator came to a halt and the door crept open for the first platform. No one got off. I turned another five degrees, this time bringing in some shoulder movement. "That you need to pee?"

He leaned down and said in my ear: "No, seriously."

This time I did the full one-eighty. "What do you mean?"

The elevator stopped again—and again no one stepped out onto the second platform. The pulleys wheezed into action and began the final ascent to the top.

Nick put his hands on my shoulders and looked me straight in the eye.

I stared back, my eyes wide and body tilted forward. Everyone observing me—Nick included—would have believed that he had my full attention. And everyone would have been wrong. As he hemmed and hawed, my mind was racing through all the possible scenarios—kind of like my mom's Choose Your Own Adventure bedtime stories.

(1) Are we here because he wants to get into my pants? *That would be pretty predictable male behavior. But let's give him the benefit of the doubt. Next.*

(2) Did he bring me here to ask me to go steady? *Next!*

(3) Did he bring me here to dump me? (Could you even technically *get* "dumped" after just forty-eight hours out in the real, post-college world?) *Let's investigate this one further.*
   (a) Was it because he hated my job, my world?
   (b) What on earth did I do wrong?
   (c) Did I have something in my teeth?

And still I gazed at him, smiled, and nodded, waiting for him to snap me out of my delirium. I had long perfected the art of looking interested and engaged when in fact any number of things could be going on behind my eyes. The skill had come in handy in my line of business. With the tape recorder on, and my head trained to nod every thirty-four seconds or so, I could safely compose grocery lists in my mind as some model deigned to let me in on the secret of what she really thought about when she was walking down the runway. But wasn't that only appropriate?

The elevator came to a halt at the very top of the tower, and without so much as an *"Excusez-moi,"* the surge of the crowd swept us up and delivered us onto the viewing platform. And there, with all of Paris lit up below us, all I could think of were the lyrics to the theme song from the movie *Arthur*. I had never seen the movie, but for some reason the song had imprinted itself in my brain, perhaps waiting for a moment like this. What happens when you get caught between the moon and New York City? Well, I was perched between the moon and Paris . . . and the time for conversation had passed. The twinkle in Nick's eye, the twinkle of the lights all around us—the best that I could do was let myself go.

So in the middle of all the tourists jockeying for

position against the rails, the moon, the stars, and the twinkling lights, Nick and I stopped midstep and made like that black-and-white Robert Doisneau photograph that graced the walls of four out of five college dorm rooms. By the time we released each other from The Clinch, the crowd had scattered, tittering about the couple that needed to get a room.

"So what were you trying to tell me?" I said, leaning back against his arm.

Nick pulled me toward him and put his hand on the back of my head. (I wondered, with some embarrassment, if he'd find any grains of sand.) Then he pressed his cheek against mine and whispered in my ear: "I think I was trying to say let's get out of here."

Nick and I had to wait five minutes for the next elevator down—our feet tapping impatiently as we remained entwined in each other's arms—and practically raced each other back across the field toward the car, giggling all the way. We must have caught Sébastien by surprise, as he was leaning against the Mercedes, smoking a cigarette, when we approached. He scrambled off the car with a start and instantly dumped his cigarette in the gutter. As he opened the door for me, I saw him raise an eyebrow at Nick. I sneaked a look back at Nick, whose face revealed nothing.

"Where to?" I said, once we were in the car.

"Let's just drive for a while," he said, to Sébastien as much as to me. And then he hit the button that raised the tinted glass between the front seat and the back.

"You bad boy, you . . ."

"Have I told you how amazing you look tonight?" he suddenly said.

I reflexively started to run my left hand through my hair. "Oh," I mumbled, "thank you." My hand stopped midsentence, as I felt some grains of sand dislodge from my hair and drop onto the seat. Oh, that's just dead sexy, I thought.

Nick slid over toward me and put his right hand on top of my left.

"Don't feel around too much," I said.

"Huh?"

"Um, occupational hazard . . . a sandstorm at the Dior show today."

Nick started laughing. That deep, sexy chuckle that seemed to emanate from somewhere inside his body, combined with the dimple etched in his cheek, made him quite simply irresistible. Which meant that I just couldn't help myself. The girl who never made the first move—well, she did.

When I stopped to catch my breath (and while I was at it, I figured I should let Nick get over the shock of my sudden aggressiveness), I eased back into the soft leather seat and gazed at my man. Or should I have said, *the* man? I surely didn't want to be overly possessive prematurely. I felt the deep, bloodred flush take seed in the pit of my stomach and begin to spread outward toward the surface of my skin.

"Where are we going, anyway?" I managed to ask. It gave me an excuse to turn away from Nick and maybe check my reflection in the window. Okay, lipstick's not too smeared, nothing in my teeth, and my face was closer to peach than beet red. Phew.

"Going in circles," Nick said under his breath.

"What's that?" I swung back around, a big smile at the ready. He was slumped in his seat, staring at his hands, which were folded in his lap. He could tell that I was looking at him, but he didn't shift his gaze for what seemed like an eternity. Finally, he leaned forward and knocked on the partition. *"La maison, s'il vous plaît, Sébastien."*

I kept looking at him blankly. But he didn't turn to face me. "We need to talk," he said, still mumbling in the direction of his lap. His words hung in the air like a spritz of musky perfume, intense at first and then slowly suffocating. I was certain that had I been able to do a quick poll of all my female friends at that very moment, they would have unanimously and independently asserted that those four little words foretold very bad things. Though I suspect that my more cynical friends would have added as an aside that the three little words seldom led to anything good, either.

My heart pounding and my right eye twitching—there it went again, like clockwork—I sat stiffly on my side of the backseat, gnawing on the inside of my cheek to prevent myself from trying to break the awkward silence, as I was wont to do, by saying something inopportune or simply inappropriate.

That was a real struggle.

Before too long—luckily for my raw cheek—Sébastien turned into a gated driveway, and after a brief pause at the guard station, we passed through. I stared out the window at the perfectly manicured hedges and flowerbeds ano rows of classical statuary and for a split second wondered how it was possible to drive through the Tuileries. In the distance sat an immense mansion, a mini-chateau, really. As we drove up to the white stone facade, what else could I do but gawk? That and ponder whether what Nick wanted to talk about had anything to do with being the long-lost heir to some throne. But that could only happen in the movies.

I turned around and looked at Nick. "We're not in Kansas anymore, are we?" I said.

"No, just Neuilly."

Ah. That suburb of Paris where French starlets and rappers moved their mothers once they hit it big.

"Well, it's in the same direction," he said. "In case you're still quibbling with my calling this close to your hotel and close to the Eiffel Tower."

"Oh, I think I've got bigger issues to quibble with at this point," I said. My surroundings had somehow shocked the tact right out of me.

Nick got out of the car and walked around to open the door for me. As I stepped onto the gravel of the driveway, he took my hand and guided me along the side of the mansion, down a path lit by a row of candles illuminating pastel-colored paper bags. The candlelight led us to a white wooden gazebo that stood at the edge of some woods.

Nick sat me down on the bench in the gazebo and began to pace.

"So," I said, after he had circled me twice.

He stopped and looked at me. "So."

"You wanted to talk?"

"Yes. Yes, we should talk."

I attempted to smile reassuringly—reassuring to myself, at least—and waited for him to say something, anything.

"I guess you've figured out by now that this isn't corporate housing," he said with a nervous laugh.

"Yeah, it didn't strike me as too corporate," I said, trying to stay cool. "Not in this economy, anyway."

"Alex," he said, stopping to kneel in front of me and put his hands on my shoulders. "I'm not exactly who I told you I was."

My heart was beating so fast, I felt like I was having an out-of-body experience. The real me was floating above us, watching the how-could-this-be-happening-to-me version of me.

"I mean, my name *is* Nick Snow, and I really *am* from New York."

Okay, so I could cross off the "he's really a prince" scenario. Damn.

"But I'm not here on a consulting job," he said.

So what was it, CIA? NSA? International man of mystery?

I could see the beads of sweat forming at his temples. His eyes looked intense, darker than I'd ever seen them. He wiped his brow with his sleeve.

"And I can't tell you why I'm here unless you sign something." He pulled out an envelope from the pocket inside his jacket and handed it to me sheepishly. "I'm really sorry about this." He averted his gaze while I opened the envelope and leafed through the pages of single-spaced type. I couldn't put two words together in my current state.

"I'm sorry, I can't understand any of this," I said, folding the papers up and handing them back to him. "Just tell me what we're doing here. Please."

Nick got up and sat down on the bench next to me. He

tossed the papers onto the table, then surveyed the landscape all around us. The night was still, silent.

He gently took my hands in his and gazed down at them. "Alex, I didn't want to lie to you. I really didn't. But I had no choice. And I have no choice now."

"What on earth are you talking about?" I said, genuinely bewildered. "Have my journalistic instincts failed me? Are you . . . *married?"*

"Oh, God, no," he said, smiling for the first time in a long while. But just as quickly he turned serious again. "No, it's worse than that, in fact. I'm—"

My heart stopped, my veins flushed with icy cold. I closed my eyes and silently braced myself.

He let out a deep sigh and started again without looking up at me. "Screw it," he said under his breath. "Alex, I'm a contestant on a reality-TV show."

What? My eyes fluttered open and I stared at him. I was certain I had misheard him. Those words just didn't belong together, had no business being in the same sentence, much less one uttered by the man I had just spent the last two nights falling hard for. I shook my head, as if I were trying to dislodge the truth from the muddle.

As he ran his hands through his hair, I noticed that they were both shaking. "Remember what I said that first night," he said, with a hopeful smile, "about my plan for the ethical treatment of models?"

"Huh?" I looked at him blankly. "What are you talking about?"

He shook his head. "Okay, let me start over," he said, grabbing my shoulders. "I just need to tell you everything. This show. It's for American TV. Oh, God. It's about . . . it's about dating models. It's called *The*

Modelizer. I have to live here for six weeks and date these models."

At those last three words, I couldn't stop myself from bursting out laughing. "Oh, that's really funny. You really had me going there, with your poker face and serious tone and . . ." And then I got a glimpse of his downturned face and realized that he sure didn't look like he was joking. "You *what*? You *what*?"

"I'm so sorry, Alex," he kept repeating. "I just didn't know how to tell you . . . but now here's the truth. I'm pretending that I'm minor European royalty"—for a split second, I almost gloated that I was half right after all—"and I have to convince the models that in order to marry me and become my princess, they have to gain weight because my country treasures plumpness. If the one I pick agrees, I win."

"What? What? *What?* This has got to be a joke. Wait. Am *I* part of this joke?" It was as if my brain had hit a scratch in the groove that coordinated speech. I couldn't think of anything else to say. In fact, all I could think was: *Where are the cameras?* I spun around and scanned the ceiling of the gazebo, but the only bug to be found was a moth that fluttered by. Then I squinted into the woods to see if I could find any telltale flashes. But there was nothing but darkness.

"Don't worry, there's nothing here," Nick said, sounding oddly calm. "This part of the grounds is off-limits."

He really was serious, I thought. This really isn't a joke. I wanted to cry. Or maybe laugh.

"I know you've probably lost all respect for me," he said. "But I really was hoping to continue on this journey with you . . ."

Oh my God, did he just say, "continue on this journey"? It was true then. He *was* reality-TV material. My shock and disbelief were slowly boiling into anger . . . and jealousy. But I was too confused to redirect any of those emotions into a cogent argument.

"Alex, you can hate me for wanting an adventure, for wanting to be on TV," he said, "but don't think I'm doing this because I have some model fetish. Look, if I really wanted to date models, if I was really just a modelizer, would I have been spending all this time with someone like you?"

"What?"

"I—oh my God, that didn't come out the right way . . . I didn't mean that you aren't just as beautiful and . . ."

"Stop. Just stop. Please." I got up, stood still for a second, and then started to sprint. I didn't know where I was going; I just needed to get away, clear my head. As I turned the corner around the garden, I came upon the swimming pool, and next to it, a Jacuzzi—occupied by three emaciated-yet-busty girls, two blondes and a redhead, who were chatting away and sipping champagne. *Oh God, it is true. It is true.*

They must have just spotted me then, because they suddenly stopped talking and began staring vacantly in my direction. I froze, caught in the glare of three supermodel wannabes—something all too familiar from my run-in with Katyarina. What, did they teach that in modeling college? I turned tail and kept on running, onto the terrace and through the double doors into the mansion.

Behind those walls was a parallel universe. A mahogany-paneled gallery ran the length of the terrace outside, but the gilt frames contained not paintings but

TV screens, broadcasting what seemed to be real-time activities from elsewhere on the estate: There were the girls in the Jacuzzi. And there was Nick, walking toward the house. I turned away and kept walking, opening door after door, wandering from one room into the next. The library, with its heavy velvet drapes and wall-to-wall bookshelves, actually did have oil paintings on the wall—but I half expected to see eyes darting back and forth behind cutout eyes in the Louis XIV portrait. I couldn't shake the feeling that I was being watched everywhere I went, that I was never alone. How could Nick stand to live here?

Nick. I wanted—I needed to exorcise any thought of him from my brain. I sped up, jogging through the hallways. The mansion was even bigger than it looked from the outside, and I could have sworn, as lost as I was, that I hadn't been in the same room twice. I opened one door off the instrument-filled music room and found an occupied bedroom: two suitcases open on the dark red Persian rug, revealing what were, I couldn't help noticing, even in my current state of mind, more cosmetics and skincare products than my mother and I owned, combined; five cartons of Marlboro Lights with airport duty-free labels on them; countless pieces of lingerie, all Cosabella; and a few skirts that would have been micromini even on me. I shuddered at the telltale signs of the species known as *Homo modelus* and slammed the door behind me.

The next door led into a heavily draped room that was lit only by the day-glo screen of a video camera, which was propped on a tripod in the corner. I had seen that green hue before . . . Where was it? It looked so familiar . . . Oh my God. I flashed back to all the wars I'd watched on TV—the wars waged in darkness. The eerie streaks of green that rained down on the screen as the bombs fell over Baghdad. This, I realized, was a night-vision camera. And then, before my sense of decency could overcome my quick-to-quip instinct, I thought: Wasn't most of Paris Hilton's sex tape suffused in the same green haze?

With that image in my head, I hastily exited the dark room, flushed with anger as much as embarrassment, and continued my way through the maze like a panicked lab rat. Around the next corner, I saw a door that was open a crack and tiptoed in. There was another video camera on a tripod, and behind it was a burgundy velvet curtain that partitioned the room. The camera was labeled "Confessional Booth 1." And the red light was on. The tape was rolling.

As desperate as I was to find my way out, my curiosity got the better of me. I inched closer to the camera and silently peered at the monitor. A teary-eyed brunette was reclining on what looked like a red leather lip-shaped sofa, wrapped in a white bathrobe and dabbing at her eyes with a Kleenex. "I was weak," she was saying in a distinctly Chicago accent. "I couldn't control myself. And now Nick must think I'm, I'm . . ." She stopped to blow her nose. My jaw dropped. I couldn't possibly tear myself away. I needed to hear what I imagined would be sordid and sleazy, and would prove in one fell swoop all of the horrible things about Nick that had just been running through my mind, as much as I knew it would hurt me. It was like the time I forced myself to watch that live Webcast of Carnie Wilson's gastric bypass surgery. Gross, but riveting nonetheless.

The brunette wiped her nose again. I watched her

every twitch, her sniffling nose, her picking at her fingernails . . . She looked down at her hands. "Nick must think I'm, like, totally not committed to the game." My left eyebrow involuntarily shot up. Not what I expected to hear, to be sure. "I saw there was only one chocolate croissant left in the kitchen and of course I ate it. And . . . and . . . I couldn't help it, I wasn't even thinking, I just automatically made myself throw it up!" she continued, gnawing on her cuticles. How many calories were in a cuticle, I found myself wondering. "I bet one of the other bitches ate the rest of the croissants . . . Those fat, back-stabbing bi—"

So what Nick had said about the show . . . it was true.

I backed out of the room and continued on my way. Deep in the heart of the mansion again, I was hopelessly lost. I wandered through a few more doorways, and as I stood in a drawing room, trying to focus and figure out which direction I had just come from, I heard their voices. I peeked through the keyhole and saw them sitting at a dining table. The main course seemed to be cigarettes, washed down with champagne.

"Oi, I saw some strange girl out in the garden," said one glassy-eyed model. It was the redhead from the Jacuzzi. A Brit—an Essex girl, to be exact.

"*Non*, you cannot be *zerious*," replied a tall, thin blonde, taking a drag from her cigarette and tilting her head, with its perfect bone structure framed by perfectly blown-out hair, so she could project the smoke up, over the redhead and toward the ceiling. She was clearly French. "Zat's so strange . . . Has anyone seen *Neekolasss?*"

"Totally weird," said a disembodied voice. Even though I couldn't see her, I could fairly well guess she was tall and thin—it was still early in the contest, I figured—and unnaturally buxom. She seemed to come from somewhere deep in the heart of what we in the business called Silicone Valley—Southern California. "He's, like, disappeared the last few nights. Is this, like, part of the game? Like, did they tell us but maybe I wasn't paying attention? . . . Hey, do you have any zit cream? Dammit, I'm starting to break out right on my chin . . ."

I couldn't take any more. I tiptoed away from the door and moved toward the exit on the opposite side of the room. I cringed as I slowly turned the knob, silently willing it to not make a sound and praying that it was my way out of there. After the past week's events, I figured I was due in the answered-prayers department. And sure enough, the door miraculously led back into the gallery I had originally entered. Relieved—but at the same time hoping I hadn't expended my whole allotment of good luck—I ran along the wall and shot out the double doors, off the terrace, and into the garden.

Somewhere halfway back to the gazebo, I ran smack into Nick, who wrapped his arms around me.

"Alex! Please, Alex. Please listen to me."

"No, I don't want to." I shut my eyes and hung my head. "Just let me go. Let me go home. I want to get out of here. Now."

"Alex, they mean nothing to me," he whispered urgently in my ear.

I opened my eyes wide in disbelief. "Why are you whispering? What, are there microphones everywhere too? And what were those papers? What did you want me to sign?"

"Release forms," he mumbled sheepishly. "The

show's producers wanted permission . . . There were cameras in the car and . . . "

"Oh God. Oh God. I cannot believe this." I was starting to sniffle. This was about to get ugly, I could tell. "I'll ask you one last time: Am I part of the joke?"

"Alex, the game's fake, that's TV. Meeting you, getting to know you, enjoying our time together—that was real. I swear."

"I'm sorry," I said, trying to compose myself. "I can't believe anything you tell me." I extricated myself from his arms and stumbled away, toward the light of the candles along the path back to the driveway. Sébastien was still standing by the Mercedes, putting out another cigarette. And next to him were the two SUVs I had seen earlier that night at the Eiffel Tower. I laughed at my own naïveté. They weren't the prey, the target of my prying eyes. *I* was the target of *theirs*.

Sébastien gave me the same sympathetic look he had offered me earlier. And this time I understood. As he shut the door behind me, Nick ran up and pounded on the door until I rolled down the window. I sat frozen, looking straight ahead.

"I'm sorry, Alex, you have to know that. Please forgive me for not telling you the truth earlier. Please forgive me. Please, please, please."

"I . . . can't . . . think," I said, trying desperately to hold back the sobs. I covered my face with one hand, and with the other, urgently pressed at the button to roll up the window again, until the tinted glass shaded me from his sight.

And as Nick stood and stared, Sébastien pulled away and drove me to my hotel.

Chapter Ten

BY THE TIME I STUMBLED DOWN the hallway toward my room, I was a blubbering mess. I had managed not to lose it in front of Sébastien and the elevator man, but once I turned the corner, all bets were off. I removed my heels, one at a time, and looked at myself in the full-length mirror on the wall. My face was puffy from the crying—the bastard!—and my hair was a disaster. Though that second part was, to be fair, no fault of Nick's. I was a sorry sight, squeezed into the sexy Alaïa dress for no one to see but the elevator man and me. The tears started flowing again as I slumped down to the floor, hugging my knees close even as the dress hugged my thighs to within an inch of their life. Well, I thought absently, Nick *had* complimented me . . . but how was I to believe anything that lying, conniving, untrustworthy . . . *man* . . . told me?

I let out a string of swearwords I hadn't uttered since that one time I couldn't find a cab in Milan during men's

Fashion Week and had to walk, blistered feet in blistering July sun, from the Dolce & Gabbana showroom back to my hotel. In three-inch heels. That I hadn't broken in yet. Or more accurately, that hadn't broken my feet in yet.

The thought of a bunch of women competing for one guy left me indignant. Not for the reason you'd think, though. Shoes, I thought in my anger—now, shoes were worth fighting over. Yeah, that last pair of jet-beaded, black suede Manolos marked down 75 percent at Bergdorf's and in your size, or even half a size too small, for that matter. Those were worth fighting for. Not some man. Not some lying, conniving, untrustworthy . . .

And why did these TV shows have to make all women look so bad? Then again, these were six-foot Barbies we were talking about. That bothered me more than I would have imagined—that is, if I could have ever imagined such a preposterous scenario. I had never felt insecure around models before, not after the first thirty seconds of talking to them, anyway. But it didn't matter how *I* thought I measured up against them. And it didn't matter how the majority of the male species thought I measured up. (By the looks of the popular men's magazines and beer commercials I had seen, I didn't stand a chance.) No, what mattered to me was the opinion of that one particular guy who I'd thought had liked me for my brain . . . and the unstatuesque body that went with it. So did DD win out over IQ in the end?

And what about *him?* Did TV win out over IQ, too? Which was worse: If he was doing it because he wanted to be able to tell his buddies for the rest of his life that he once dated models? Or if, as I assumed was the case for most of these reality-show contestants, he just wanted to be on TV, to get his fifteen minutes of fame? Now, I *knew* from experience that being on TV wasn't what it was cracked up to be. Not when you were splayed on a runway unable to extricate yourself from a supermodel's leg. And wasn't that what reality TV was, an on-air train wreck for all to see?

What bothered me most, of course, was that if he could so glibly lie to the girls on this show, what was keeping him from lying to me too? Was I part of the scam?

I was starting to run through every moment with Nick, to see if I could in brutally clear-eyed retrospect find some hint of deception, when I heard the sound of the elevator door opening on my floor. I scrambled to my feet and padded down the hallway to my room. As I hurriedly slipped the key into the lock and let the door slam behind me, I remembered that I wasn't alone. Shit, I said under my breath. What was I going to tell Mom?

"Honey, is that you?" Her muffled voice was coming from the bathroom.

"Oh, hi, Mom, I'll be right there," I called out as I turned on the light and looked at myself in the mirror. My eyes were still puffy and my skin blotchy. Good God, she was going to see it immediately. I ran over to the minibar and cracked open a bottle of Vittel, which I splashed on my face . . . only to realize that I didn't have a towel. My eyes shut to keep the makeup-muddied water from dripping into my contact lenses, I wandered over to the bed, where I had dropped my bathrobe three hours before—that is, when I was still giddy and blissfully ignorant. Idiot me. I shook off the thought, trying to keep the tears from falling again, and patted my face against the terrycloth of the robe, leaving a big smudge of makeup on the left sleeve. Then I unzipped myself from the dress and wrapped the robe around me. I rushed over to the bathroom door and knocked.

"Mom, are you decent?"

"Of course, honey!" she said with a laugh. "I'm just paintin' my toenails."

I turned the knob and stepped into the doorway, one foot in the bathroom and one foot out—just in case I had to make a quick getaway because I couldn't control my urge to cry like a baby so that Mommy could kiss my boo-boo and make it all better.

Not that I would know what to say to her. After all those subliminal messages in my formative years about not letting a man get in the way of living my life to the fullest, I was always too nervous to talk to my mom about men, in those rare moments when one existed in my life. I always assumed that she'd never approve until the day I had visited every country in the world or won a Pulitzer or hit middle age, whichever came first. Whenever I had boy troubles, I would get her advice and comfort indirectly, by making up some thickly veiled scenarios. Real love-life angst: A guy I liked asked my friend out on a date. Translation into the parallel-universe language I spoke with Mom: I had lost a plum assignment to a colleague. So what if the resulting advice seldom made much sense? The ego-stroking pep talks *did* make me feel better.

As I stood there silently reminiscing about that speech, in which she told me I just had to go out there and prove them wrong—show them what they were missing—I started to feel my mouth and throat thickening.

"Hi, Mom," I said, trying to sound light and carefree. God, I felt like I was trapped in a commercial for one of those "women's products." "I thought you were out like a light. When did you get up?"

"Oh, just about fifteen minutes ago. I betcha it's the jetlag . . . or I reckon I'm just too worked up about our date at Chanel to sleep!"

She didn't look up as she focused on putting the finishing touches on her tastefully beige pedicure, but I could tell she was grinning ear to ear. Seeing her this excited did make my boo-boo better. Well, almost. Actually, not even close.

"Did you just come in? I heard the door." She still didn't look up. She was applying the quick-dry top coat.

"Oh," I said, caught off guard while trying to craft a metaphor for my current problems. What on earth was comparable to finding out your crush was on reality TV? "Umm," I said, now racking my brain on two fronts. "Uh . . . Oh! I just had to run out and get some ice. Uh, for a, uh, uh, some sort of insect bite. Yeah, really weird, I think that's why my face is all blotchy and my eyes are puffy."

Oh, that was good and terrible at the same time.

And it got the attention of my mom, who put down the bottle of polish and padded over, her feet awkwardly spread by the pink foam toe separators we had bought by the gross at the nail-supply store the last time I was home. "Lemme see," she said, scrutinizing my face. "I don't see any bite marks," she concluded after a minute. "But I brought some calamine lotion. It's in my purse . . ."

"I'll get it," I said, making a beeline for her bedroom. What was the harm?

I caught another glimpse of myself in the mirror as I walked back into the bathroom with a travel-size bottle of calamine lotion in one hand and some Q-tips in the other. I was a mess. My mother must really be jetlagged if she couldn't see through this.

Oh, but she could.

"So," she said all too casually as she sat me down in front of her on the floor and started dabbing, "what's really goin' on, honey? It's a boy, isn't it?"

I had crossed the Rubicon, committed to bangs, declared orange the new black. In other words, there was no turning back.

I gulped, but that didn't keep the words down where I wanted them. And once the sniffles started, nothing stayed inside. Against my better judgment and two decades of practice, I spilled my guts. Without once making eye contact, I told her everything—well, everything short of a kiss and a grope or two, and leaving out the worst details about Nick's show—and by the time I'd finished twelve and a half minutes later, I felt utterly small and naked and chilled to the bone. Like when you're having a perfectly normal conversation with a chatty, not-even-close acquaintance and suddenly, before you even realize it, you're babbling on about some horridly embarrassing personal hygiene problem.

Of course, this was my *mother*. The woman who'd changed my diapers and cleaned my teenage bathroom, who had taught me everything—and yet nothing. Since my adolescence, she had never once tried to engage me in "the talk." Mom and I had subscribed to the "don't ask, don't tell" policy long before Bill Clinton did. And now look what I'd just done: I'd blown the closet door off its hinges.

So what did she do? She sighed. And in the split second I dared to look up at her, I could have sworn I spied a tear welling up.

"Honey," she began, "you don't know how long I've been waitin' for you to confide in me about boys. But I am so, so sorry that it had to be somethin' like this. Come here, honey." She pulled me close and hugged me, my face brushing against her hair and cheek. My head resting on her neck, I breathed in a familiar smell—a mix of Chanel No. 19 and Oil of Olay, which she still used nightly, no matter how many jars of Crème de la Mer I bought her. It took me back twenty-some years, to every bedtime story that ended in happily ever after for Princess Alex, even if there was no Prince Charming. And that was when the tears flowed unabated, uncontrollably. After a moment I pulled away to get a tissue. When I came back, there was Mom, her face and hair one big mess of calamine pink. And for the first time in a long while, it seemed, I giggled. Still sniffling, I made the internationally understood gesture for "You've got something on your face," only I couldn't stop at pointing at my cheek; I had to keep going and move on to my hair and neck.

Mom tilted her head toward the mirror and gasped.

"Oh my stars," she said, rubbing at one pink smudge on her left cheek. "Now, how are you gonna take me seriously when I look like *this?*" Under other circumstances, this might not have been all that funny, but in the state I was in, I found it so hysterical that I couldn't stop laughing—which caused my mom to laugh in turn. So we both howled uproariously, until tears started rolling down our cheeks. Which brought us back to where we'd started.

"Mommy . . ." I hung my head as she wiped away my tears. "I just never thought you'd want to know. I was afraid you'd be disappointed in me . . . that I could waste my energy and be such a fool over a *man* . . . And, well, I chose a real good place to start, didn't I? I sure didn't break you in easy . . ."

She untied my hair and quietly began to run a brush through the mass of tangles. "Honey," she said finally, "what in heaven's name gave you the idea that I thought men were a waste of time?" She chuckled softly. "Didn't I marry your daddy?"

I turned around to look at her. "Of course you did. But, no offense or anything, weren't you always telling me I could do better? I mean, not better than Daddy. I mean, well, didn't you raise me to change the world or something? World changers don't have time for silly boys . . . or husbands and families, for that matter . . ."

"Oh my Lord," she said. She furrowed her brow something fierce—something I'd learned from her *never* to do. "Is that what you've thought all these years, Alex? If that's what you thought, I hope like hell you've been rebellin' against me."

I spotted the tiniest grin on her face when she said that. She might not have asked, and I might not have told, but she knew I was my mother's daughter.

"Well, *maybe.*"

"Alex, for the record, I woulda been pleased as punch had you gotten yourself married straight out of college."

"Really?"

"Okay, maybe not *really* really," she said, smiling sheepishly. "But if that had made you happy, well, yes, really. Honey, my point has always been that I never wanted you to feel like you had to choose, like I did when I was in my twenties. I wanted you to do whatever you wanted—everythin' you wanted. I'm proud that you've had a full life and that you've seen the world. But I'll also be proud the day you decide to settle down with someone. Not that settlin' down means *not* havin' a full life and seein' the world. Maybe *settle* isn't quite the right word. So many bad connotations . . ." She sighed. "Honey, I just never wanted to be the typical mother, pressurin' her daughter for grandkids . . ."

"Well, thank God for that!" I said, reaching out to her for a hug. "I guess maybe I just heard half of what you were saying . . ." As my mom's words continued to sink in, another thought brightened my face. "Sooo," I ventured, "does this mean Daddy isn't disappointed that I didn't go back to school for a PhD or at least another master's?"

"Now, don't press your luck, honey," she deadpanned. "I feel like it's part of my marital duty to be his proxy and say"—she cleared her throat and lowered her voice an octave—" 'It's never too late.' "

I grinned back at her. "Well, I guess I can look to you for inspiration, Mom. You did have it all in the end, didn't you?"

"Yeah, I guess I did." Her smile had expanded to a wide grin. "And you can, too, Alex. You have time. Remember that."

"Yeah, time to cross men off my list, one by one . . ." I said glumly. "Mom, how could a guy seem so great and end up being so . . . so . . . typical?"

"This may come as a surprise to you, Alex, but I'm not so fuddy-duddy. I've seen some of these reality shows on TV. Your dad makes me watch 'em . . . Oh, heck, I'll be honest, he only led me to them. I got myself hooked."

"You what?"

"Yes, I'm not ashamed. I watch those shows. And you know what? They're entertainment, just like everything else on TV."

"So what are you trying to tell me?"

"I can't believe I'm sayin' this, but . . . how do you know this fella's not just playin' a role on his TV show? Maybe what you saw when you met him *was* the real deal. I mean, this is the guy who actually drove you to talk to me about men. That's gotta have some significance!"

Her attitude totally took me off guard, and it was a good ten seconds before I could respond. "I guess you might be right . . ." I said slowly. "But are you sure you aren't just in a hurry for grandkids?"

Mom shot me the evil eye. "Am I gonna have to ground you?"

Without another word I leaned in for a hug.

By the time we had left the bathroom and retired to our beds, it was close to four in the morning—and our appointment at Chanel was at ten o'clock sharp. Mom didn't mind that she was missing out on her beauty sleep, which she figured she wouldn't have gotten anyway, considering how excited she was.

Still, when my alarm went off at eight-thirty, it wasn't pretty. I must have flung the clock so violently across the room that it accomplished half its purpose: It woke up my mother two rooms away. She called out dibs on the bathroom ("Just like in college!" she said perkily), which was fine by me, because it gave me another fifteen minutes or so of shut-eye. Yes, my eyes were shut, but my brain was in TiVo mode, rewinding through the highlights and fast-forwarding through the lowlights of the last few days.

As I tried in vain to hit the delete button somewhere between the Eiffel Tower and my chat with my mom, there was a knock on the door. "Mom, did you order room service?" I called out. All I heard in response was the shower running, so I reluctantly pulled on my robe and made my way to the door.

"Qui est-ce?" I said, leaning against the door in exhaustion.

"A delivery for Mees Simons, *s'il vous plaît.*"

Confused as to why they would consider breakfast a delivery, I opened the door and watched, mouth agape, as five bellboys rolled in cart after cart filled with long-stemmed red roses—there must have been a good twenty-five dozen.

"Il n'est pas un salaud . . . 'E eez not a bastard," each of the bellboys said as they marched back out of the suite, the last handing me an envelope.

Despite my sincerest attempt to remain stern, I had to giggle. I had never in my life seen such an extravagant display of . . . misguided groveling. Well, okay, maybe not *entirely* misguided. I'd always had a weakness for roses. I stared at the envelope—thick Smythson stock again—and considered whether I should just throw it out as a matter of principle. My pride wrestled my curiosity to the ground and pinned it—and so I threw the envelope, unopened, into the wastebasket by the desk. Thirty seconds later, though, Curiosity did a fierce scissors kick and knocked over Pride, and I plucked the envelope out.

I picked up the heavy silver letter opener on the desk and tried to be nonchalant (for whose benefit I couldn't say) as I sliced open the envelope in one violent thrust. Lucky for Nick I wasn't armed last night, I thought melodramatically.

The card inside was ivory, with a red embossed kicking bull at the top. How appropriate for the master purveyor of bullshit. No matter what my mother was trying to tell me—she had obviously gotten soft in her three decades away from the dating scene—I was determined not to let him off so easily.

I bit the inside of my mouth to brace myself and started to read.

> Dear Alex: What will it take for you to believe in me again? How can I make this all up to you? I'm sorry . . . three thousand times over, I'm sorry. Please give me a chance to explain. Please call me. 06.44.50.21.11. Anytime. Nick.

The bastard. I could see his puppy-dog look now. And it was cute.

I shoved the card into the top desk drawer, where I had so delicately placed his two earlier notes. I slammed the drawer shut and just stood and stared at all the fragrant buds surrounding me. Steady, girl . . . I had to keep reminding myself not to break so soon, even as the scent of all those roses intoxicated me.

"Who was that?" my mom said as she pushed open the door from the bathroom. She gasped. "Oh my word!"

Dressed in her best off-the-rack Chanel suit, topped off by a tidy towel turban wrapped around her wet hair, she walked over toward me, stopping here and there to sample the scents along the way. "Alex, you have to admit: The boy is *tryin'*." She leaned over, her left hand carefully propping up the turban on her head so it wouldn't keel over on top of me, and kissed me on the cheek. "What does he have to say for himself?"

"Nothing convincing," I said stubbornly, doing my best to hide a smirk.

"I don't suppose he wrote his phone number on the card?" she said mischievously.

"Maybe."

"And I don't suppose you've already committed it to memory?"

"Maybe." I smiled. "And maybe he deserves a chance to explain himself—but Mom, you know I can't cave in *yet.*"

She winked back at me. "Like I said, you have plenty of time."

As consumed as I was by Nick's alternate reality-TV reality, I was determined not to spoil my mother's big moment. We walked out of the hotel hand in hand, Mom in her head-to-toe Chanel, and me in a cream cashmere vest with the tiny ruffled tiers (Chanel, in honor of our morning appointment), Christian Dior gray wool trousers (apropos of our lunch date with Lola), and a blue and orange nautical-themed Hermès scarf around my neck (always appropriate).

Unconsciously I scanned the street for Sébastien—if that was even his real name—and his black Mercedes, but there was nothing there but some white taxis and the odd Mini Cooper. Stricken by my moment of weakness, I lifted my chin, slid my Dior sunglasses on, turned sharply in my three-inch Manolos, and strutted over to the first taxi in the queue.

In the cab my mother and I both got progressively giddier as we neared the House of Chanel. Of course, she hadn't the foggiest idea where we were or how long it would take us to get there, but she must have felt it in her bones. It was like the swallows returning to Capistrano. She just *knew.*

By the time we pulled into the rue Cambon, it was my turn to experience that mixture of dread and excitement and anxiety—all too similar to that damned feeling of falling in love. Only it evolved into mostly just dread. In all the madness of the past few days and nights, I hadn't even considered that here I was, taking my mother to the site of my greatest humiliation. (I thought of last night with Nick.) Okay, make that my greatest humiliation caught on camera. (And then I thought of Nick's rigged car.) Make that the greatest humiliation caught on camera not involving a guy I was interested in.

I was shocked that I had almost forgotten about my moment of shame—and I was hoping against hope that everyone at Chanel had forgotten, too. Or at least that my mother's order today would be enough to call it a wash.

I nervously stepped out of the cab, on the heels of my altogether too perky mom, and paid the driver. We stood for a moment on the narrow street that had always struck me as much too modest for such an immense historical landmark. We were like pilgrims to the Holy Land. Mom gazed up at the facade of the *maison*, took a deep breath, and pushed open the door.

I nudged my sunglasses flush on the bridge of my nose—as if that would help me disappear—and meekly shuffled in behind her.

After we announced our intentions, we were guided to the top of the stairs where Madame Alice, the head of the salon, and Madame Suzanne, Mom's very own personal *vendeuse*, were waiting for us. Mom took to Madame Suzanne instantly (as did I, if only because she didn't give off any hint of knowing what had happened to me last time I was here)—which was a good thing, because Madame Suzanne was about to know her more intimately than her gynecologist did. We had done our research about what goes on in a couture fitting. Basically, you're in your skivvies for much of the time, while a veritable crowd of people clinically dissect you with their laser-sharp eyes, as if you were some laboratory specimen, to determine how to hide your flaws and then—what glamour!—proceed to poke, prod, and meticulously measure every inch of your body. And that was just on the first date.

Needless to say, Mom had spent much of the morning fretting over the *other* lacy La Perla set she had left at home, and then wondered whether she shouldn't have gone out and bought her first-ever girdle . . . And why, oh why hadn't she tried that Killer Abs class at her gym? But when the moment came for her to enter the fitting room, she put on a brave face and told me I could wait outside, and she would bring the show to me when she tried on the samples. "We still love the red-flecked cream tweed coat edged with chiffon, don't we?" she whispered as she was led away by Madame Suzanne. Half a dozen of the atelier staff—the quaintly named *petites mains* who painstakingly put the garments together by hand—briskly fell into step behind them.

I was left in the waiting room, which was devoid of all that was froufrou. Clearly it had been designed for husbands and bodyguards. I couldn't get comfortable on the stiffly padded cream sofa, so I absentmindedly picked up the new look book from the mahogany end table. Oh my God, I realized as I turned the pages, it was from this week's show. I shut the book, and my eyes, for a moment before continuing, masochist that I was. I thumbed through it quickly until I saw her. Katyarina. It must have been just seconds before our collision. She looked so calm, so cool, so unsuspecting . . . Holy shit. There I was, a tiny speck in the corner. I turned the page, half expecting to see the next frame from the camera, and then the next and the next, as if I were looking at one of those children's books that replicated a silent movie when you flipped through it.

Luckily for my fragile state of mind, the powers that be at Chanel had thought it out better than I had. Still, when I came to my senses, I realized how equally embarrassing it would be to be caught studying my own ignominy. So hoping no one would see me, I was furtively slipping the book back on the table facedown, far away from me, when my mother twirled in, Madame Suzanne smiling primly at her side.

"What have we here?" I asked.

"Numéro quinze," said my mom, who was hamming it up for the *petites mains* who had helped pin her into the runway sample and were now hovering by the dressing room. The suit jacket was made of wool that was as soft to the touch as a baby rabbit, in an alabaster color that lit up my mother's complexion. The gently rounded, fluttering collar framed her face nicely, and the three-quarter sleeves accentuated her narrow wrists. The red-flecked tweed A-line skirt (which, as I recalled from the couture show two months earlier, had been a mini on the model) ended just below the knee with a tiny trim of chiffon. It was a variation on the outfit we'd selected from Mom's printouts, and in fact it was more flattering than the long coat would have been on her five-foot-four frame. As much as we petite women might dream, Madame Suzanne had been insistent that the long coat "would not do, Madame!" She was right, of course. The suit was a classic style that would age well in my mother's closet—and, I mused, could even be worn by her granddaughter someday. Yes, I had faith in Chanel to survive the number of years that it would take for me to find a guy, date him, move in, marry him, celebrate a couple of anniversaries, and *then* give birth to a daughter—plus twenty years or so. (I had to draw the line at letting a teen, even my hypothetical teen, wear Chanel.)

"Well, what do you think?" Mom said anxiously.

"I think it's a keeper," I said. "Does it just *feel* fabulous on?"

She walked over to me and lent me a sleeve to touch. "Well, other than these cuh-razy tight sleeves—I had no idea how tiny those models are! This is so beyond . . . I mean, just feel this!" We both collapsed into giggles as we stood there, Mom in her couture suit and me feeling it up. "The frightenin' thing is," she said, "I could really get used to this! Your daddy can thank his lucky stars that I didn't let myself come here before . . . because he would need to start playing the lotto if he wanted to ever retire!"

I gave her a big hug and attempted a tight smile. "Mommy," I whispered in her ear, "you know you deserve this. And I am so happy to be here with you today."

Despite everything else that was going on in my life, I really did mean it.

It took another hour for my mother's exact measurements to be taken for the toile—the muslin pattern that would be fitted onto her body at the next appointment, which Madame Suzanne promised, with a wink and a smile, to push ahead of schedule to Monday morning, just before Mom flew home. At some point during the six weeks it would take for one of the *petites mains* to sew and garnish the outfit from start to finish, Mom would have to make another trip to Paris for a third and final fitting. But she wasn't complaining.

We left Chanel just past noon, completely intoxicated, as if we had just been through some alcohol-fueled initiation into an ultra-exclusive secret society. Which, in a way, we had been—minus the drinking-till-we-puked part.

Mom had long forgotten the initial mortification of standing in her underwear for the crowd and was flaunting her new vocabulary, praising the "fabulous *vendeuse*" and the "remarkable *petites mains*" as we got into a cab for the short trip to the House of Dior. Now that she was an expert at being a couture client, she would be able to appreciate the behind-the-scenes tour that Lola had been promising to give her for months, long before Mom had even gotten up the nerve to broach the subject with my dad. Oh, poor Daddy, I thought again, not for the last time that day.

My mom took the lead, strolling into the *maison* with a mantle of confidence resting on her shoulders, where the Chanel toile had been a short time before. So there *was* some truth to what those in the know had rhapsodized about: Wearing couture suddenly made you stand straighter and taller, move a little more . . . alluringly. What I couldn't be sure of was whether it was because of the 100 percent perfect fit or the 100 percent attention paid to you (never mind that you were in your undies at the time).

After checking in on the first floor, we were escorted by a stunning brunette—at first I couldn't tell whether she was a house model or a publicist—to an all-beige sitting room where the decor was understated in a way that ran completely counter to the house's new runway reputation. Perhaps, I thought, a blank slate was needed before the visual overload we were about to experience. Lola, we were told as we sat down on an overstuffed sofa, was still with another client—"*Another* client!" Mom mouthed at me giddily—and would be with us shortly.

The minute I sank into the sofa and the flow of adrenaline ebbed, my thoughts began to sneak back to Nick. What would he say when I eventually did call him? How long should I make him wait? Wasn't he trying hard to make it up to me? Wasn't it a little pathetic but also really endearing? Didn't it *feel* real?

After just a few seconds of my spaced-out silence, my mother inched closer and put her arm around me. "Thank you for comin' with me today," she said. "I was hopin' that a little fun would get your mind off things—since you're holdin' out and all."

"Oh, Mommy," I said, leaning my head on her shoulder. "I'm sorry if I've been distracted. I don't want to be. I'm trying not to be. This day is supposed to be all about shopping!"

"That's what I like to hear!" Lola said by way of announcing her arrival. She breezed into the room in her all-black fashion uniform of a crisp cotton man's shirt unbuttoned low, tight trousers with a sharp crease down the front of each leg, and strappy three-inch Louboutins, and kissed me on both cheeks before turning her attention to my mother.

"And you must be Mrs. Simons—I'm so excited to meet you finally. Alex has been telling me all about your adventures. So how's Puffy?"

Mom giggled. "Oh, him. He couldn't keep up with us, y'know?"

"Like mother, like daughter!" she said, winking at me as she led us out to the elevator. "We have a reservation at L'Avenue at one o'clock, so let's snoop around for a bit first."

We got off on the next floor and followed Lola into what looked like the costume closet at a theater, but was in fact the home of Dior's latest couture collections. All along the walls of the surprisingly small room were rails on top of rails of feather-flocked ballgowns with six-foot-diameter skirts and day suits spun from Chantilly lace. I could hear my mother's breath quicken, and indeed it was awe-inspiring to behold such creations in close proximity. I imagined the only comparable feeling might come from standing on scaffolding high above the floor in the Sistine Chapel and being allowed to reach out and graze Michelangelo's fresco of the creation of Adam.

To serious art lovers, that would sound like a grossly overreaching comparison. And I might have thought that once, too, until the first time I attended a couture show. Sitting in the front row in the cozy confines of Valentino's *maison* on the place Vendôme, I marveled over the exquisite embroidery not just on the outside of evening gowns, but also on the inside of day garments, flashed through a skirt's high slit or a loose, unbuttoned jacket. And then when Lola took me into the Dior atelier for the first time, I could actually trace those same details with my own fingers, like some painfully precious Braille that translated into the four and five zeroes on the price tags. And at that moment, those prices actually made sense. Almost maybe.

"Go ahead, Mrs. Simons, you can touch *everything,*" Lola said. As my mother wandered around the room in a trancelike state of ecstasy, Lola pulled me aside. "I got a call from Jacques last night. He couldn't find you and he said he absolutely *needed*"—she raised both her eyebrows sharply—"to meet today. What happened to you?"

"Oh," I said. Despite my desperate attempt at looking and sounding *not* desperate, I felt my face drop, so I knew I couldn't keep it from Lola for long. But I wasn't sure I was up for rehashing the whole affair at that moment. "Um, long story," I said, mustering a faint smile. "But I really want to talk about L-H. What did Jacques have to say?"

"I'll get back to you and your long story in a minute," Lola said, cocking her head, "but Jacques sounded frantic. He didn't want to talk on the phone. I told him we were meeting for lunch today, so he's going to stop by. Maybe he can make heads or tails of what Bartolome is up to."

"Well, good. I suppose it's about time I focused on my story," I said furtively. "So I'm glad. Will you be ready to leave for Switzerland Monday? My mom's flying out that morning." Not wanting to make eye contact with Lola, who knew me far too well, I started digging around in my Vuitton bag. Which must have looked pretty unconvincing, given that the tiny purse held exactly three things. Where was my huge Speedy when I needed it?

"Sure," said Lola, apparently oblivious to my bad acting. "Most of my appointments are done, and someone else is dealing with the glossies this season, so I should be fine to take off on Monday." And then she remembered. "But what about—"

I cut her off and gave her a Cliff's Notes version of the night's events. "Let's not talk about that right now, okay?" I gave her a pleading look. "Let's have some fun with my mom and we'll talk more later."

Lola nodded at me and gave me a sideways glance that telegraphed both concern and curiosity. I set my jaw and raised my eyebrows. "Shall we?" I said, as much to myself as to anyone else in the room.

I walked over to my mother, who was fingering the delicate lacelike cutouts along the hem of a suede dress. "This is just so beautiful I might cry," she said without looking up from her precious find. "Did you ever see such an extraordinarily beautiful thing?"

We worked our way around the room clockwise, huddling over each heavenly creation as Lola waxed poetic over the intimate details of how it had come into being and who had a copy hanging in her closet. My mother couldn't have had a better time. Not only did she get to play dress-up for grown-ups, she also got to add juicy new details to her mental dossiers on her favorite characters from *W*.

We could have spent the whole afternoon—the whole weekend, really—in that room, but we had one more seminal moment to add to my mom's Paris experience: lunch at the fashionista hangout L'Avenue. The two-story restaurant with the velvet-and-gold decor and the Costes brothers' stamp of chic stood just down the street from both Dior and Nina Ricci, so it practically served as a cafeteria for those employees with expense accounts. As a well-liked regular who didn't merely fit right in with the glamorous clientele but was, in fact, the mold, Lola was greeted with a smattering of air kisses all around. The maître d' himself escorted us to our table on the restaurant's second floor. I always felt the urge to suck in my butterfly-filled stomach and move shoulders first as I ascended the curved staircase at L'Avenue—it was not unlike parading down a catwalk; the audience was about the same. Heaven forbid, I pondered as I slowly mounted the stairs, if you tripped or collided with a waiter—that would be as bad as getting tangled up with a model at a . . . oh, crap. I reached out for the wall and scurried the rest of the way up.

Seated at a corner table, we were perfectly situated for

my mother to partake in some people-watching. Not that Lola and I wouldn't feel compelled to do it too—discreetly, of course—but since it was my mom's first time, we gave her the seat of honor, with her back against the wall, which gave her a commanding view of the entire room. Lola and I, seated on either side of her, would have to turn our heads a few degrees (almost imperceptibly, perhaps timed to a languid yawn, and with no sudden moves) in order to follow all the action.

On this afternoon, there were plenty of people to see and be seen by. At one table in the back—in the area where you sat when you ostensibly didn't want to be noticed, but then naturally drew the most attention by sitting there—were the estranged husband of the Monegasque mini-mall mogul's youngest daughter and his new older-woman conquest. A table over from them, a French pop singer whose name I couldn't remember moved food around on her plate as she listened intently to her date, a smarmy-looking, silver-haired older man. I couldn't place him either. "Some billionaire with a dubious source of income. He came in with her for a fitting this morning," Lola whispered. And with impeccable timing, she added a beat later, "His wife was in on Thursday."

We were all still giggling over that bit of gossip when I gazed across the room to the staircase, and that was when the whole space-time-continuum thing seemed to go amiss. I saw her first, moving up to the top of the stairs—a tall, striking redhead. Why did she look so familiar? Was she another pop singer whose song I could hum but whose name still escaped me? . . . Oh no. Not the hot-tub scene! I gasped and quickly ducked behind my menu just as his face came into view.

It was Nick. With one of his models from the mansion.

"Alex?" My mom looked at me, behind my menu, then over at the new arrivals, then back at me. "What's going on?

"Oh, the turbot looks really good," I babbled instead of responding. "Though the sauce may be too rich. What are you having? Lola? Mom?"

I could see them both staring at me as I lowered the menu just a quarter of an inch so I could sneak a glance. Luckily Nick and his date were being seated all the way across the room, but despite my rapidly offered prayers to the seating gods, the redhead sat down with her back to our table, and he took the chair facing us. I quietly groaned as I slipped the menu back in front of my eyes. I scooted my chair as far diagonally as I could, so that I was leaning on the table with my left elbow, my hand covering the side of my face that might have been visible from Nick's table.

"Alex, honey, what has gotten into you?" My mother looked around the room and zeroed in on Nick.

"Mom!" I spat out under my breath. "Please! Stop! Staring!"

She did—for the second in which she turned to Lola. Lola shrugged in ignorance, and then the two of them nearly gave themselves whiplash by swiveling their heads in unison in Nick's direction.

"Will you *please* not stare?" I growled.

"What, at that cute boy with the redheaded girl?" Mom said.

I scrambled to raise the menu again, this time to cover both of us. "Yes, over there. *Please* stop looking over there. Please, please, *please*." But rather than avert her gaze, she kept her eyes peeled as she dug in her purse for her glasses. Finally, exasperated, I squeezed my own eyes shut and heard myself saying, "It's *Nick.*"

Lola and Mom both gasped. And craned their necks. And stared.

"Oh yeah," Lola said, a big smile crossing her face. "I knew I'd seen him before . . ."

"Cu-cut it out! You guys! Stop it! Stop it!" I frantically whispered.

"Oh, Alex, the pictures in the papers didn't do him justice," Lola said appreciatively. "But am I still allowed to say that?"

"He really *is* quite good-lookin'," my mother chimed in.

"Mom!" I screeched, shocked as I was at our new open-door policy on girl talk. Getting giddy over couture was one thing, but this—this I had to get used to.

"Will you please cease and desist?" I groaned. "Please pry your eyes away from him. Please, before he notices. Lola, is there a back way out of here?"

"No, there isn't," she said, finally looking away from Nick. "Sorry, darling. We'll try to behave now. I'm simply famished." She opened her menu with a flourish and pored over its contents with gleefully exaggerated studiousness. My mom, having instantly bonded with Lola at Dior, mischievously followed suit.

"All right already . . ."

They ignored me and merrily went about discussing their appetizer choices.

If I couldn't beat them, I'd have to join them.

"Okay, okay," I said, still hiding behind my menu, "so what are they doing over there?"

Lola jumped at the opportunity to give me the play-by-play. "Okay," she said, discreetly peeking around the side of her menu, "he's looking at his menu. She's looking at him. He's not saying anything."

"Honey, he looks like a sick puppy dog," my mother said.

"He deserves it," I said stubbornly, my brow furrowed. I stared at my menu for a minute, then said in a tiny, hopeful voice, "Do you really think so?"

I lowered my head and glanced over at Nick's table. He did look uncomfortable, I confirmed with some satisfaction—which I instantly tried to brush off. I mustn't care, I told myself. No, I needed to think about other things . . . like where could the TV cameras be hidden, as in those old Folgers coffee commercials. *They've secretly replaced the usual beautiful people with two reality-TV-show contestants . . .*

I quickly scanned the room again, and found myself eyeing a woman in her thirties who had placed her very large jute handbag on the table rather than on the empty seat next to her. Her companion, a man in a dark suit, looked as nondescript as a Secret Service agent: that is, conspicuously nondescript. Bingo. Of course, I would have known for sure had I not been so immersed in Nick on our dates; these same people had probably followed us too. While I fought off the memories of said dates, Ms. Conspicuously Nondescript caught me looking at her and nudged Mr. Conspicuously Nondescript. I could have sworn they both smirked at me. I gave them my best scowl and turned back to my menu.

When our waitress—catwalk-ready like all the staff at L'Avenue—came by to take our order, I pondered if she, too, had tried out for *The Modelizer*. Why might she have been rejected, while the redhead got on the show? Did they look for diverse personalities? Hair color? Eating disorders? Or maybe the most important characteristic was just a high enough level of cattiness. I imagined that the producers might have envisioned wrestling matches, with orange Jell-O if possible, or maybe old-fashioned pillow fights . . . in lingerie. I closed my eyes indignantly and instead tried to think happy thoughts, of couture gowns and *petites mains* . . .

Lost in my pleasant reverie, I didn't notice that Jacques had arrived until he had walked right up to me and put his hands on my shoulders. Startled—I almost thought it was the redhead, or worse, Nick—I jumped out of my chair. Jacques took the motion to be an invitation for an embrace, so he wrapped me in a full bear hug and proclaimed with great emotion how glad he was to see me. I must have gasped a little too loudly, and Jacques must have proclaimed a little too loudly, because suddenly everyone on the second floor of the restaurant was watching us. My eyes shot around the room in panic, and as I tried to hush Jacques down into the empty seat at our table, I spotted them: Nick's bright hazel eyes, staring through Jacques and right at me.

"Jacques, have a seat, sit down, join us," I mumbled, trying to get the situation back under control. "Oh, Jacques, this is my mother," I said. "Mom, this is Jacques Billings. Do you remember . . . ?"

"Oh course I remember," Mom lied. She wouldn't have been able to pick my high school French teacher out of a lineup, so I was glad I had filled her in on the whole story of what I'd done that week. This was hardly a good time for a lengthy explanation. "Glad to see a fellow Texan," she added. "Paris is teemin' with us, actually!"

Jacques smiled at my mother and reached over and squeezed Lola's hand. I could still see the sadness in his eyes, which were now underscored by dark circles.

"What's going on?" I whispered to him while Mom and Lola made small talk. I put my arm protectively on his back. "I'm sorry you couldn't reach me yesterday . . ." I luckily controlled my impulse to sneak a peek at Nick.

Jacques nervously looked around the room before moving his head in close to mine. "I heard from someone," he said, barely audibly. "A model. I don't even know how she found me, but she told me that she knows everythin'." He shut his eyes, and his mouth quivered.

"Knows what, Jacques?" I tried not to let my imagination get too far ahead of me, but things were already sounding bad.

"She knows what happened. What happened to Luis-Heinz. And where they're keepin' him."

"What? Who? Why?" My jaw dropped. I suddenly felt guilty for not taking Jacques's darkest fears seriously all this time. All this time I'd been wasting on Nick . . . But dammit, I thought, did it have to be a *model*?

"I wish I knew, because I'm worried sick," Jacques continued. "She wouldn't tell me over the phone. She said she wanted to meet tonight. That's why I've been so frantic lookin' for you. You have to come with me . . . I don't know how I could do this on my own . . ."

"Of course, Jacques," I said, trying to sound positive. "Of course I'll go with you tonight."

I could feel Jacques's pulse slow down a bit, and his breathing become a little less constricted. But he was still clutching on to me. I could only imagine what the gossipers in the restaurant were thinking . . . I wondered what Nick might be thinking. I stole a glance at him. He was watching, all right. I turned my eyes away from Nick and gave Jacques's arm a squeeze. "Things will work out fine," I told him—and myself. "I just know they will."

He nodded. "I think I need a drink," he said.

"You and me both," I replied.

Two vodka gimlets later, Jacques seemed to calm down considerably, and even found mild amusement in how Lola and my mother were torturing me about Nick. "Oh, he *is* cute," Jacques managed to interject when they brazenly pointed "Mr. Hottie" out to him.

The free-flowing alcohol apparently helped loosen me up, too, because somewhere between my steak au poivre (ordered *saignant*—literally, bloody—which nicely encapsulated my state of mind) and my espresso, I had decided to send Lola to the restroom with a detour past Nick's table to do some spying, and she was taking up the reconnaissance mission like a couture counteragent.

We watched her wend her way through the room, stopping to air-kiss a Dior client here, a fellow publicist there. And at just the right moment, as she parked herself just to the left of Nick's table, she engaged a waiter in what, from where we sat, looked like a heartfelt, but ultimately mindless, conversation. "Oh, she's good," I muttered. "Way too good."

But then, to our slightly tipsy alarm, first the redhead and then Nick stood up. "What, are they leaving already?" I said under my breath, secretly taking glee in their aborted date—maybe even fancying myself the reason why—until she headed toward the restroom and he sat back down. "Oh, he's got nice manners," my mother murmured as Lola abruptly ended her chat with the waiter and followed the redhead down the stairs, stopping first to flash a silly, sloppy grin at us.

The rest of us were beside ourselves by this point. "What in heaven's name is Lola gonna say?" my mom wondered. "Are all publicists trained for spyin' . . . ?" She started giggling.

"Maybe she can go undercover on that show now." I laughed. "She can be the mole. The secret twist. She can turn them all against him and—"

"Ahem."

I was in midguffaw, midthought, perhaps even midinsult when I noticed that Jacques and my mother were both staring somewhere past me, above my head. It could only mean one thing, and I could feel myself rapidly turning crimson, starting with my ears. Or should it have been Nick whose ears were burning? How lucky that I could just turn around and ask him.

But instead I sat motionless, mortified. It was Nick who spoke first.

"Alex?" he said quietly.

I bowed my head and started stroking my hair forward, around my face, as if that would somehow render me invisible.

"Alex, I'm sorry to interrupt," he tried again.

I bit my lip, and seeing that my tablemates had deserted me and were now pretending to be deep in conversation with each other about whether to order dessert with their espressos, I turned my head partway and gazed up at him out of the corner of my eye. "Oh, hi," I said, as nonchalantly as I could muster.

He knelt down beside the table to look me in the face. "Alex, please let me say again how sorry I am," he whispered. "And God knows I am truly sorry that you have to see me here like this." He rubbed his eyes and then clasped his hands in prayer position over his nose and mouth. "Look, I have a *contract*," he said urgently. "I didn't do this to meet models. I just wanted to be in Paris. I wanted an adventure. I signed up on a whim and now I can't get out of it. If I had a choice . . ." He shook his head and sighed. "But I don't. I have to finish this. I'm not even sure I'm supposed to be talking to you like this . . ."

My head was spinning: Don't get sucked in so easily just because he's cute and he's giving you that *look*, that hard-to-resist look, and his mouth is saying "I'm sorry," and his eyes are saying "I'm yours, all yours." *No. Must. Not. Back. Down.* But I allowed my gaze to meet his eyes—and there went my resolve. "Nick," I said softly, "I want to talk to you, I do. Now just really isn't the right time . . ." I blinked a few times as my brain caught up with my heart. "Here's my cell number," I said, scribbling it down on a receipt I probably needed for my expenses, but what the hell? This drop-dead-gorgeous man was trying to make it up to me. I gave him—thankfully for my pride—only the smallest hint of a smile. "Call me tonight, okay?"

Before I knew it, Nick had given me a quick peck on the lips and retreated to his table. Cheeky monkey, I thought, my face flushing as I remembered that I'd had an audience all this time.

Chapter Eleven

"HAVE I GOT A STORY FOR YOU," Lola said breathlessly as she floated back to the table.

"Um, have *we* got a story for *you*," my mother said. "Don't you, Alex?"

My flushed face was now completely red.

"What? What did I miss?" Lola looked at me.

"Nick came by," I mumbled. "That's all."

"And he kissed her in front of all of us. And she agreed to talk to him later," Mom reported, adding in her best imitation of me, "That's all."

"You little hussy!" Lola joked. "A round of drinks on me!"

I looked up at Lola coyly, and took the opportunity to glance at Nick's table, where the redhead was brimming with excitement and Nick was once again standing up to help her into her seat. And just before I could turn away, she winked in our direction. Flustered at getting caught staring—really poor form when you're people-watching or, well, spying—I looked around the table. Who, *me?* "Did she just wink at me?" I asked.

"No, darling, she was winking at *me*," Lola said matter-of-factly. "Now, didn't I tell you I had something very interesting to share?"

To my surprise, it was Jacques who good-naturedly said, "Pray tell."

"Well, my friends, I do believe I may have another career if this whole fashion thing doesn't work out." She grinned. "Publicity, spying—two sides of the same coin. Hey, fashion is *competitive*. It's all about information."

"Oh, so that's why every designer will say that navy is the new black at the same time," my mother exclaimed.

"Something like that," Lola said. "We can discuss later. Anyhow, I followed the redhead into the ladies' room, but I didn't want to freak her out, so I didn't say anything at first. I just pretended to check my makeup for a *really* long time." Lola rolled her eyes. "So when she's finished doing her thing, I ask her if she's got any eye-drops. Of course she does. *Of course.*" I wasn't sure why *of course*, but I didn't want to interrupt.

"So I started chatting her up, asked her if she was a model, because I was a fashion publicist," Lola continued. "Now, I just want to digress for a moment here and say that had I been a man, she would have thought I was coming on to her and stalked right out. That really is a bad opening line. Trust me, I know." Lola fell silent, closing her eyes dramatically as if she were remembering some horrible "Hey, baby" moment. She shook it off and resumed her tale. "But luckily for us I'm a woman and she fell for it. She told me her name was Siobhan, and yeah, she's trying to be a model. In fact, she's confident she's going to be famous, because she's going to be on TV. Oh my God, you will not believe what they're doing on this show. Oh, she told me *everything*. It was as if she hadn't eaten in days and was gobbling up everything in sight. Only it was the reverse, so, like, everything came out." Lola wrinkled her nose. "Eww, that was kind of a gross image, sorry. And actually, it's not true, because they *are* eating. At least they're trying to, but it can't be easy to overcome years and years of conditioning." While my mom and Jacques exchanged puzzled looks, I nodded, gratified. Thank God he had told me the truth about the show.

"See, these models think Nick is a prince of some tiny country that they wouldn't have any way of knowing wasn't real, and in order to be his princess they have to gain all this weight because his country worships fat women," Lola announced, looking extremely pleased with herself as Jacques's jaw dropped and my mother gasped.

"Honey, did you know that's what the show was about?" she said.

I looked down at my lap, up at the ceiling—anywhere other than my mother's eyes—and scrunched up my face. How was I to admit to her, now that the truth was out, that I'd known something I had been too embarrassed to tell her in the first place? "Um . . . yes?"

Luckily, Lola was moving into her play-by-play. "Oh my God, look at her now, scarfing down the bread." So of course we all turned and gawked. "Anyhow . . . I asked her who the cute guy at her table was. This is where it gets good."

As the rest of us pushed aside our espresso cups and leaned on our elbows, faces propped in our hands, Lola went off on another tangent. "You know, she's not bad-looking." She saw me glaring at her out of the corner of her eye. "Hang on, Alex, I'm not finished. I was just about to say that she looks kind of like Geri Halliwell, just stretched out another ten inches or so. Oh, and she sounds like her too."

Lola was obviously enjoying herself much too much. She cleared her throat and proceeded to do her best Cockney-cum-*East Enders*-cum-dying-parrot impression. "'Oi, 'im, Nick, yah, 'e's cute,' Siobhan said, and I quote," Lola said triumphantly, "'But blimey, I 'spect 'e's gay. 'E 'asn't so much as snogged any one of us—never mind shagging. All me mates warned me there'd be a twist on the show!' End quote. Ahem. Now, from what I've gathered from Miss Simons—and I hope I'm not grossing you out, Mrs. Simons—I don't think he's gay! But Alex, I do believe the unexpected twist was *you.*"

I think I might have actually said "Pshaw." I was tickled pink by Lola's assessment—or maybe tickled red, I mused as I self-consciously felt my cheeks for any telltale warmth. Nick's really got to stop doing that to me, I thought. Hmm . . . was making me blush all he'd have to make up for in the end?

He likes me, he really likes me.

And that's all it took? I had to have a good think about this.

Well, what was I really angry about, if what Siobhan told Lola was true? So he was doing something stupid on TV; hell, I'd been there and done that. Okay, to rephrase: He was *voluntarily* doing something stupid on TV. Then again, there were some people in the world (including that Pulitzer-obsessed—and I didn't mean Lilly—part of me) who considered my vocation just as ridiculous. After all, my job required reading a publication called the *Catwalk Caterwaul*. Who was I to talk?

So just what was his crime? He didn't tell me everything from the get-go, which made me feel a bit . . . foolish, embarrassed. But he was the one making a fool of himself on television, not me. After all, *I* never signed any releases. Ha! If they ever aired the footage of our dates, they would have to cover my face with one of those blurry blue dots. I chuckled to myself. No one would believe my mother when she bragged that her daughter was the blue dot. I shook my head at the ridiculousness of it all.

"Let's get out of here," I said as Lola paid the bill. But as I rose from my chair and headed out, I just couldn't stop myself from making quite the exit. First I strolled by the Conspicuously Nondescript couple and smiled broadly for their hidden cameras, and then, straightening my back, I found myself walking past Nick's table, perilously close, so that my bag brushed the back of Siobhan's chair. I nonchalantly paused to adjust the Hermès scarf around my neck *just so*, and then walked on. A centimeter closer—and had she perhaps been holding a glass of red wine and wearing white instead of black—and there might have been a throwdown the likes of which hadn't been seen since the last Miller Lite commercial. Now *that* might have made for some good TV.

"I haven't had this much excitement in one weekend since I did business with Enron," my mother said, straight-faced, as we walked out of the restaurant. "I think I need a li'l nap." She let out a li'l yawn.

While we walked to the taxi stand a block up on the avenue Montaigne, I involuntarily scanned the street for the two black SUVs. And there they were, idling in front of Nina Ricci. They were like a bad spray-on tan that couldn't be exfoliated away.

Lola had to return to Dior, if only to clear her schedule for the evening. "I went to the twentieth arrondissement with you and lived to tell the tale, so I'm not chickening out on you now," she said. "What could possibly be worse than that?"

"Well . . . ," I said slowly, "we're meeting the model at the Buddha Bar at seven."

After letting out an involuntary gasp, Lola simply looked aghast. "I had *no idea* the Buddha Bar was even open that early," she said, wrinkling her nose with distaste.

"Unfashionably early, I *know,*" I said, racking my brain for a line of thought she'd appreciate. "But think about it. We'll be out of there long before anyone who's anyone would see us."

Lola paused, and the wrinkling of her nose relaxed. I exulted at my skill in fashionista logic. "Oh, all right, that's a good point," she said finally. "And how are we supposed to recognize her?"

"She said she'd be wearing one of Luis-Heinz's dresses," Jacques said, "to prove she knew what she was talking about."

"The little thief!" Lola blurted out. "No one's gotten

their hands on those dresses but me, not even Alex!" She let out a few choice swearwords under her breath. After a moment's reflection, though, she changed her tune. "Well, I guess it's a good thing I know what *not* to wear," she mused. "How embarrassing would that be? Um, did she say what color dress?"

I sighed and kissed her on both cheeks before climbing into the waiting taxi.

As Mom dozed in the middle of the backseat—undoubtedly dreaming of the *petites mains* stitching away at her newly ordered Chanel suit—Jacques and I whispered over her like little kids after lights-out.

"So what exactly did this model tell you?" I asked, frowning the second the word *model* escaped my lips. "And can we call her something other than 'this model'?"

"Well, she didn't give me her name," he replied. "But she did—I think inadvertently—mention that she was going to a lingerie go-see. "

"Lingerie, huh?" I said slowly.

"Yes, the key to trackin' down the love of my life is a lingerie model." He sighed. "Not too promisin' . . ."

"She may be a *highly intelligent* lingerie model: lingerie model by day, biochemistry doctoral candidate by night. She did manage to find you, after all," I said, trying to sound hopeful. "How *did* she find you, anyway?"

"I don't know. The model—I mean, what's-her-face—she didn't want to talk on the phone too long."

"This informant . . . what to call her? Let's see . . ." The cogs in my brain were spinning. At *The Weekly* I had worked hard to become the go-to person for clever captions, punny headlines, punchy kickers to end stories. And I wasn't about to be stumped now. I needed to lighten the mood for Jacques. I needed to stop hearing the word *model.* I needed to live up to my reputation.

"Lingerie . . . cleavage . . . pink slips . . ." A grin slowly crept onto my face. "Okay, I've got it. 'This model' is now codenamed," I said, pausing for effect, "Deep Décolletage."

Jacques's hearty laugh filled the taxi. A little levity was just what we needed as the effects of the alcohol began to wear off and the light of day shone through the windshield. But we soon drifted into silence, and I nervously tapped my foot against the back of the front seat as my mother's head slowly nodded, bobbed, and swayed toward my shoulder. In his corner, Jacques stared out the window as he crossed first his left leg over his right, and then his right over his left, and back and forth over and over again.

Mesmerized by the metronomelike motion of Jacques's feet, I dozed off and dreamed about meeting a tall, buxom woman wearing dark sunglasses and a nightie under her trench coat in a shadowy parking garage: That was our girl, our Deep Décolletage.

But she was nothing like what I'd imagined.

When Jacques and I met Lola at the Buddha Bar—my jetlagged and overexerted mother couldn't be roused once she got back into her hotel bed—we figured we'd have no trouble identifying a lingerie model. After all, at quarter of seven, the hotspot was barely tepid, filled as it was with tourists from Germany and the American Midwest. That may have translated to tall Teutonics in leather pants—but that was just the men. And the milk-fed, rosy-cheeked blondes? All around the age of thirteen and chaperoned by their parents.

The three of us parked ourselves at the bar downstairs, in the shadow of the giant golden Buddha statue. A hundred candles illuminated the red lacquer walls and the Asian kitsch that filled the cavernous room, while an oddly blissful mix of flutes and drums and ambient music filtered through the speakers. You could barely make out the person across the table from you, much less a lingerie model–informant you'd never seen before.

Still, we all stared off in separate directions, zeroing in and then dismissing one woman after another. No one stood out; certainly no one towered over the rest as we had come to expect a model should.

In the end, I saw the dress first. The fit and flow of Luis-Heinz's creation were unmistakable. I found myself mesmerized by the way the nectarine-colored fabric clung to the hips, then swayed around the legs. Without taking my eyes off the approaching figure, I nudged Lola, who in turn alerted Jacques.

"That must be her," Lola said, who like me couldn't tear her eyes away from the dress, "unless the wench hocked the dresses that rightfully belong to me." She thought better of it and added, "And to you, Alex, and all the women of the world."

I was far too lost in my fashion reverie to notice.

And then Jacques broke the spell when he said, "Do you really think she's a lingerie model?"

"What's that?" I turned my head and looked at him. He was squinting in sync with the flickering candle at our table. He looked decidedly puzzled.

I looked back at the mystery woman—and this time I tried my best to focus on her instead of the dress. No, she wasn't that tall. Nor was she particularly buxom. But my oh my, that dress really looked good . . .

Armed with a girly-colored cocktail, she was standing perfectly still in the corner, but it was obvious she was scanning the room looking for someone. That—and the fact that she had her face mostly covered by a straw cowboy hat—convinced us that this woman was in fact our Deep Décolletage.

Jacques quickly got up from the table and made his way over to her, floating around packs of tourists like a pro (I figured he must have learned that working at the Bon Marché). I could see in her body language that she was relieved—but still nervous—when Jacques finally reached her. They exchanged a few words, then separated; he headed back toward us while she disappeared in the opposite direction.

"What's going on?" I wondered out loud, not really expecting an answer.

"God, I really want that dress," Lola said, the first sign she had snapped out of her trance—or not.

Jacques returned to the table without a word.

"Well?" I asked.

"It'll be a few minutes," he said under his breath.

As promised, she appeared a few minutes later, face still obscured by the hat, and plopped herself down in the one empty chair that we had agonized over for a good twenty minutes before situating it nearest the corner of the room. (What was informant etiquette? Would she want to face the door? Back to the door? Would she be spooked by three people?) The truth was that she hardly seemed to notice anything other than the bottle of white Burgundy that Lola had ordered. Lola poured her a glass of the wine, which our guest downed in one gulp.

"These are my friends," Jacques said to her. "They're tryin' to help me find Luis-Heinz, so you can speak freely in front of all of us."

"Ah'm glad you found me," she said, finally moving her head just so, so that her face showed from under her hat.

"I've seen you somewhere before," Lola murmured, almost to herself. "I know I have . . ."

I turned my gaze from Deep Décolletage to Lola and back.

"*Shaunee?*" we squealed in unison.

"Yeah. How'd y'all know?" She looked a little nervous.

"Oh my God, I knew it!" Lola crowed. "You're the girl I saw with Bartolome yesterday at the Dior show. You won that modeling contest . . ."

"Ah can't believe you recognized me—Ah won that contest three years ago, when Ah was jus' seventeen," she said, wanly smiling up at us from under her hat. But somehow our remembering her from three years ago—an eternity in fashion time—put her at ease. I noticed her shoulders lower, as if the tension was seeping out with every word, and she relaxed her grip on the wineglass. "Winnin' the contest brought me to Paris. Ah was the toast of the modelin' world, Ah was fixin' to be the next Kate Moss—Ah'm not so tall, as you can see. Ah think the agency secretly hoped Ah jus' hadn't stopped growin' yet." She laughed ruefully. "And they were right, sort of. Ah grew all right—sideways. Ah was so homesick that Ah ate everythin' in sight."

As she stopped to raise her glass for a refill, I took a closer look at her face. There was something about her eyes that made her seem older than her years, I thought sadly. Then I realized it was just the artificial-blue contact lenses.

"Well, before long, they sent me packin' and Ah was home in Arkansas," Shaunee continued. "And Ah was back to modelin' tracksuits and prom dresses for Mervyn's."

I glanced at Lola. She looked like she was going to cry. I kicked her under the table. We didn't have time for a big weepy night.

"But all that time, Ah knew that wasn't for me," Shaunee said, with a newly determined tone in her voice. "And one Friday night, Ah was home eatin' corndogs and watchin' my ol' high school football team playin' on TV, and there was a commercial for a new reality show, lookin' for people who wanted to change their looks 'n' their lives: *Total Makeover*. It was like a gift from God."

My jaw must have dropped somewhere down near my knees. Good God, was everyone and her mother on a reality show? Speaking of mothers, I'd have to remember to ask mine about this one . . .

As Shaunee began to recount her return to fabulousness, her voice fluttered into Mariah Carey range. (Lola, meanwhile, was sniffling into her cloth napkin.) "Ah wrote a five-page letter that very night, tellin' 'em my whole sad story, the rise and fall of Shaunee Caruth, and wouldncha know it, the producer called me the followin' week," she trilled. "Ten days later, Ah was at the Four Seasons in L.A., workin' out every mornin' with Tabu, the personal trainer to the stars . . . and gettin' ready for a few nips and tucks." Shaunee stopped to flash us all a triumphant—and blindingly white—smile. "A teensy li'l bit of lipo, breast enhancement, thigh sculptin', ab shapin' . . . got da Vinci veneers, got my hair highlighted, my brows reshaped, my frown lines Botoxed . . . and now, here Ah am! So Ah'm not workin' with the big names—yet—but Ah'm back! Where Ah belong!"

To Jacques and Lola, and for that matter Shaunee, I may have looked like I was staring at her assets, awestruck, but in truth I was ringing up the price of her makeover. Luis-Heinz's dress deserved a lot of credit for her figure, but I reckoned one model's nip and tuck was another Beverly Hills surgeon's child's college fund. After some further analysis, I silently congratulated myself for recognizing her with her new nose. And then—finally—I found myself thinking that I was kind of pleased for the little model that could. I had to admit that there *was* some good to come out of reality TV.

Lola wiped her eyes for the tenth time and reached out to give Shaunee a hug. "That is just *so* inspiring," Lola sighed. After a moment of soaking in the good modeling karma, Lola remembered the other reason why she remembered Shaunee. "Wait, but how do you know Bartolome?"

"That's why Ah'm here," Shaunee said quietly. She tossed her long hair, which was perfectly salon-highlighted into the color of Malibu sand (in three o'clock sunlight). "Ah was fixin' to give you information about your friend—and Ah don't mean Bartolome, 'cause he ain't no real friend to anyone."

We all gulped and leaned in closer.

Shaunee cleared her throat and plunged into her story. She had met Bartolome at a nightclub a few months ago.

"Look, he picked me up," she said. "Ah'm not prouda that. Ah wasn't lookin' for a boyfriend, but he said he was fixin' to make me the spokesmodel of the most amazin' design house the fashion world had ever seen."

"Bastard!" Lola muttered under her breath.

"At first Ah didn't take him real serious, but he was cute an' whatever." She shrugged. "And then one day he took me to meet your friend Luis-Heinz."

"Bastard!" Lola repeated. I realized she was in too deep a shock to come up with any other response. After all, how many phone calls, pisco sours, and wild rides had it taken her to get to meet Luis-Heinz?

"He seemed like the nicest guy, so quiet and shy," Shaunee said. I glanced at Jacques, who looked proud and worried at the same time. "And his dresses, of course, jus' knocked my socks off. When we got home, though, Bartolome told me"—she lowered her voice and put on what I guessed from Lola's grin was a dead-on imitation of Bartolome—"'that Luis-Heinz is a fool, he doesn't care about money, just cares about how women feel, blah blah blah, stupid, stupid!' Ah was *shocked.* After he drank himself drunk as a skunk that night, he told me he was gonna steal Luis-Heinz's secrets!"

"What?" That was all I, or any of us, could muster. Beneath the table I grasped Jacques's hand. I tried to give him a reassuring look; if only I felt reassured myself.

"Ah knew it wasn't right, but Ah just didn't know what to do," she said, looking apologetic. "Who could Ah tell? Who would believe a girl from Podunk, Arkansas? An' besides, he was takin' me to the Dior show."

Lola nodded approvingly—proudly, really. "It *was* a brilliant show."

"Ah was stuck," Shaunee continued. "Then two nights ago, Bartolome told me he was meetin' with some people who were fixin' to make us real rich. He told me to stay home, but Ah couldn't. Y'all know what? Ah followed him."

After switching Métro lines twice and transferring to the RER, and then cabbing it from the station, Shaunee recalled, she followed Bartolome into a warehouse in the suburbs past Neuilly—Nick's neck of the woods, I thought to myself. For a second, I allowed myself to wonder when he was going to call—but then I was back to focusing on Shaunee's story. Once she spotted Bartolome walking into a room with some strange men, she sneaked around the warehouse until she saw a frightened-looking Luis-Heinz being hustled into a storeroom by two muscle-bound men. ("They looked like they could be Britney Spears's bodyguards," she said helpfully.)

And what did she do? Run home? Call the cops? No, she followed them—and at this point in her story, my positive opinion of her crystallized right in front of my eyes. This girl was one fearless Southern woman. She was up there with my mom and Liza Rowland. I wondered if I would ever belong to that group.

Shaunee brazenly pressed her ear to the door and overheard a Frenchman telling Bartolome that he and his colleagues would pay ten million euros for Luis-Heinz's designs. They would have to keep Luis-Heinz, too. (Her high school French, I thought to myself, apparently was much better than mine. Then I glanced guiltily at Jacques.)

"So this lingerie company really thought that Luis-Heinz's dresses were going to put it out of business?" I mused.

"That's crazy," Jacques said. "All Luis-Heinz ever wanted was to make the world beautiful, one woman at a time. He never wanted to be a conglomerate!"

Lola quickly snapped to attention. "And I wasn't going to let him, either! His dresses were going to be *exclusive*."

Shaunee just shook her head. "No, it's bigger than that," she said. "This small-time company, Les Deux Lapins, which Ah can't even believe Ah ever was gonna let Bartolome make me their spokesmodel"—she sniffed daintily—"they wanted to blackmail the big companies in the industry. They were fixin' to threaten them, say they'd come out with these designs and put them outta business, unless they paid them millions. See?"

I could see that Lola's blood was boiling at the thought of Luis-Heinz's going mass market. Jacques, clearly overwhelmed by this development, was slumped in his chair. Besides being even more impressed by Shaunee's French comprehension, I was shocked by the twisted logic of these lingerie lightweights. It seemed pretty unlikely to succeed. But that didn't help Luis-Heinz any.

"So where's Luis-Heinz?" I asked Shaunee.

"Still there, Ah hope," she said. By some miracle—or by an oversight typical of French businesses, depending on your opinion of French businesses—Bartolome and the Frenchman and the two heavies had left the room, not bothering to lock the door. Shaunee had watched them walk across the warehouse, discussing what they were going to eat for dinner, and slipped into the room. And there was Luis-Heinz, with a rack full of his beautiful clothes.

"His hands were tied, and he looked so relieved to see

me," Shaunee recalled. "But then Ah tried talkin' English and then French, and he just shook his head, had no idea what Ah was sayin'."

"Oh, L-H!" Jacques sighed. He looked forlorn. "I really have to stop speakin' Esperanto to him. He has to learn!"

"Ah untied his hands, and he was tryin' to say *somethin'* to me, but Ah jus' didn't understand. So once his hands were free, he wrote down his name, and your name, Jacques, and your phone number . . . and then he handed me this dress and pushed me out the door."

For the first time since Shaunee started talking about Luis-Heinz, I noticed that I had blinked. Lost in her story, I just sensed she was telling the truth. Now that I had come to that realization, I had to figure out what we were going to do about it. But Jacques beat me to it.

"Where's the warehouse?" he said urgently. "We're goin' there tonight."

Tape recorder: check. Tiny notepad that they handed out at the Missoni show: check. Mechanical pencil: check. (I had learned the hard way, while chasing a Saks security guard down the courthouse corridors at the Winona trial, that No. 2 Ticonderoga pencil leads break and pens run out of ink.) Cell phone equipped with text messaging in case we had to be quiet: check. Oversize Marc Jacobs bag to carry everything in, with the added benefit of the heavy hardware that meant it could be used as a weapon: check.

Just before ten, we were finally armed and ready.

Against my better judgment—of course, at this point, I had to wonder just what "better" meant—I had acquiesced to my mother's demand that she tag along. "Who would suspect a middle-aged woman in Chanel was the lookout?" she reasoned, once she was wakened from her nap by our loud rummaging and packing.

"Haven't you got enough stories to tell all your friends back home?" I said before I finally relented. "But who's going to stay here, to take the call if something goes wrong?" I gulped at the sound of my own words. Mom and Lola looked at each other.

"Oh, all right," Lola said, pouting something fierce. "I'm it." She looked around. "So do I have dibs on your wardrobe if you don't come back?" she added with a wink.

Jacques and I had synchronized our clothes—black turtleneck, black pants, and black leather trench, as if we were rejects from *The Matrix*—and our watches. (As it turned out, we had the same Cartier Tank Française, the one with the subdials I hadn't bothered finding out how to use.) Meanwhile, Mom replenished her Chanel bag with Kleenex, moisturizer, eyedrops, a bag of M&Ms (king size), antibacterial hand lotion, Benadryl, and some plastic sandwich bags—stuff we might never need, but it was comforting nonetheless, and boy, did I need some comfort. I was quaking in my Jimmy Choos—the low heels. They may have been the least of all the evils I had with me, but where were my Prada *Sport* shoes when I needed them?

So there we were, my mother, my French teacher, and me. This, I swore to myself, would *not* be mentioned in the article, or the book or the movie adapted from it. Not even as an extra director's cut feature on the DVD. Who would believe me anyway?

About as unintentionally conspicuous as we could be, the three of us marched in formation through the hotel lobby and out to the cloudy night.

We were parked in the backseat of a cab for a good thirty seconds before I realized I didn't know exactly where we were going. I rolled down the window and beckoned to the hotel doorman—so rude of me, I cringed, but these were desperate moments—and asked him if he knew where the warehouse for Les Deux Lapins might be. At first his eyebrows leaped up in alarm, but wouldn't you know it, Parisians know their fashion like London taxi drivers know their roundabouts.

"Bien sûr, mademoiselle," the doorman said, leaning into the driver's half-open window as he launched into the most precise directions I had ever heard. The driver intermittently nodded in agreement.

"Are you writin' this all down?" my mother whispered. I shrugged helplessly. They had lost me at the first right turn.

"I'll pay him to wait for us," I said, trying to give her a reassuring smile.

The doorman gave the taxi a friendly tap on the roof, and wished us Godspeed.

It couldn't be that bad, I told myself—certainly no worse than the wild-goose chase to Luis-Heinz and Jacques's place. I leaned back into the seat and tried to relax. By the sounds of the directions, we were in for a long ride.

Twenty-five minutes later, after walking through an unlocked, unguarded gate, I was hiding behind a cart full of bolts of Lycra and lace.

In the taxi, we had come up with a plan of action based on Shaunee's intel: Mom and I would stand guard in the main room of the gloomy concrete block of a warehouse. Though the open space was as big as a football field, it certainly felt claustrophobic when one was positioned in the middle of two dozen carts of fabric, all shades of black and white and gray.

Meanwhile, Jacques would go in search of the storeroom where Luis-Heinz was being held. Where we *hoped* he was still being held. We hadn't really considered the possibility that he wasn't there anymore, much less come up with a Plan B—until the thought popped into my brain as a piece of lace grazed the top of my head. Oh crap, I muttered, brushing the thought, and the lace, away. I tried to think happy thoughts—of Jacques reunited with Luis-Heinz. Of Lola reunited with those dresses. Of me reunited with . . .

I was startled out of my reverie by the vibration of my phone, which I had clipped onto my belt—an ugly but necessary fashion faux pas since I hadn't thought to pack my roomy new chocolate-brown woven-leather Bottega Veneta bag, the one with the little cell-phone pocket conveniently placed halfway down the suede lining, just high enough to be easily accessible but low enough to be hidden from sticky fingers. I had set the phone for text messaging only, since I couldn't exactly go into my first stakeout with a phone that could ring at any inopportune moment, now could I?

My mother watched as I scrolled through the message

log, so she must have seen my game face turn to one big, goofy, smiling mush.

"Nick?" she whispered.

"Yeah . . ." I grinned. "But what am I going to tell him when we're in this . . . in this . . . *situation?*" Just talking about it made me skittish; I poked my head between two rolls of fabric and scanned the warehouse. No signs of life. I retracted my head like a snapping turtle. "I've got to text him back *something.*"

Mom raised her eyebrows. "Textin'? Like what the McDuffs' ten-year-old daughter does with all her friends? Doesn't anyone just talk anymore?"

"Umm . . . not if you don't have to," I confessed. God knew how much easier it was to say no to Roddy via e-mail.

"You know, Mrs. McDuff is convinced that the shorthand kids use these days for instant messaging and whatnot is makin' them borderline illiterate," my mother threw out with a surprising amount of disapproval. She had a way with her segues. "And you—you work for a news magazine! You're a *writer!*"

"Yes, I am, and yes, she's probably right," I said. "But these are extenuating circumstances. So what should I say?" I clutched the phone in my right hand, thumb at the ready, as Mom watched over my shoulder.

"Tell him that you're busy right now," she said tentatively.

I scrolled down to Nick's message and found the option for responding to it. Then I let my thumbs do the talking, painstakingly hitting the number keys until the right letter came up. I wondered whether doctors were quickly discovering a new teen epidemic, to go along with mononucleosis and acne: thumb sprains, thumb pulls, or even thumb paralysis, brought on by repetitive stress.

Injuries be damned, I hunted-and-thumbed: GOT YR MSG BZ NOW TALK 2 U L8R.

"Wow, that's rather impersonal, isn't it?" my mother whispered.

Tap-tap, tap-tap-tap, tap-tap, tap-tap-tap. GOT YR MSG BZ NOW TALK 2 U L8R XOXO.

"Better?" I asked her.

She peered at the tiny screen. "Amazin'. It's stranger than I ever thought. What *language* is this? Is this Phonebonics? How did you learn all this?"

"Have no idea," I said. "Maybe from the models I meet. They're at about the same educational level as Mrs. McDuff's daughter." I giggled. "So are we ready to send this message or what?"

Mom nodded, and I did the honors. No sooner had I clipped the phone back onto my belt than it vibrated again. I unclasped the phone and looked at the new message: MUST C U WHERE R U.

As much as I wanted to see him too, this was hardly the right time . . . was it? Before I could reconsider the rashness of my actions, and before my mother, who was doing her every-other-minute scan of the warehouse, could see me, I punched in ON ST8OUT 2 LAPINS WAREHOUSE and hit Send.

Bad, bad girl.

Chapter Twelve

"WHAT THE—"

The rest of the sentence seemed stuck somewhere between my brain and my throat. I stood paralyzed, my eyes blankly flickering, like a television on the fritz. A flash of light, and the blurry lines were swallowed up in a spark. And then nothing.

"What the—" I tried again. And once again that's as far as I got. It was as if the thought were too unbelievable to even be expressed. When the doors of the warehouse burst open, and there stood Nick with his camera crew in tow, there I stood, dumbstruck. I mean, I had texted him where I was. That he showed up fifteen minutes later didn't surprise me exactly. *But what were the cameras doing here?*

And then the weight of one pair of inquisitive eyes started to slowly sink in.

"Is that who I think it is?" my mother asked quietly.

"Oh. My. God," I whispered. "Oh. My. God." I ducked behind a cement column and squeezed my eyes shut. Must . . . calm . . . down, I thought. Deep breath. "Ommmm . . . ommmm . . ."

My mom grabbed me by the shoulders and shook me like an old bottle of nail polish until I returned to my natural, non–Milk of Magnesia color. "What on earth is goin' on here?" she hissed.

"Uh, gee, it's Nick." I shrugged helplessly. "All I know is that we're staking out this warehouse, hoping to find my missing designer, and suddenly my *Charlie's Angels* scenario has turned into *This Is Your Life* . . ." I was hyperventilating. Deep breaths, I thought. "Okay, so I told him where we were. But I didn't think he'd come!"

My mother gave me a suspicious look—which I countered with a sheepish one. I looked her straight in the eye, and lowered my voice still further. "Do I look okay?"

"You look absolutely wonderful," she said, shaking her head disapprovingly.

I peeked out from behind the column at Nick and Mr. and Ms. Conspicuously Nondescript, who were openly brandishing their cameras this time. While Nick was poking around the warehouse, the pair seemed to be having a heated discussion.

"What is he thinking?" I said to myself.

"Honey, Jacques should be comin' any minute now," my mom said. "Or else we're supposed to go in after him." There was fear in her eyes, but that was offset by the excitement in her voice. My dad had told me years ago that when my mom was pregnant with me, she watched way too many James Bond movies. Figured.

"Let me think," I said. I took another peek. Nick was

now just fifty yards away, and Tweedledum and Tweedledee were following him from opposite ends of the room. I guessed they needed different camera angles for a cinema verité effect. Geez. We're *entertainment*, I thought.

"Alex! I'm here!" Nick called out.

Crap. What was I thinking when I hit Send? I rubbed my temples. I had to think fast . . . I wished that I had packed a compact so I could check my makeup . . . Hang on. Priorities! How about trying to shut him up so that the baddies—wherever they were—wouldn't know we were holding a veritable flash mob in the warehouse? Sheesh.

I took a deep breath, pressed my lips together to spread out what was left of my lip gloss, and stuck my head out farther into the open space. "Over here!" I yelped, making eye contact. I put an index finger to my mouth and with exaggerated motion, whispered, "Shhhhh!"

And what did Nick do? He gave me one of those glistening, glorious smiles, and started to jog over to me. Jogging might have looked dorky for someone else. But not for him. Nope.

I shut my eyes. Nick was like the anti-Medusa: Everything he looked at turned to Jell-O. And that was the last thing I needed right then.

"Alex," he said, never losing eye contact. "Alex. I got your message. What on earth is a stateout?"

"Huh? A stateout?" I said.

He reached out for my hand and finally blinked. And as his eyes cleared, he noticed that we weren't alone. "Oh, hello again," he said, acknowledging my mother with a smile. "This is all kind of unconventional, isn't it?"

"Mom, Nick. Nick, my mom," I said nervously, shifting my weight from one leg to another. I stared at my feet for a while before daring to look up to see how the introductions were going.

My mom was silently sizing Nick up—I figured she felt it was her obligation, in my dad's absence. He anxiously smiled back at her.

"Stateout?" I repeated, puzzled. "S-T-8 . . . Oh, crap, I meant *stakeout*. That text messaging is kinda imperfect, huh." I attempted to smile confidently, or at least not look how I must have sounded: completely and utterly ridiculous.

"Oh," he said. "Well, okay . . . so you're on a *stakeout*?" He started glancing around the warehouse nervously.

"Umm, yeah, long story, but my friend Jacques is hunting for his boyfriend back there somewhere, see, because he was kidnapped . . . and . . . and we hope there's no one else here . . . like bad guys or something . . ." As I trailed off, I raised my eyes to his and, startled by the sudden intimacy, I thrust some hair forward to cover as much of my face as possible.

"Right . . ." Nick said. Was it concern or confusion that made him stick with me and not lose eye contact, despite my imitation of a home-schooled seventh-grader with an overactive imagination?

"Uh . . ." Flustered by his intense gaze, I lowered my eyes and pretended to scan the room. And then I saw the cameras. "Damn!" I said under my breath. I couldn't believe that I had completely forgotten they were there, right behind Nick, and filming away. How about that—you really *can* get used to them, I mused, off on a tangent. So that must be why people act so foolishly on TV . . . And that thought jolted me right back into the present reality, which was far too real and surreal at the same time.

"Uh, we can't have these cameras rolling like this," I said firmly. "And what are they *doing* here, anyway?"

"Huh?" Nick seemed completely taken aback. He turned and looked around, finally spotting his faithful followers. "Oh! Them." He shook his head. "I didn't even remember they were here." (I was right! I thought triumphantly.) He looked at me plaintively. "You know it wasn't my idea," he said. "They just follow me everywhere, and there's not much I can do about it. Contract and all . . ."

And in that instant, as I stared into his gentle eyes—with only, I swear, the quickest of glances at the way his jeans fit him—I knew that this was the moment of truth. Never mind my plans to keep him hanging. It was time to relax and learn to live with his reality (TV), and in the process, be a very happy, albeit at times temporarily annoyed, girl. Hadn't I heard just that evening how good reality TV had been to Shaunee, after all?

"Right, your contract," I said, trying desperately not to give in to the urge to kiss him right then and there, in front of my mother and the cameras and everything. It was *really* hard.

"Alex—" I heard my mom calling. Our moment of truth would have to wait.

I whipped my head around and saw Jacques first, his heavy brogues clop-clop-clopping along the cement floor. He was practically dragging a pale, thin man with cropped black hair and an aura that even Miss Cleo's most novice psychic could read as "delicate, creative soul."

It had to be Luis-Heinz.

And those two beefy men barreling through the double doors at the other end of the warehouse? They had to be, for lack of a better word, the baddies.

And there we were, caught right in the middle of the action.

"Shit!" I said, long delayed. I looked behind me and saw that my mom had ducked behind one of the many carts littering the warehouse. "Good, stay there," I mouthed at her. I doubted that she could see me, but verbalizing what seemed to be a plan made me feel reassured nonetheless.

Nick grabbed me and pushed me behind another cart before walking purposefully toward the scrum developing at the other end of the warehouse.

What was *this* all about? Was he trying to play the hero? I looked around to get the lay of the land. At the far end, the camera crew had propped themselves in position to catch all the action. They must have thought they'd died and gone to reality-TV heaven. Had they had any idea that news might be breaking out? (But maybe I, of all people, shouldn't be such a journalistic snob about it. Who knows, maybe they'd burned out on covering wars and famines and stumbled into this line of work. Uh-huh.)

And there in the middle, Jacques and Luis-Heinz had reached Nick, who was now standing between them and the big bad guys—emphasis on *big*—and seemed to be doing some negotiation.

I quickly evaluated the bad guys. Shaunee was right: They were definitely celebrity-bodyguard material. Or maybe NFL defensive line material. I gulped. Each must have weighed at least three hundred pounds. And, good

God almighty, what was that bulge in Big Guy #1's pants? No, not *there*. Was that a gun?

And suddenly *This Is Your Life* had segued into *The Sopranos*.

"G-gun . . . gun . . . gun!" I croaked out—for whose benefit I wasn't sure. Was there any way Nick could hear me from here?

"Hey there," he was saying to Big Guy #2, in back-slapping, beer-guzzling guy mode. "I think I must have made a wrong turn somewhere. We were . . . we were looking for the Hôtel Costes?"

Oh God. I rolled my eyes. What was he doing? Like they were going to buy *that?*

Big Guy #1 took a step forward. Nick, in turn, took one step back. It was like a slow, methodical dance. Jacques and Luis-Heinz instantly followed suit, quaking like thirteen-year-olds getting up the nerve to ask a girl for the next dance.

Big Guy #2 grunted and patted the bulge.

"Yeah," Nick continued, showing no sign of fear, "I'm meeting a bunch of models there."

I instantly felt a dagger piercing my heart. Why, oh why did it always have to come back to *that?*

Another step forward for the baddies. First Nick, then Jacques and Luis-Heinz continued to dance backward, toward the exit—and, I could only hope, toward the waiting SUVs that had been following Nick everywhere. Why would that change now?

Big Guy #1 took a daring lunge forward. "I don't believe you," he said in French-accented English.

Nick et al. countered with a few steps. Slow, slow, quick-quick, slow—was that the paso doble, or was it the cha-cha? I couldn't be sure; despite my parents' best efforts at schooling me when I was young, everything I knew about formal dancing came from the movie *Strictly Ballroom*. And no one was wearing spangles and Lycra tonight.

Now they were faced off, Nick just past me, and the baddies almost directly in front of my cart.

"Seriously, man," Nick said, his hands on his hips. "You see that cameraman back there?"

Jesus, what was he doing? They're gonna freak!

Nick pointed to Mr. Conspicuously Nondescript at his post near the rear exit. "See, I'm on a reality-TV show," he boasted, adding with a chuckle, "and it's about dating models."

I could see Nick's eyes from where I stood, and I was shocked to see that they looked positively lecherous. I shuddered. He was far too convincing. I was seeing the side of men they usually hide until at least five months into a relationship. All for the greater good, I had to remind myself. All for the greater good.

As if he could sense my dismay, Nick caught my eye for a split second and winked.

Relieved, I looked back at my mom. She was about to burst with her pent-up giggles. I shot her a pouty supermodel glare—and then I stuck my tongue out. Didn't she realize this was a dangerous situation, not a joke about my love life? Crap, had *I* forgotten that this was a dangerous situation? The butterflies crept back into my stomach. This was real, not made-for-TV! Well, actually, it *was* being filmed for TV, but it was real and . . .

"Yeah, there are ten hot—we're talking beer-commercial hot—models waiting for me at Costes," Nick was saying. This did not sound like him at all. Or at least I hoped not. He'd better be a really talented aspiring actor in real (i.e., non-reality) life.

The three parties continued their dance down the length of the warehouse, Nick now leading, even while dancing backward.

"*Vraiment?*" said Big Guy #1. "Why should we believe you?"

Nick called out to the cameraman. "Hey, Marcos," he said, "come over here and show them those hot-tub scenes."

Oh God. Not the hot-tub scenes . . .

Mr. Conspicuously Nondescript scurried over with his compact digital camcorder, all the while frantically pushing the rewind button as he kept one eye on the playback screen and one eye on Nick.

"*Regardez,*" Marcos said breathlessly, as he shoved the screen in the Big Guys' faces.

I couldn't see what was being shown, but I could have sworn that the bulge in Big Guy #1's pants shifted.

"Zat's zee sheet," Big Guy #1 said. "*Merde*, zeez girls are 'ot," said Big Guy #2. They were both completely engrossed in whatever was happening on the screen. I could only imagine that it involved bikinis.

Nick was grinning insanely, his eyes wide as he glanced over at me.

I narrowed my eyes back at him. What was he trying to tell me? He mouthed something at me.

"Gun?" I mouthed back. "Yeah, I know." Duh!

He shook his head and mouthed something again.

"Done?" I lip-read. What the hell was he saying? My brain was rolling through the alphabet like a grade-school poet seeking rhymes.

"Run," I heard a whisper coming from behind me. "Run," my mother repeated. *"Run!"* She was scrambling over to my perch, but I was already a step too slow. She stopped and cowered with me behind the cart of fabric.

The big guys had apparently seen enough to be convinced that this TV show existed, and that Nick could lead them to the promised land of hot tubs and hotter babes. Now they were debating amongst themselves how, not whether, they were going to get to what they were surely envisioning as a model orgy. I thought I heard one of them ask the other if they looked okay. *Men!*

We two women, meanwhile, huddled behind my cart, discussing amongst *our*selves how we were going to get out of there. Nick couldn't possibly intend to take the baddies to Hôtel Costes, could he? How would we lose them? And would Nick's model army really be there? Were the big guys going to forget all about the fact that they were supposed to be guarding Luis-Heinz?

They were men. There were models involved. An imagined, if not promised, orgy. Yup. We would have a safe getaway.

Still, I didn't want to take any chances, and Mom agreed. We had to suss out our escape route.

I looked over at Nick, hoping for some sign. Some mind-reading, perhaps. He had his cell phone out, as did both big guys. What, were they exchanging numbers? Jacques and Luis-Heinz, I noticed, had retreated almost all the way to the exit, and were now squatting by Ms. Conspicuously Nondescript. (She was wearing Hush Puppies, I noted. Very practical. I looked down at my own pointy shoes and cringed.)

I breathed a sigh of relief at the sight of Jacques and

Luis-Heinz, so close to freedom. For some reason it made me want to break out into Abba's "Fernando." Wasn't there some lyric about crossing the Rio Grande? What were Swedes doing crossing the Rio Grande, anyway? As I nervously hummed to myself, I realized that I must be losing my mind.

I nearly jumped when I suddenly felt my hip vibrate. Was all this excitement getting to me or what? I smiled guiltily. Nick *did* look awfully good.

And then I snapped out of it and realized that it was my phone that was vibrating. There was an envelope on the screen: new message. "I GOT THE GUYS U GET YRS," I read in a slow whisper. "DONT WORRY."

"Does Y-R-S mean *yours* or *years?*" my mother asked absentmindedly. "I'm tellin' you, it's confusin', this new language . . ."

I had to admit, she made me stop and think for a second. Then I shook it off.

"Okay, so what's the plan?" my mom said.

"Let's use this cart for cover," I said firmly, trying to sound decisive and authoritative. "Just in case. And then we'll make our way to Jacques and Luis-Heinz. Nick said he'd handle the big guys, so we just need to wait for them to leave, and then we're home free. Okay, ready?"

"Good thing I've been takin' Pilates classes," my mom said.

I smiled at her and kissed her on the cheek.

"Promise me you won't tell Daddy about any of this," she said.

"Promise," I said. "But after this you deserve *two* couture outfits."

On a whispered count of three, we put our weight

into it and pushed. And still the cart didn't budge. Had there not been big guys with a gun involved, I might have taken a moment to celebrate my natural conclusion that in this one instance I was, quite literally, a lightweight, a ninety-eight-pound (give or take a dozen pounds or so) weakling, even. But there was no time for that.

"These bolts of fabric are heavier than I thought," I muttered. "I swear I'm not gonna buy lingerie from this company, ever."

I slowly raised my head above the cart and looked out from between the bolts of Lycra and, as I registered when some fabric grazed my face, polyester blends. I was most definitely blacklisting their lingerie.

Nick and the baddies were on their way out of the warehouse, with his crew in tow. The door slammed shut, and a minute later I heard the sounds of the SUVs revving up and driving away. We were in the clear. Feeling victorious—and confident that nothing truly bad could happen to Nick in the presence of two TV cameras, anything involving models in bikinis notwithstanding—I did a silent Tiger Woods double-pump, ready to high-five any and all comers. I skipped over to the corner of the warehouse where Jacques was crouching, his arm wrapped tightly around the elusive man I'd been hunting all week. (No, the *other* one.)

"Saluton, Luis-Heinz!" I said, attempting to sound declarative but more likely sounding questioning—blast my excited upspeak. *"Esti sana?"*

I felt a gust as everyone whipped their heads in my direction, in one seemingly synchronized movement. My mom shot me a puzzled look. "Oh, just a little Esperanto

I picked up." I shrugged. "You can find just about anything on the Internet."

When dawn broke the next day, I was at my laptop, transcribing the last part of my interview with Luis-Heinz, as translated mostly by Jacques and when necessary by miming and drawing stick figures. Jacques and Luis-Heinz were nestled like two peas in a pod, fast asleep on the sofa, safe and together.

Mom had long ago retired to her bed, exhausted after reenacting the rescue mission for Lola, who in her excitement at seeing Luis-Heinz alive and well just about forgave us for leaving her behind.

But now the cursor blinked mercilessly at me from the screen as my sleep-deprived brain searched for a headline for the story. Deep Décolletage would make an appearance in this story, so the headline really had a lot to live up to. "Runway Runaway"? Nice alliteration, but not quite accurate. "Off the Rails"? Let's see: a lingerie cabal, a mysterious designer, an informant who models in her skivvies. Well, yes, it *was* off the rails—and then some. Of course, at least some of the "and then some" part would have to remain off the record. After much internal debate over my ethical obligation to tell the whole truth versus my desperate need to not completely embarrass myself, I had compromised. The dashing hero would make his appearance, but there would be no plug for his TV show. Of course, knowing Roddy, he already had the lowdown on the show, and my journalistic debate would be moot. He'd probably want the models in the lead paragraph.

I absentmindedly released my hair from the sloppy bun I had it in, believing that would somehow help me think better. And suddenly bells were going off.

Actually, it was the doorbell.

Still playing with my hair, I walked over to open the door. The minute I saw Nick standing there, I realized that I had been more worried about him than I had admitted to myself. I wanted to jump into his arms, but then I remembered my resolve to play it cool—for at least a minute or two.

"The party's over already?" I asked casually.

"Got broken up by the cops, actually," he said, looking down at me with a coy smile. "Those two lunkheads made such a scene when we got to Hôtel Costes that I didn't even need to sound the silent alarms. And after I told the police where I'd found them, they gave up their bosses in a minute . . . But your friends are still going to have to go in and file a complaint, you know."

I nodded and smiled with relief—for Luis-Heinz and his safety, and for me and my aching feet. I would be spared having to chase after Bartolome, once Shaunee talked to the police too.

Besides, I had other prey to face now.

"So were you really meeting your, ahem, harem there?" I asked him.

"Nah, I just knew that's where they always were. Not too many surprises from them," he said. He cocked his head. "Unlike you."

I blushed, and he stepped closer.

"So you found your man?" he asked, under his breath.

Does he mean what I think he means? I was completely flustered, but I cleared my throat and told myself not to sound too excited. "Yeah, I found him," I said, choosing not to engage in his line of questioning. I gestured at the sleeping Luis-Heinz. "And I'm finishing up the story now. You've just filled in some blanks for me, so all I need now is a headline."

He looked pensive for a moment. "How about calling it 'In the Nick of Time'?" he said with a smirk, stepping even closer, until there was nothing but microns of air between us.

So much for not engaging. "How about giving me a kiss?" I smirked back.

And he did.

And in the midst of our clinch, I thought of the scene in *To Catch a Thief* where fireworks light up the sky outside as Grace Kelly and Cary Grant kiss inside a hotel room. That moment in moviemaking should rightly be seen as cinematic cheese, but in fact it made me—who, I supposed, should rightly be deemed cheesy—melt every time I saw it.

I slowly opened my eyes, blinked, glanced around the room, and then turned my gaze back to Nick's flickering hazel-gray eyes. "Is someone filming this?"

A few days later—after my mom had gone back to Texas with a Vuitton trunkload of stories to tell her pals and a Luis-Heinz dress tucked into her carry-on for good measure—Nick and I borrowed the Vespa from Jacques's nephew and went on our first date that didn't involve surveillance cameras.

That is, once we ditched Nick's "chaperones."

With the wind blowing tangles into our hair, we shimmied the scooter in and out of traffic on a scenic route to the Jardin des Tuileries, kicking up a wheelie as we finally lost the camera crew in the black SUVs somewhere near the Musée d'Orsay.

Sporting my new seashell-beige Luis-Heinz creation and coordinating three-inch python Manolos, I wisely stayed on the scooter while Nick got off to push it through the garden's gates, over the dirt and gravel paths, and past the fountain where children were launching their toy boats. Nick parked me near an empty stone bench beneath a perfectly manicured tree and helped me from my perch before running off to buy some crepes at a nearby outdoor café.

"All they had was strawberries and powdered sugar," he said, proffering the crepe in his left hand temptingly. "And Nutella," he mumbled, almost as an afterthought.

"Nutella, please," I said sweetly, immune to his powers of suggestion. "A celebration calls for Nutella."

"Oh, all right," he said. "I *guess* I can let you have a bite of mine."

As he started to laugh, I grabbed him by the waist, distracted him with a mind-erasing kiss—and plucked the Nutella crepe out of his right hand. And once I got what I wanted, I unhanded that man and happily nibbled away at what was rightfully mine.

"Sorry, did you just celebrate my freedom by liberating my crepe?" he said, trying his best to sound indignant.

"Mmmm-hmmmm!"

We were in fact celebrating, over crepes and that bottle of Cristal that had come compliments of P. Diddy, even though I was heading back to London the next day and we were only in the beginning stages of working out how to have a Eurostar relationship. But none of that mattered at that moment, not when Nick was about to be released from the evil clutches of the models.

After that rather, um, eventful week, the producers of *The Modelizer* had decided that Nick was a bit too much of a wild card to be a contestant on their show, and that they would have to ship in the understudy, pronto. And then it would be goodbye, camera crew, we hardly knew ye. Why the producers came to their conclusion I could only guess: Was it, say, the Givenchy show altercation? The incendiary interview in the *Catwalk Caterwaul?* The lack of hot-tub action with the models? Or maybe that whole misadventure with the baddies?

In fact, it was his performance at the warehouse that convinced the producers to keep him on as—what else?—a consultant. Which, it turned out, he really, truly was. (And one day I would find out what that really, truly meant.) The producers liked that Nick could think on his feet, so they placed him in charge of the show's plot twists. Even I had to admit that in the smart-and-shallow pantheon, that sounded like a pretty cool job.

But Nick wasn't the only one doling out plot twists. Serious smooching aside, I decided that I couldn't let him think he was completely off the hook just yet. And there was really only one appropriate form of penance I could mete out.

I was taking him shoe shopping.

After we finished our crepes and he kissed off the last

remnant of Nutella from my chin, we hopped back on the Vespa and headed to the Bon Marché. I got goosebumps as I walked into the venerable department store, hand in hand with Nick. He was about to be initiated into a sacred rite that most men would never be privy to. Nor would most want to be, but whatever.

Nick sat still and, as far as I could tell, with only a minimal amount of eye-rolling, he patiently watched me try on thirty-one pairs of shoes: the same Manolo pumps in seven colors, four Louboutin sandals in different skins, Chanel boots (ankle and knee lengths), Dior stilettos, and so on, and so on, and so on . . .

And horror of horrors, after two leisurely hours, I didn't buy a single pair.

But don't think that I'd lost my shopping touch. I knew I wasn't going to leave Paris empty-handed. I got the story, and I got the guy. And God knows I already had the accessories.

About the Author

Julie K. L. Dam is a senior editor at *People* magazine, where she currently oversees the magazine's music coverage. She lives in New York City. You can check out her blog at www.somelikeithaute.com.